Forbidden Romeo

An Enemies to Lovers Fake Dating Dark Irish Billionaire Mafia Romance

Kiana Hettinger

This book is an original production of Hardmoon Press.

By Kiana Hettinger

Forbidden Romeo is a Dark Irish Mafia Romance Standalone.

Mafia Kings: Corrupted Series

#0 Cruel Inception

#1 Corrupted Heir

#2 Corrupted Temptation

#3 Corrupted Protector

#4 Corrupted Obsession

#5 Corrupted Vows

#6 Corrupted Sinner

#7 Corrupted Seduction

Standalones

Stolen Bond

Brutal Oath

Forbidden Romeo

Your Exclusive Access

Thanks a million for being here. Your support means so much to me.

The best way to keep in touch with me is by signing up for my newsletter – sendfox.com/authorkianah (I promise I won't spam you!) and by joining my readers' group, Kiana's Kittens – facebook.com/groups/KianasKittens

You'll receive bonus chapters, inside scoop, discounts, first access to cover reveals and rough drafts, exclusive material, and so much more!

See you on the inside,
Kiana Hettinger

Author's Note

When Jack and Aimee's story came to me, I was itching to write something with a lot of angst, love, lust, chemistry, betrayal, and the icing on this delicious enemies-to-lovers is the good old family rivalry. These two didn't fight *me* as much as they fought with and for each other.

I hope you find someone who fights with and for you.

K

Table of Contents

Prologue

Jack

Thump. Thump, thump. Thump. Thump, thump.

My fists pelt the training pads in perfect rhythm. It's been a while since I've been able to lose myself to this particular beat. I've missed the simplicity of hitting a mark with deadly accuracy over and over.

Thump. Thump, thump. Thump. Thump, thump.

It's soothing, almost as if every thought in my head is melting away. The only thing I need to focus on is the impact. Withdraw. Impact again. My muscles remember the pattern well and stretch and contract comfortably.

Thump. Thump, thump. Thump. Thump, thump.

The last hit has my trainer stagger back a step. Good, I can still catch him off guard. When you've been out in the field as long as I have, there's always a worry that you'll start to forget the basics of the ring.

Thump. Thump, thump—

"Jack!"

Graham's voice snaps through my concentration like a knife, and I turn to look at my brother with no small amount of irritation.

The bastard has the nerve to smile right back. "Thought we were on the job?"

"Aye, if you bothered to show up on time," I quip back before dismissing the trainer with a wave.

"You know me," Graham replies, walking up the steps to lean casually against the ring post. "I'm a busy man."

"Yeah? What's her name this time?"

"Lorrel," Graham pretends to think about it. "Or maybe Lorraine?"

I shake my head at him. We both know he's about as good with women as he is in the ring. That is to say, not at all.

"Fancy a quick spar?" I challenge just to throw him off.

Graham merely indicates his pristine three-piece. "Not on your life, mate. Come on, put a shirt on; they want to open the doors."

"Fine," I say, already ducking under the rope and grabbing a towel.

Ideally, I'd be after a shower around about now. But, with Graham finally here, I get the feeling I'll be skipping it.

We stride up the stairs to the VIP box, narrowly avoiding the streams of people coming in to watch the evening match. It must have gotten later than I thought it was. I don't bother with a shirt until after we've escaped the rabble and taken a seat overlooking the entire arena.

"Padraic wants an update," Graham says in a low voice. A force of habit more than anything else, I think—it's not like any of our men stationed around the box would flinch at the name.

"Impatient as always," I mutter back.

"I assume you have one? Or did you drag me all the way to Luckies to remind me you can still take me in the ring?"

"Doesn't it make you feel nostalgic?" I tease.

Graham grimaces. "No."

The fighters enter the ring at that moment, and the crowds start cheering for the favorites. It's just a preview, so there's not as much ceremony as the bigger games, but the kids they showcase seem to get scrawnier every year.

"I hope Padraic has a decent lineup for the annuals," I comment as the bell rings. "These two aren't worth the walk to the bookies.".

"Jack. Concentrate, please."

I snort—*like father, like son.* "Got a tip from the ticket office that Maguires have been here every night this week."

Graham's expression darkens. "Staking us out?"

"Or something. Seems like one hell of a risk when they already know this place is swarming with our people."

"How has no one caught them yet?" Graham says, glancing at the armed members of the Dead Eyes stationed at every exit of the arena below.

"Luck of the Irish, I guess," I reply bitterly.

"We're more Irish than those fucking British sympathizers," Graham spits to emphasize his point. As if any of us need reminding that Graham is proud of his family name.

I simply nod at this and lean back in my chair. "Well, I guess their luck is running out tonight, then."

"You got an ID on them?"

As Graham says this, a young man dressed in the Luckies uniform approaches the box. I turn to him with a smile—perfect timing. "Sal, has our guest of honor arrived yet?"

"Yes, sir," Sal confirms and passes me a folded note before scampering away.

I unfold it quickly, noting the contents before passing it on to Graham: *F23*

"Seat number?" Graham confirms unnecessarily—I'm already scanning the crowds.

Then I see it, the flash of red hair that's so unmistakably Maguire, my toes begin to curl. Not to mention that the man is staring right at us, despite the fact one of the scrawny fighters has just managed a knockout.

"Seems we have an admirer," I comment and stand up with a stretch. "Fancy a walk, Graham?"

Graham seems to spot him, too, and frowns. "Why do I recognize him?"

"I thought you said all those ginger twats look the same?" I say as the ginger twat in question stands up too.

"He's too confident, Jack," Graham says as we watch him leave the arena without any of our men seeming to notice. "Send the boys after him first."

I groan a little. "Don't want to ruin your nice suit?"

"I'm serious."

"Come on, when was the last time we roughed up a Maguire together?" I counter.

Graham stares up at me, unwavering. "They're clearly planning something. And you're just itching for a fight."

"When have you known the Maguires to demonstrate they have more than two brain cells to rub together?" I glance back at the arena; the man has disappeared from sight. It's now or never. "Padraic will give you the 'Best Son' award if you bring him in yourself. Bet it'll come with a little gold trophy and everything."

"You're his son, too," Graham snaps back, but I can see his resolve wavering.

"Barely," I reply. "Besides, you know you're going to get credit for this anyway, may as well earn it."

It's a low blow that I'll definitely pay for later, but I know it will work. Sure enough, Graham is on his feet a moment later, giving me a look that promises an untimely end.

"Let's walk," Graham Duffy announces, and his entire demeanor changes. He slips seamlessly from his lighthearted mask into his true self—the legitimate heir to the Dead Eyes mob and son of one of the most powerful men in New York City. Graham Duffy isn't a man you tease about women or his chances in the boxing ring; Graham Duffy is a man you run from.

Despite everything, I'm just glad I get to walk by his side.

On our way out, I pick up a knife and pistol from the surrender box and conceal them casually—knowing full well that Graham is probably carrying an arsenal already. He whispers to the men at the door, no doubt telling them to trail us, before gesturing to me to follow him out the front door.

New York is never quite dark, yet stepping into Hell's Kitchen at this time of night always has me on high alert. With the fight in full swing, the street outside the underground arena is eerily quiet.

"Andy said the guy headed north when he left," Graham comments as we begin stalking the streets.

"Alone?"

Graham nods, and we wordlessly head north a few blocks. Every person we pass speeds up a little to move out of our way, and I note each one of their faces, the color of their hair, whether their eyes linger on us or are glued to the floor.

Then, in the distance, I see it again—a flash of red hair disappears around a corner. I nudge Graham, and we make our approach.

Rounding the corner, Graham already has his gun in his hand. It's a darker alley with a wire fence blocking the other end. Piles of trash litter the floor, and fire escapes loom over us on either side, making the space feel even narrower.

I hear Graham click off the safety, and I do the same.

I scan the windows and the fire escapes as Graham presses forward, but there's no movement at all. Not even a rat.

Suddenly, a man steps out of the shadows in front of us with a crooked smile on his face.

"Well, I'm honored Padraic thought me worthy enough to send his true-born son. For a while there, I thought I'd be stuck with the bastard," the man croons.

This close, we can finally get a good measure of him. He's much bigger than I would have liked, and his long, ginger hair is tied back from his face. He doesn't look armed, but that's not saying much.

"Connor Maguire," Graham replies coolly. "Thought I recognized you."

"In the flesh," Connor says with another smirk.

"How's business, Maguire?" I say. "I'd say sorry for your loss, but all things considered, your father was a daft old sod."

That wipes the smirk off his face.

Graham cuts in before he has a chance to reply. "You have our attention, Connor. What do you want?"

"More than you can offer." Connor glares at me. "My father let things slide for too long."

I snort at this. "So you're here to what, assert your dominance?"

"I'm here to tell you things are going to go a little differently from now on," Connor snaps back.

"If that's all, Connor," Graham says, sounding more than a little bored, "thank you for wasting our time."

Graham nods at me, and we begin to walk away. Only to hear the telltale sound of Connor cocking his gun. I turn to see him pointing it directly at Graham, and my blood begins to boil.

"You're going to stand there and listen to me, Graham Duffy," Connor hisses.

Graham doesn't look phased at all by the barrel of his enemy's gun. He takes a step forward. "We both know you're not going to shoot me, Connor. Or did you miscalculate? There's two of us and only one of you."

Connor raises an eyebrow just as something flickers in the corner of my eye. My attention snaps back to the fire escapes. Five... seven... no, ten men climb through the windows, armed to the teeth and pointing their weapons directly at us.

Jesus fucking Christ.

"Where the hell did *you* get the money for all this?" The words leave my mouth as I think of them.

"We made some new friends," Connor replies, his smirk now plastered back on his face. "Friends who share my… enthusiasm for restoring the family name."

Fuck.

Graham and I exchange a glance. We need to get out of here now. Or at least stall them until our own reinforcements can arrive.

"You made your point," Graham says evenly. "Make your grand speech so we can go tell Padraic you're a big boy now."

Connor lets out a long sigh and waves off his men. "The thing my father struggled with the most was efficiency. I have to hand it to you Duffys, you run a tight business. Your setup at Luckies is impressive; even I struggled to get past your goons. But, in the end, it just wasn't efficient enough to stop me."

Connor pauses to examine his gun, and I can feel the hairs sticking up on the back of my neck.

"You're right," he continues. "I'm here to send Padraic a message."

He looks at us both slowly. Then his gaze lands on me, and his expression turns icy cold.

"But the thing is… You only need one person to send a message."

The gun echoes.

Time stops.

I glance down at my body, half expecting to see blood already blooming from my chest. But there's nothing. I'm fine. I look back up at Connor because the bastard fucking missed me. All this talk and he *missed*.

But he's not looking at me anymore.

He's looking at Graham.

14

"No."

I run to him, not caring that I'm turning my back on an armed Maguire. Graham looks as shocked as I feel, his face white and drained of color.

"No!"

I lower him to the ground, applying pressure to the wound. Dear God. There's so much blood already. It seeps through my fingers and splatters across the floor.

"No!"

Distantly I'm aware that reinforcements have arrived. That the Maguires are scattering. That Connor has disappeared.

But all I can see is Graham, his mouth opening and closing, eyes unfocused and rolling wildly.

"J-Jack?" he finally manages to whisper. Suddenly, he's not Graham Duffy anymore. He's the boy I played with as a child. The teenager I would bully in the boxing ring. The man I fought and killed for. My brother. My best friend.

"I'm here," I whisper back.

"You better fucking kill them for this."

The light disappears from his eyes.

I roar.

Chapter One

Jack

You go to enough funerals, and you realize they never look like they do on TV. The sky isn't pouring with rain; there's no sea of black umbrellas or a shady character observing from a distance.

All the shady characters are right here, and only half of them have the decency to wear black.

Any other day, I'd beat Lars O'Neil for showing up in jeans but, lucky for him, I just want this day to be over. Padraic insisted on an open casket at the wake. God knows I'm relieved to finally see Graham lowered into the ground. Seeing his face again, hearing his last words echo through my skull over and over.

You better fucking kill them for this.

My hand itches towards my holster. I should be out there hunting down Maguires until I have Connor begging for his life at my feet. I should be avenging my *brother*. I don't have time for this parade of politics. I said my goodbyes to Graham days ago; the funeral is just a way for Padraic to show anyone bothering to pay attention that we're still a united front.

The priest drones on and on. I'd happily wager that none of the Dead Eyes have ever crossed the threshold of a church if there wasn't already a dead body inside, but traditions are traditions.

Last time we were here, Graham's mother was the one on her way out. She was a shrewd woman who never took a liking to me, but Graham struggled that day. I snuck him out of the cemetery for a smoke at the end of Pier 88. We spent the rest of the day there, just drinking and throwing rocks in the grimy water below.

It's my fault.

I have to take a moment to steady my breathing. There are too many witnesses, and I'll be damned if any of them see me cry.

In better circumstances, I might even be impressed by the turnout. All the Duffy factions are represented—all the families that slowly broke away and formed their own gangs after we emigrated. Two hundred years later, their loyalty to the oldest Irish family in New York remains. A legacy Graham was going to continue proudly.

Now… I glance at Padraic. The man hasn't spoken to me since the day I brought Graham's body home. He's a brute at the best of times, but today he looks borderline disgusted by the resting place of his only true-born son.

Of course, Padraic Duffy would see this primarily as an inconvenience.

The priest finally drones to a halt, and Padraic steps forward to throw a handful of dirt on top of Graham's coffin. It hits the wood with a delicate patter. Despite the gentle sound, it seems to echo across the cemetery— finally breaking the silence of the crowds.

I watch as Padraic takes one last look at his son before he turns away, disappearing into the midst of his men. Huh. Perhaps he's not as interested in the politics of funerals as I thought.

"Jack Duffy."

I grit my teeth as I turn away to see Lars approaching me with a smirk slapped across his face.

I take a moment to school my expression into something more neutral. "O'Neil."

"My condolences," the mobster says without an ounce of feeling.

I simply nod and turn away.

Today isn't about networking, and God knows I don't need to be cozying up with Lars fucking O'Neil.

"It's a pity," Lars continues despite my apparent lack of interest. "The Duffys are left without a true heir."

"That's not your concern."

"I'm not the only one wondering if Padraic's bastard will get a nice little promotion out of all this," he replies with a knowing look in his eye.

I bite my tongue. It's not the first time someone's thrown the word "bastard" around to make me uncomfortable, and it won't be the last. "I suggest you leave the gossiping to your wife, O'Neil."

"The hell you know about my wife?"

"Only what she told me in bed last night," I quip back. He really walked into that one.

Lars' face colors. "Now's not the time to make an enemy out of me."

I take a step forward lazily, squaring up to the man who barely reaches my chin and letting him size me up properly. "Are you seriously threatening me at my brother's funeral? Get out of my fucking sight."

Lars falters, torn between saving face and backing down. He barely manages to get a gulp in before an elegant hand clamps his shoulder and pushes him away.

"You wouldn't be causing trouble now, would you, Jack?"

Kate brushes past without a second thought—the only person who's ever been able to sneak up on me. Her mourning clothes are immaculate, refined, and probably thousands of dollars more expensive than they needed to be.

But Graham's cousin was as close to him as the rest of us. There's a tightness to her expression that I think only someone who knows her as well as me would notice. A strain on her otherwise perfect composure that means something is brewing under the surface. Something that, right now, makes her very fucking dangerous.

Luckily, she's staring right at Lars O'Neil.

"Lot of nerve you've got, O'Neil, showing your face here." Kate's blonde hair swishes over her shoulder as she tilts her head at him curiously. Like a predator examining a meal.

Lars, ever the hot-blooded male, misses the cues to get the hell out of Dodge and smiles at her. "What's wrong with my face, like?"

"The O'Neils were Maguires only a generation ago; that's enough to get you killed these days," Kate replies, absently stroking a fingertip over her clawlike nails.

"We split from the Maguires thirty years ago."

"Aye," Kate concedes before fixing him with a fiery glare. "But your family still sold us out to the British, and that still makes you a Maguire to me."

"Still yapping about the famine, are we? God, you do sound like Padraic," Lars whines.

"I'm sure my uncle would love to hear you've decided it's not worth 'yapping' about."

Lars has the decency to look a little nervous before glancing at me. "Ferocious one, isn't she? Maybe Padraic will do us a favor and name her instead."

The knife is at Lars' throat before I have time to react. I don't want to know where Kate was hiding it, but she's suddenly pulling him in close as if they're locked in an embrace.

"I'd prefer it if you didn't talk about me like I'm not here," she whispers sweetly in his ear. "Everyone's a little on edge today, and I would *hate* it if something happened to you."

"Bitch!"

"Shush now. Or they won't let your family hold an open casket by the time I'm finished," she purrs as she drags a nail across Lars' cheek for emphasis.

I glance around us—several people have noticed our little altercation, and it's only a matter of time before someone reports to Padraic. That's the last thing I need today.

"Kate," I say sharply in warning.

To her credit, Kate suddenly releases Lars from her grasp. He scuttles backward a few steps, clearly furious.

Just as he goes to open his slimy little mouth again, a rage comes over me like I've never felt before. Suddenly it's like I'm back in the ring, everything around me fades into the background, and my only focus is the target in front of me.

"I hope your next words are an apology, O'Neil. Or else it won't be Padraic who comes after you. It will be me," I say quietly, staring the man down.

Lars seems to finally acknowledge he's walked into the wrong fight. The color drains from his face as he stares at me, breath coming out in short puffs. Fight or flight.

He takes a step back, then another.

"You didn't need to do that, Jack," Kate says as we stand there watching Lars make his feeble retreat.

I cast a side glance at the cold expression on her face, and my chest begins to ache—it reminds me so much of Graham at his own mother's funeral.

It's my fault.

"I couldn't let you tear him apart. We're supposed to be a united front, remember?"

That, at least, earns me a small smile. She turns to me. "Padraic wants to see you."

"Right now?"

She nods without looking me in the eye, and I frown. Lars was right about one thing—we're the only ones left with any claim to the Duffy empire. If Padraic wants to meet with me this close to the funeral… my mind jumps into overdrive.

"I'm sure it's nothing," Kate says stiffly. She's always been vocal about her desires; becoming heir was never one of them. That said, Padraic dotes on her more than anyone I know.

"And if it's something?" I say cautiously.

Finally, Kate looks up and holds my gaze. Her brown eyes bore into mine—the same eyes I've seen every day since we were children. For the first time, I realize I don't know where I stand with her anymore. I can't remember a time when Kate and I haven't been at each other's throats (literally on more than one occasion). Still, Graham was always the mediator when it came to the three of us. Without him, we're just two people that know too much about each other, yet somehow not enough to be considered friends.

"There are worse things, I suppose," Kate says finally.

I bow my head slightly. Whatever the outcome of this mess, Kate's blessing is invaluable.

"Just don't let it go to your head," she says before turning away.

***

"Padraic," I say in greeting as I enter my father's office. He has numerous rooms just like it across the city, all laid out in the same regal way as his home office. I'm not sure he's changed a thing since he inherited them from his father, nor he since he inherited them from his.

At least the chairs have been reupholstered, a fact I'm grateful for, as Padraic indicates for me to sit down.

"To what do I owe the pleasure?" I say casually while trying (and failing) to see through his stony expression for any indication about where this conversation may go.

He allows me a moment to stew before finally replying, "I'll cut to the chase, Jack. My son is dead, and I've been left without an heir."

I bite my tongue to stop myself from informing him he's pointing out the obvious and merely nod.

"This could cripple our entire family, two hundred years in the making," he continues.

"I know," I say quietly. "I've already made plans to make the Maguires pay for what they've done."

Padraic narrows his eyes at me. "I do not blame Connor Maguire for this."

It's my fault.

It's like he reached across his desk and pulled my heart straight out of my chest. Rendering me completely speechless, unable to move, unable to *feel.* The words I've been telling myself this last week are finally spoken aloud.

I take a gulp and try to regain some composure, "Connor–"

"I didn't invite you here to listen to your excuses, boy. The Maguires will be dealt with in due course, but *you…*" Padraic's voice takes on a venomous twist. "Tell me, were you or were you not assigned to the task of flushing the Maguires encroaching on our territory?"

"I was." I have to break eye contact and stare down at my hands.

"And did you, or did you not, request my son join you on this task?"

"I did."

"And when my son asked you to send others to investigate a suspicious lead, did you deny the request?"

It's my fault.

A phantom knife twists in my gut. "I did."

"Why?"

"I thought we'd be able to take them–"

"No. You were being reckless, immature, and irresponsible," Padraic cuts me off. "These are qualities I cannot have within my ranks."

I look up in pure shock. Genuine fear shoots through my veins—this family is my entire *life*. It's the only thing I've ever known.

"Padraic, you can't," I say.

Padraic merely sneers at me. "You don't tell me what I can or can't do."

It's my fault.

"I'm your son," I whisper.

He laughs. It's a cruel dry sound that comes out more like a bark.

"You're no son of mine. As for the Dead Eyes… That's a privilege you must *earn* should you ever wish to regain your position within my ranks."

I shake my head. "This is my family."

"No, Jack. This is *my* family."

Chapter Two

Aimee

"Roisin, you dumbass! You locked me out again!" I bang on the apartment door while awkwardly trying to balance the cardboard box on my hip. A strand of messy red hair falls in my eyes, and I blow at it fruitlessly.

Today really isn't going as well as I'd hoped.

Roisin wrenches the door open a second later, and I immediately offload the box on her.

"Hey!" she whines as I breeze past her into the apartment. *Our* apartment.

"I carried that thing three flights of stairs; you can carry it to your room," I reply, falling onto the only free space on the couch. The rest is occupied with a combination of shoes, Christmas decorations, and a sewing machine I'm pretty sure is broken.

"I thought we were going to leave this behind?" I shout to Roisin when she disappears behind her bedroom door.

"What?"

"The sewing machine," I reply, picking up the offending object.

Roisin reappears a moment later with her arms folded across her chest. "I'm going to fix it!"

I roll my eyes at her. "Uh-huh. When?"

"When," she says as she strides over to snatch it away from me, "I have time."

"It stays in your room," I counter.

Roisin simply sticks out her tongue and retreats, no doubt going to dump her newly acquired goods in her room, never to be touched again.

I stretch my arms out in front of me, letting the muscles crack and pop in all the right places. "Let's not move again for a while. I'm so tired."

"Was that the last box?" Roisin shouts from the other room.

"Yeah. Table won't get here until next week, though."

"Looks like we're eating on the floor then," she says, walking back into a room with an old blanket that she lays across the ground for us. She steps away from it a moment with a frown. "Hmm… something is missing."

Playing along, I slide off the couch and onto the floor as she rushes off into the kitchen.

It feels weird to be back in New York after all this time, but the tiny apartment already feels like it's welcoming us home. There's something about an unfurnished space that screams "fresh start," but the hustle of the people below, the sirens a couple blocks away, and the horns of the cabs narrowly avoiding each other reminds me so much of Harlem it can be unnerving.

But this is Brooklyn.

And, in Brooklyn, we can just be two sisters making their way in the world.

I'm brought out of my musings by Roisin, who promptly hands me a glass and pours me some white wine. It's an old, chipped tumbler, but somehow, the alcohol has never tasted so good.

"Have I told you how much I love you today?"

Roisin laughs as she takes a seat next to me. "You could stand to say it again."

"Love you to pieces, Roshe," I say sincerely as we clink our glasses together. "Can you think of anything more quintessentially 'New York' than drinking on the floor of your new shabby apartment?"

"Hey, it's shabby chic!"

I roll my eyes at her as I take another sip. "We'd be paying half this rent if we were back in LA."

"Well, LA isn't New York, is it?" she replies with a dreamy glance out the window. "There's so much we could do here, you know?"

I feel my hand tightening around the tumbler. "I feel like you've glamorized it in your head."

Roisin looks back at me, annoyance written all over her face. "Why wouldn't I? All those movies we used to watch. This place is all I've ever dreamed of."

"I just want to manage your expectations," I reply as pragmatically as I can.

Roisin glances down and bites at her bottom lip.

I know what she's thinking—it took her months to convince me to come here after she got into Julliard. If I'm not enjoying myself as much as she is, she'll blame herself for forcing me across the country.

We must have had this conversation a thousand times before we moved. She knows I have reservations about coming here, even if she thinks it's for the wrong reasons. Ever since she got back from rehab, she's been a saint—even if she can still drink like a particularly parched fish. I trust her completely, and I know she won't ever do anything reckless.

But the problem with being back here isn't Roisin; the problem is everyone else. Everything she can't remember about why we left five years ago.

"You don't need to coddle me, you know?" Roisin says quietly. "I know you know this place better than I do, but you don't need to worry about me slipping into old habits."

I take her hand in mine and offer her a smile. "I'm your sister. Worrying about you is kinda my job."

"Well, don't," she says as if it were that simple.

"I trust you, Roisin–"

"--It's just everyone else you don't trust. I know, Aimee," Roisin teases.

If only she knew how true that was.

I force back a smile and ruffle her ginger hair.

"Hey!"

I snort at the disgruntled look on her face. "You know what would make this perfect?"

"What?" Roisin replies as she fixes her hair.

"Chinese."

I love the way her eyes light up at this; it's like we're kids again, and I just suggested we sneak out to the park. Yet somehow, I became the responsible one out of the two of us.

"I can run out and grab something if you want?" Roisin says, already moving to stand up.

I pull her back down. "This is New York, Roshe. The food comes to us."

"But where…"

I give her an incredulous look. "Bold of you to assume I haven't already made a list of the best takeout joints within five blocks of this place."

Roisin squeals and gives me a side hug. "You're the best!"

I make the call, reciting our usual order from memory, as I watch Roisin lie happily on the blanket. Taking photos, scrolling social media, and messaging her new college friends she hasn't met in real life yet. At that moment, I decide that it's all worth it. Whatever turmoil I'm putting myself through about being back in New York, it's worth it to see her like this.

Besides, it's not like either of us will be out there actively looking for trouble. Someone would need to put a gun to my head before I ever stepped foot in Harlem again. My residency is on the other side of town, and from what I remember, our family home was practically falling to ruin before we left. With any luck, it might have collapsed completely by now.

Food arrives promptly, and Roisin practically skips to the door to pick it up. She returns with two brown paper bags while examining something brightly colored in her hand.

"Did you see your lanyard already arrived?" she says, throwing it to me.

"Yeah…" I catch it and take a look at the plastic card. "They kept my name the same, though."

She groans and sits back down on the floor, distributing our food to its rightful owners. "I don't get why you want to change it anyways. It's not like Connor is actually going to find you. I'm sure he has better things to do," she says bitterly.

I glance at her. We don't often talk about our family, and right now, it's a topic a little too close to home. Literally.

Instead of addressing it, I grab my chow mein and dig in heartily. "Maybe I just don't want to be harassed when you make it as a famous actress."

She pokes me with her chopsticks. "Aren't you excited, though? You've barely spoken about it."

"Of course, I mean residency in a New York ER is super competitive and everything, and I'm honored to have a position."

"But?"

I hesitate, "But… I don't know, it's easy to be honored about something, isn't it? I think actually doing it will be a lot harder. Besides, I'll have interns now. I'm not used to being the kind of person people look up to like that."

"Hey, I've been doing it for years, and look how I turned out." Roisin puts her food down to look me in the eye. "A bullet wound is a bullet wound; it doesn't matter if you're in LA or New York."

I pout at her. "You don't know that. They could have different bullets here."

"And if they do, you'll be able to handle it, Aimee," she replies, but it comes across as more authoritative than reassuring.

I raise an eyebrow at her, utterly unconvinced.

"Don't make me hold you down and give you a pep talk!"

I shudder. "I'm good, honestly."

"Then say it."

"Say what?"

She puts both hands on my shoulders for purely dramatic effect. "Say that you're the best goddamn doctor the world has ever seen."

"That's not really true…"

"Say it."

"Fine! I'm the best goddamn doctor the world has ever seen!"

Roisin grins. "We're young, free, and single in New York City. We can be whoever we want to be."

When I don't repeat her words, she hits me playfully in the arm.

"We're young, free, and single in New York City. We can be whoever we want to be," I say monotonously.

"And you can be the kind of person little interns will cower from in fear," Roisin continues.

"Nope." I shake her hands off me and go back to my noodles.

Roisin sits back moodily. "Okay, fine, but you'll tell me if any of them are cute, right?"

"Roisin, real life isn't like *Grey's Anatomy*. Physicians are usually just tired and skinny."

She lets out a long, drawn-out sigh. "Can't a girl dream, though?"

"Dream away," I concede with a giggle.

Yep, she's going to do so well at Julliard.

"May I propose a toast?" I say after a moment, raising my tumbler in the air with the gravitas of someone holding a fine chalice. Roisin imitates me immediately.

"To new beginnings."

"And hot physicians." Roisin clinks my glass.

Chapter Three

Aimee

"Dr. Maguire, we have a nine-two-two trauma call coming in. How fast can you get there?"

I look up at my attending from where I'm sitting, finishing up a chart for a young man with a back injury. She looks back with an expectant stare. Dr. Lous is a firm woman who I discovered quite quickly has a distaste for pagers.

"Two minutes," I reply distractedly, scribbling faster.

"Take one," Dr. Lous says as she walks on from the room without so much as a goodbye.

I curse under my breath, handing the chart over to the nurse to finish.

"Kyle, you're with me," I say to my intern as I leave the room and head over to our station. It didn't take long to learn the layout of the hospital, and it helped that I'd examined the floor plan on more than one occasion before we even left LA. It never hurts to know how to get out fast.

A moment later, I hear the telltale scurrying of feet behind me. "I haven't done a nine-two-two before."

"You ever done a nine-one-one?"

"Yes, but—"

"It's the same thing, just less people in the room," I say firmly.

Kyle, at least, seems reassured by that. Out of all the interns, he's been the most consistent with trauma calls—and right now, I need every pair of hands I can get. The four years I interned in LA were some of the hardest days of my life. But the sheer volume of calls in this place is overwhelming. I only took two weeks off to move here, but I can probably count the times I was at the gym on one finger. God knows I'm paying for that now.

When we enter the room, the nurse is already there setting up. I've seen her enough times this week to recognize her behind her mask—which reminds me to pull mine on too.

"Any word?" I say in greeting.

"Bullet graze to the shoulder. ETA is about two minutes," the nurse replies, not stopping her preparations.

Kyle pulls on his mask with a frown. "Is a bullet graze a nine-two-two?"

"No," I reply. "Dr. Lous must have misheard."

The nurse snorts. "Lous needs to get over her whole pager thing."

I smile at that. "Could I get your pager then?"

"Sure," she says, reeling off her pager number for me to memorize. "You're the new resident, right?"

"Aimee Maguire," I reply automatically. "And yes, I've seen you around."

"My name is Aisha. Anesthetist."

I nod my head, "That'll be easy to remember, at least."

Her eyes crinkle above her mask. "You have good taste in interns."

We both turn to examine Kyle, who just stands awkwardly in the corner of the room. He's an impressively tall guy with a flop of curly, dark hair that doesn't look like it'll start receding any time soon.

"Thanks," I reply. "My sister is looking for a boyfriend. If he survives the trauma calls, maybe he'll survive her."

Aisha makes a thoughtful sound. "Maybe. But I heard he had a thing going with a couple of the girls in pediatrics."

"A couple? Jesus, Kyle," I say, more to Aisha than the man in question.

Kyle splutters, "I'm right here!"

Lucky for Kyle, our patient arrives before we can harass him anymore. He's a sturdy-looking man in his middle years, blood smeared across his clothes. The medics drop him on the bed, relaying his condition and treatments so far.

"We've cleaned it already, but we can't stick around, I'm afraid. There's been a shoot-out," one of the medics says to me apologetically.

I wave him off. "We can handle it, thanks."

The man in front of us is holding on to consciousness like a trooper. From a distance, it's hard to imagine him in a gunfight. His expensive, dark suit trousers suggest that, at one point, there was a matching jacket and tie. The bullet probably ripped through it like it was nothing.

"Kyle, double-check for an entry wound or shrapnel. Aisha—"

But the nurse is already approaching the patient, anesthetic in hand. I recite her pager number in my head—we need to be friends.

"W-what? What is that?" The man stirs as Aisha lowers the needle.

"It's just local anesthetic," she replies, administering it quickly before he has a chance to protest.

To his credit, the man doesn't flinch. "I don't want to fall asleep."

"You won't," I confirm. "Kyle?"

"Looks clean," he replies and moves over for me to check.

It's a nasty graze, but the man was lucky that whoever it was missed. A couple inches lower, and he'd be in real trouble.

"Good job, Kyle," I offer the praise sincerely, and I can tell he's grinning behind his mask.

My pager goes off again, and I glance at it. Another 922—the medics must be bringing in the next patients from the shoot-out.

"You know, about your sister…"

I smack his shoulder. "There's another nine-two-two coming in. Go bother someone else."

"But—"

"You must have sutured a graze a dozen times. Make yourself useful and actually learn something new," I snap. Aisha stifles a laugh next to me as she hands me the needle, ready for stitching. "Aisha and I have got this."

Kyle groans but thankfully does as he's told, leaving the room without another comment.

I turn my attention back to my patient to find him examining me curiously. I raise an eyebrow at him as I prod around the graze site. "You feel anything?"

"I thought he was the doctor," he says.

Great, he's one of those.

"Surprise," I say sarcastically, prodding a little harder. "Any pain?"

He shakes his head, and I get to work stitching him up. There's something quite soothing about the process—if Kyle has done this a dozen times, I must have done it a hundred. I take pride in my steady hand and neat stitches; it was one of the first medical procedures I ever learned.

Even if I wasn't strictly speaking a medical professional at that point. I mean, who is at fifteen? I knew what a bullet graze like this looked like before I went to medical school.

The one thing about Maguires is that we know what we want.

Roisin was always going to be an actress, Connor was always going to be… well… But me? I was always going to work in the ER. After all the pain and suffering my family has caused, being able to treat and heal people feels right.

I get about halfway through when I feel Aisha hovering behind me. "You okay?" I ask.

Just as I say this, there's a yell from down the corridor. Shit, it must be a bigger situation than we thought.

"Go," I dismiss her. "Sounds like someone else could use you."

"Sure?" she replies, already taking steps toward the door.

"I'll page you if I need you."

"Thanks, Dr. Maguire."

I turn back to my stitching to see the man looking at me curiously again.

Has this man never seen a doctor with tits? Annoyed, I sit back, remove my mask and grab the glass of water Aisha left on the side for me (may she ever be known as St. Aisha).

When I glance back, the man is still staring.

"Must have been one hell of a shoot-out," I say conversationally, hoping that discussing his battle scars will distract him enough to look away. I'm practically sweating under the intensity of his gaze.

"Maguire…" he says quietly. "Is that a family name?"

Shit. I try to keep my composure.

"My husband's," I lie smoothly, thanking the gods of hygiene that I'm wearing gloves so he can't check for a ring.

There are only two groups of people in New York that might be interested in my surname. If I were to be discovered, I don't know which group would be worse for me. Or Roisin.

"What happened today?" I try again.

The man huffs out a laugh. "Nothing I'd want to worry your pretty little head about."

"So, you knew your assailants?" I deduce. I don't really want to know the answer, but any insight into what Roisin and I can avoid could be invaluable.

"Aye," the man replies, and I flinch. Irish. It's been a while since I've heard anyone use that mannerism. "You worried I'm some kind of murderer?"

I clear my throat and go back to work. Quickly. "Even if you were, it wouldn't change how I treated you."

"Noble," he comments. "I've not met many noble Maguires."

My needle works even faster.

There's no way, out of all the people in New York, that I ended up treating a goddamn *Duffy*. I dig in a little harder than I need to, and the man winces.

And then his face splits into a wide, cruel smile. "Met a few ginger Maguires though. Daresay that hair of yours is infamous around these parts."

I stand abruptly, cutting the suture as I do. "Someone else will be in in a moment to complete the dressing. I'm needed elsewhere."

The man simply laughs as I make my escape.

My hands are shaking as I walk down the corridor, and I fumble for my pager.

How could I be so stupid? I just completely blew my cover. I can't believe I listened to Roisin and didn't get my name changed—it doesn't take a genius to add up that Maguire, plus red hair, equals mobster.

If the families weren't looking for us before, they definitely would be now.

I need to move. Fast. Before that guy is discharged and the wolves descend.

Thankfully, I spy Aisha just as I finish typing in her number. She approaches quickly, looking more than a little worried, "Are you okay? You're white as a ghost."

"I need you to do me a favor," I say quietly. "I promise I'll make it up to you."

"What?"

I glance over my shoulder, back toward the room I was just in. "That guy in there? He needs dressing; I've got to speak to Lous."

Aisha gives me an odd look. "Of course. I thought for a second you were going to ask me to hide a body for you. Are you sure you're okay?"

"If he asks about me, you don't know me. You don't know my name or how long I've been here," I whisper urgently.

This sobers her up instantly; she glances over my shoulder, too, and replies simply, "Okay."

"Thank you," I say and give her a look that I hope expresses the depth of my gratitude before moving on to Dr. Lous' office.

The attending physician is hunched over her desk, tapping away on an ancient computer as I enter. It seems her distaste for technology stretches beyond just the pagers.

"Maguire," she says after she glances up at me. "How's the nine-two-two?"

I don't bother correcting her. "Under control. I'm here because I need to file for a name change urgently."

"You get married in the half-hour since I last saw you or something?" Lous says dryly.

"Or something."

Lous looks up at me properly. "Listen, I don't know how you did things back in LA, but administration here is more of a marathon, not a sprint. I'm not sure they understand the term 'urgently.'"

"I thought maybe if it came from you–"

"I have a thousand other things to do before I even get half a second to myself. Unfortunately for you, that time will be spent napping and not arguing with the admin department," Lous replies matter-of-factly before softening a little. "I'm sorry, but you'll have to take it up with them yourself."

"I have a stalker!" I blurt out suddenly—the story forms in my head milliseconds before the lie leaves my mouth. "That's why I moved from LA. But I just saw him here today. I think he's tracked me down somehow, and I don't know what else to do."

Dr. Lous stares at me in shock. "Why did you not make the request sooner?"

"I did," I reply. "But I think there was some kind of admin error. My lanyard came through with my old name, and I haven't had a chance to change it."

The older woman pinches her nose and reaches for her phone. As she punches in the number, she says, "Give me your lanyard and leave out the staff exit. I want you back here tomorrow morning to collect your new one. Understood?"

"Yes, thank you," I say, not having to fake the relief that fills my voice.

She waves me away, and I retreat.

As I quietly make a beeline for the exit, I squash down the guilt of lying and abandoning my post when I know the team needs me. But if the shoot-out did involve the Dead Eyes, there could be even more people who would be able to identify me.

I leave the hospital behind me and make my way to the subway on foot.

All I can do is hope that my name change will be enough to throw them off for a while until I can think up an excuse to change hospitals. Maybe Lous will be able to give me a referral letter. However, she was right about one thing—admin takes a long time. For now, I'm going to have to make do.

As I'm thinking this, I pass by a beauty supply shop, and I pause.

There's one more thing I can try.

Back home, I immediately run to the bathroom and lock the door behind me.

Thankfully, Roisin is still in class. Otherwise, I know she'd murder me for even attempting this. But, as I coat my hair in the dark, semipermanent dye, I know it's the right thing to do. We've been here less than a week, and already my worst fear has been realized. There's no way Roisin will be able to make it through school at this rate.

I rinse and dry quickly and stare at the new reflection looking at me in the mirror. Her brown eyes look somehow duller now that her hair matches their shade. My fair skin looks paler in contrast too, and Lord knows I'll need to work on my tan before the summer. But it's a start.

Besides, no one cares what you look like when you're giving them life-saving care, and it's not like I moved here to start dating, either. I can live with being brunette.

My reflection offers me a tentative smile.

It's going to be okay. It *has* to be okay.

What the hell have I gotten myself into?

Chapter Four

Jack

I feel like a shadow lurking everywhere I go. Torn between defying Padriac's orders, leaving to set things straight, or sticking around so no one dumps my things on the curb.

Padraic slapped me under house arrest while he arranges his next steps. A part of me hopes that once he calms down, he'll reconsider. But the realistic side of me knows he's not going to let this go for a very long time.

Besides, he's right. Graham's death is on my hands. That's not something I'll ever be able to forgive myself for. At least here, I can lose myself at the gym or spar one-on-one with one of the men who aren't embarrassed to be seen alone with the disgraced Duffy bastard.

For the third time in as many days, I make my way down to the gym to let off some steam. Andy is usually around at this time, and he's at least willing to spot for me. My father's preferred confidant has always been a fair and pragmatic man. We've never been friends, but at least he knows I'm worth more to the family alive than crushed under the weight of a barbell.

But when I open the door, the place is completely empty.

I snap into high alert. The Duffy mansion boasts almost twenty bedrooms, not to mention the conference rooms and all the lounges.

Padraic's rotating entourage alone means there are at least five men stationed here at all times. In short: The gym is never empty.

So, where the fuck is everyone?

I grab my phone to find out what's going on when a text comes through.

KATE: *where r u?*

JACK: *???*

KATE: *2nd floor boardroom.*

My gut twists into a knot, and I stare at the message until my screen goes dark. It doesn't take a genius to put two and two together.

Padraic called a meeting, and no one bothered to fill me in.

This feels juvenile, even for Padraic. I've been sitting at his left side since I was fourteen—regardless of how he feels about me, I'm the best lieutenant he's got. It grates on my pride, and I'm tempted to throw up a middle finger and leave because of the disrespect.

But this is just a game to him; he's testing me to see if I'll act out and give him another opportunity to kick me when I'm already down. He told me the only way back was to prove myself, so I can't give him that opportunity now.

Begrudgingly, I head to the second-floor boardroom in double time and slip into the back.

The boardroom is already filled with tension and the aroma of Cuban cigars. Around the polished mahogany table is the top brass of the mob's organization. Padraic is at the head, of course, surrounded by his trusted advisors and most senior lieutenants.

The men in my father's room have already taken their usual seats and are whispering quietly with each other between Padraic's statements. Only Ray seems to notice me entering. He grimaces before casting a weary glance to the head of the table, where Padraic sits stoically. The chairs at his side that Graham and I usually occupy are visibly empty.

I don't take his bait, going instead to stand in the corner where I notice Kate is lingering too. She gives me a quizzical look when I approach her, and I shake my head. No, I didn't get the memo.

Kate tuts under her breath and turns her attention back to Padraic. The Dead Eyes boss has already begun debriefing the room about the funeral. His eyes glaze over when he notices me standing there, but he doesn't falter in his report.

"Conan and the Long Roads are siding with us. Maguires raided their warehouses last week, and they're keen to get this little uprising under control as much as we are."

"With all due respect, Padraic, don't you think it's more than a little 'uprising' at this point?" Ray points out. "We've had reports of numerous assassinations, and he's managed to infiltrate some of our most secure properties."

Padraic slams his hand on the table. "This *boy* is still wet behind the ears, and you're telling me he's getting the better of you?"

"I wouldn't say—"

"Incompetence is what this is. All of you. Caleb Maguire was a drunk and a fool, and it made you all soft and lazy. I want you to lock down each of our properties until you've reviewed every single security measure. Am I clear?"

Ray looks down at the table. "Yes, sir."

"Vigilance. I will kill the next man who tells me they let a Maguire slip through their fingers." Every man in that room knows that there's at least a fifty percent chance Padraic will make good on that threat.

Buzz, a rising lieutenant who's clearly spotted an opportunity, glances at me with a twisted smile. "I heard there was a run-in with the O'Ncils at the funeral."

"Why am I only just hearing about this?" Padraic snaps. "Who dealt with that?"

Buzz looks at me pointedly, daring me to raise my voice. The man has never liked me, but clearly, he's decided I'm fair game to torment now that I've fallen out of favor.

"I did," Kate suddenly pipes up at my side. She gives me a small nod that I return cautiously. I've never known her to take the fall for me before, but maybe she's just reading the room. Padraic is never productive when he's flying off the handle like this, and God knows he has a soft spot for Kate.

True enough, Padraic's entire stance relaxes a little. "And?"

"Just testing his luck," Kate replies. "Seems the other house heads are coming to their own conclusions about our… family situation."

Andy, who's been quiet until this point, finally speaks up. "Which is what exactly, Padraic?"

Padraic levels every man in that room with a stare so intense I can practically hear the sweat dripping down their foreheads. Only Andy, as always, seems unfazed by this.

"Our family might be grieving, but we remain a united front. I will not tolerate speculation until all those involved have been brought to justice," Padraic growls.

But Andy only doubles down. "Why not name Jack as heir and get this over with?"

I stiffen at that, aware that all eyes are suddenly shifting to me. The men murmur to themselves as Andy and Padraic lock eyes. It seems there's a fairly even split on the matter.

"As much as I appreciate your support, Andy," I say calmly, immediately snapping Padraic out of his fury, "I am no longer in a position to have a claim on this family."

This causes more heated debates to begin across the table.

Padraic's mouth tightens at the uproar, and he regards me with a look of disgust. "Enough," he barks a moment later. "I will not discuss this matter any further. My son's body is barely in the ground; the matter of succession can be dealt with when I'm goddamn ready."

Andy looks like he's about to push his luck but thinks better of it.

"Gentlemen, the Maguires have embarrassed us. It's time we hit back, and we hit hard." The room murmurs in agreement before Padraic continues, "I have it on good authority that one of the Maguire sisters was spotted at Lenox Hill ER. If one of the sisters is back in town, it could mean Connor has plans to strengthen their alliance with their new 'friends.' I want her here, alive."

As he says this, a memory stirs in the back of my mind. A fundraiser for one of the Italians we attended once as kids. I remember standing with Kate in the corner of the grand ballroom, much like we are now, as Graham was paraded around like a prize cow. Neither of us was thrilled to be there, but we were still unwilling to miss out on a party.

I remember watching from a distance as Graham was introduced to a scrappy-looking ginger boy and his father. It was one of the only times I ever saw Caleb Maguire—a man who could barely stand, even at the beginning of the evening, speaking too loudly about things others thought distasteful and getting kicked out before the night had begun.

Graham was ushered away from his kids quickly, but not before Kate had the chance to sneer at the two girls that followed Connor around like puppies. The youngest couldn't have been more than ten years old, and not once did she let go of her sister's hand.

We had intel they'd gone missing about five years ago, along with rumors of Caleb's descent into madness. But, if one of them was back, I'd wager the other wasn't far behind.

And I've always been a betting man.

"Kidnapping someone's sister, especially someone like Connor's, is gonna start a war," Ray points out. "We don't want to risk losing everything we've built here."

Padriac's eyes narrow. "This is already war. We can't allow them to walk all over us like this. We need to take the fight to them."

The group falls silent for a few moments, each lost in their own thoughts.

Finally, Padraic stands and walks to the window, looking out at the bustling city below. "All right, here's what we'll do. Andy, I want you to start gathering information on Lennox Hill. I want a positive ID on this girl. We'll be patient; we won't make any moves until we know exactly where she is and what we're up against."

Andy slowly nods his head in agreement. "It's unlikely she'll cause any trouble, but nobody approaches her alone."

"Buzz, I want you to put a bounty on her too," Padraic says before adding, "I want her *alive*. If the Italians catch her first, I want them to know I'm willing to renegotiate Pier eighty-eight if she arrives at my doorstep in one piece."

Buzz smirks at this, no doubt thinking through the loopholes of *alive*. I cringe a little at the thought but push it out of my mind.

Padraic turns to Kate. "I want you ready to intercept this girl when the time is right."

"I thought Andy just said we weren't going solo on this one," Kate replies.

"Fine." Padraic waves her off. "Pick someone and make your preparations together."

"And if I pick Jack?" Kate says defiantly.

If it were anyone else, I think Padraic would have blown a fuse at that moment. But he manages to restrain himself and focuses his wrath on me, pointing a rigid finger in my direction. "If any of you see this man leave the compound, you drag him back here. Are we clear?"

The room silently turns to look at me again, and my jaw clenches. Scolding me in front of everyone like I'm a teenager.

"You can't expect me to stay here when my brother's killer is still out there. I'm more use to you on the streets," I growl back.

"I expect you to follow a goddamn order," he roars.

No one breathes as they wait for my reply. I look around the room for an ally, anyone else who might be willing to stand up to Padraic Duffy. But Ray is staring intently at the table. Even Andy looks uncomfortable. The only other person who holds my gaze is Kate, who simply shakes her head.

I take a step back, then another, before looking back at Padraic.

"Of course, sir." My voice is strained, but at least it's respectful. "May I be excused?"

Padraic grunts in confirmation before launching into a new topic of discussion. I tune it out as I leave, wholly consumed by the anger and frustration coursing through my veins.

I make it about halfway down the corridor before a voice stops me.

"Jack?"

I turn to see Kate approaching me. "Thanks for sticking up for me in there," I say sarcastically.

"I took the fall for Lars, asshole," she hisses back.

"I didn't ask you to do that."

Kate considers me for a moment before heaving a heavy sigh. "You never know when to pick your battles, do you?"

"He was treating me like a child."

"He's grieving the loss of his son."

"I'm grieving the loss of my brother!" I snap right back.

Kate grabs my arm and holds me fast, sharp nails digging into my skin. "I want revenge for Graham as much as you do, but you're not going to achieve anything if you lose your head."

The warning is clear, but underneath… I stare at her a moment longer to be sure I understand. I have an ally in Kate, after all.

And when we finish with the Maguires, they'll regret ever crossing us.

Chapter Five

Jack

I walk into the lab the next day, relieved to find Ray alone, hunched over his computer as always.

He greets me with a small, sarcastic salute as he spots me. "Jack."

"Hello, Raymond," I reply formally.

"You need your Internet history cleared again?"

I smirk; at least *he* hasn't changed since my demotion. I was starting to get a little bored with people avoiding me.

"That reminds me, how is your sister?" I quip back.

Ray rolls his eyes and keeps typing away. I take this as my sign to pull up a chair.

I lean as casually as I can against his desk. "I need to run a name," I say innocently.

Ray's fingers pause. "What kind of name and where?"

"Schools and colleges here in New York. Anyone around the age of twenty to twenty-five."

"Jack…" Ray stops altogether and turns to look at me. "I can't help you. You heard Padraic—whatever you're planning, I don't want to be a part of it."

I nod at this and pretend to give it some thought. "What if I don't tell you I'm planning anything?"

Ray narrows his eyes at me. "Why schools?"

"I thought you didn't want to be a part of it."

"I don't."

"Okay, then."

"Fine."

There's another pause, and I wait patiently for Ray to crack. After about a minute, he lets out a deep sigh.

"Even if I help you find a lead. *If*," he reiterates with emphasis. "There's no way you're getting out of here without anyone noticing. Not without somehow managing to persuade Andy to give you access to the basement so you can–"

I reach into my pocket and dangle the basement keys in front of him.

"You fucker," Ray gasps.

I smile at him sweetly. "Your discretion would be appreciated."

"You can't do this to me. Padraic will have my head."

"There are two Maguire sisters," I whisper, and Ray's eyebrows shoot up. There's nothing like a valuable piece of information to barter with, and Ray is a connoisseur.

He turns back to his screen and shuts down the windows he was working on. "Two?"

I nod. "The younger one should still be in college."

"That's a leap, Jack. How do you know they came back together?"

I shrug, "That's why I came to you. If it's nothing, it's nothing."

Ray glances around toward the door then back at me. "Fine. But just one look."

"That's all I ask."

He gets to work bringing up all his search engines and plugging in all the school databases he can. In no time at all, he's typing in "Maguire" and hitting Enter.

157 results for "Maguire."

Damn it.

Ray gives me a dry smile. "You want me to print you off the full list?"

"Can you filter these?" I say desperately.

"I said one look," Ray mutters. But he continues to show me the options anyway.

I point at the screen. "There, let's look at those who enrolled in the last month."

Four results for 'Maguire.'

My heart starts to beat faster in my chest as I scan through the names.

Ezra Maguire. Columbia University.

Joel Maguire. Barnard College.

Matthew Maguire-Smith. Rochester Institute of Technology.

Then, finally:

Roisin Maguire. Juilliard.

I stare at the name, committing it to memory. "Well, she sounds Irish enough."

"You really think it's a lead?" Ray says quietly, running the name through social media. A blurry profile picture of a redhead pops up, and he clicks on it. Private. Damn. Ray could break through the encryption, but I don't think he'll let me push "one look" that far.

I bring up my own phone and type 'Roisin Maguire New York' into my preferred search engine. "Probably not."

A link comes up to an event happening tonight. "Hey, Ray?"

"Hm?" he replies as he logs into a few burner accounts, no doubt to try and get Roisin to accept a friend request.

"Did that say she was at Julliard?"

Ray looks at me. "What did you find?"

I turn my phone toward him, and his jaw drops.

***

I lean against the brick building opposite the theater, smoking a cigarette. I don't usually smoke; it's just a bad habit I picked up from Graham to help with the stress.

The show had already started by the time I got here—sneaking out of the Duffy mansion had taken longer than I'd anticipated. But swearing Ray to secrecy was an easy enough task, especially when I promised him he'd be the first person to know if the lead was warm.

Everyone else descended on the hospital, but so far, it seemed like the trail had gone cold there. If I'm right and I can bring Padraic not one but *two* Maguire sisters, he'll have no choice but to reinstate me as a lieutenant. Especially if everyone else fails to deliver even a lead.

I finish my cigarette just as the crowds begin to exit the building, and I scan the crowds for anyone who looks even vaguely familiar. As predicted, the off-Broadway musical about comic book characters attracted a very particular kind of audience. More than a few are sporting synthetic red hair, making my task all that harder.

I switch tactics and bee-line for the stage door. It's down a quiet alley, and thankfully, there are no crazed fans waiting outside already. I do a quick scan of my surroundings as I approach. No cameras. Good. I reach for the handle and find it unlocked.

Could it really be this easy? I'm just going to walk straight in?

Only, as I push down the handle, the door swings open, and I come face-to-face with a startled brunette.

"Oh!" she huffs as she regains her balance. With my arm as her anchor. "I'm sorry, I didn't think anyone would be coming in."

She snatches her hand away as soon as she realizes her mistake and looks up at me—another apology on her pretty lips.

But the words don't come out.

Our eyes meet, and it's like someone has blown the air out of my lungs. Her soft features gawk at me, no doubt a mirror of my own expression. Eyes like melted chocolate stare deep into mine. I'm transfixed by the dimple in her mouth, the kindness of her expression, and the way her dark hair falls perfectly around her face. I've never seen anyone so lovely in my entire life.

Her heart-shaped face suddenly fills with color, and she looks away, releasing me.

"It's quite all right," I say slowly, hoping she might look at me again.

I'm rewarded with a smile so sweet it makes my chest ache. She steps to one side and holds open the door. "Did you want to come in?"

"Yes," I say, stepping forward automatically before reconsidering. "Well, maybe not."

"Maybe not?"

It's like someone has put this woman in my path just to mess with me. She has the most distracting face; I can barely remember why I'm here. My money is on Graham's ghost. Asshole.

"I'm looking for someone," I reply finally.

The woman brightens at that. "Maybe I could help? I'm not part of the show, but I know a few people."

"Great. Excellent," I scramble to remember the right name. "I'm looking for Roisin?"

If I wasn't staring so intently at her eyes, I might have missed the way they dimmed ever so slightly as she repeated the name. "Roisin?"

"Yes."

The woman points past me back into the theater. "The cast has gone out for drinks already, but I can show you to her dressing table if you want to leave a gift or something."

"She's gone?" Damn it. I look back down the alley toward the busy street. "Any idea where they went for drinks?"

"Sorry, no," the woman says brightly. The smile on her face doesn't waver a fraction. "The show is on tomorrow, though, if you want to see her in person. Although I have to warn you, you might have some competition."

51

I do a double take. "What?"

The woman looks me up and down. "Competition, you know, for Roisin? The last guy came with flowers."

I blink at her before it clicks into place. "Right."

"She's not usually interested in fans, but… I imagine she'd make an exception for you," she says casually.

I tilt my head at her, unable to resist a follow-up. "And why is that?"

The woman's cheeks color again, and something inside me growls in satisfaction.

"You know, um…" She takes a second to recompose herself. "Comic book fans don't usually look like you."

"Well, I could say the same about you."

Her eyebrows shoot up in surprise. "Oh… well…."

As I take a step closer to her, I tell myself it's because this woman clearly knows Roisin, and she's my best lead to finding her. I tell myself it would be a perfect opportunity to get to know the enemy before I strike. I tell myself I'm a professional and not going to get another opportunity like this.

But the problem is I want more of her. From the moment she touched my arm, my body has been begging for her to touch me again.

There is nothing professional about the way I corner her and lean an arm against the doorframe above her head.

"I'm not into actresses," I say with a smirk. "I just represent a large family… organization that is interested in potentially moving her career somewhere more public."

Her jaw drops. "Y-you're an agent? I'm so sorry… I thought…"

"It's okay," I brush her off quickly. "I'll be back tomorrow. Dinner plans can always be rearranged."

She raises a perfect eyebrow at me. "Dinner? That's… You're quite sure of yourself."

"I'm good at what I do."

It's a gamble, and I wrack my brain to figure out where we are and how I can pull a reservation out of thin air. But if it plants a seed that takes root… I could be one step closer to finding Roisin by the end of the night. Spending more time with this woman is just an added bonus.

"Which is what, convincing women to have dinner with you?"

"Persuading women that an evening with me could change their life."

She bites her lip a little as if concealing her amusement. "If they need persuading, you're probably not as good as you think."

I smirk at her. "Would you like to find out?"

There's a beat where I just stand over her, challenging her to move closer. The air between us is thick with intense electricity. For a moment, I think she's going to give in to me and close the distance between us.

But something rational flickers across her eyes, and she ducks out from under me quickly, clearing her throat. "Well, I wish you luck tomorrow."

I straighten up with a sigh. It was worth a shot. "Will I see you then?"

"I have to go back to work," she admits, albeit dejectedly.

"Well," I say without moving an inch, "I suppose this is goodbye then."

"Yes… um… goodbye… er?"

I reach out a hand for her to shake. "Jack."

She takes it. "Aimee."

I don't let go of her hand. The feeling of it slotted perfectly in mine is intoxicating. I don't want to say goodbye to her; I don't want to leave now, knowing I might lose her in the crowds of New York and never see her again. It's such a strange and impulsive idea—but I've never been one to resist temptation like this.

I give it one last shot.

"You know, I would hate for this dinner reservation to go to waste…."

"I would love to," Aimee blurts out.

It's adorable, optimistic, *hopeful*. Everything I'm not, but everything I *want*.

I feel my face split into a huge smile.

"Then it's a date."

Chapter Six

Aimee

One minute I was watching a very mediocre musical and making small talk with a sound technician, cursing out every movie that ever told me New York was just a romantic fantasy waiting to happen.

The next minute I bump into the most attractive man I have ever met. A gorgeous, leather jacket-clad casting agent is shamelessly coming on to me in the middle of an alleyway.

I'm tempted to look around for cameras because this right here isn't real life. Handsome strangers don't just waltz up to you and offer to take you out for dinner on a whim. Surely Roisin or someone is paying this guy?

But as we walk through the streets of New York together, it becomes apparent that whatever this is, it's really happening. I don't miss the way the women we pass do a double take at Jack as they walk by. Yet the man himself has barely taken his eyes off me.

"So," I say, raising an unimpressed brow at a blonde woman who's practically gawking at him. "Where are we going?"

"My family owns a hotel just up here," Jack replies as if telling me the weather.

It's my turn to gawk at him. "Sorry, did you just say you *own* a hotel?"

"My father does," he clarifies.

I shake my head. "Please tell me it's like a cutesy little B&B with no air-con and not like—"

We come to a stop outside a sleek skyrise with a concierge out front. Jack looks at me expectantly.

"—some sleek sky rise with a concierge out front," I finish with a mutter.

"I can find us a B&B if you'd prefer," Jack teases. "But I promise you, the restaurant here is better than anywhere else in the city."

I scowl at him. "Does your family pay you to do promotion?"

He laughs loudly at this and simply takes my hand and walks us up to the door.

Before we enter, he comes to an abrupt halt and looks at me with an unreadable expression on his face. "Could you, er… wait here a moment?"

"Why?"

"I just need to sort something out with reception."

I nod as innocently as I can as he turns away and approaches the front desk. I count three seconds before quietly following behind.

Was it growing up in the mob that made me suspicious? I wonder. Or is it something I'm naturally prone to? Either way, this guy is already too good to be true. In my experience, that's usually because they are.

The inside of the hotel is a tasteful fusion of high-end minimalism and historical pieces. Huge Renaissance-style masterpieces litter the walls, and I take a seat by the interior fountain to eavesdrop on Jack's conversation.

"Good evening, sir!" the cheerful receptionist greets him in clear recognition. At least he wasn't lying about knowing the place.

I watch as Jack nods in response. "Evening."

"My apologies, we weren't expecting you."

I lean forward a little.

"Don't apologize; this is an impromptu visit." Jack brushes it off. "I need a table for two in the sky lounge, somewhere discreet."

"Of course, sir, I'll let them know you're on your way up."

I watch as Jack pulls something from his jacket and places it on the counter before leaning in closer to say something I can't quite make out.

The receptionist merely smiles in response. "Have a good evening, sir."

With a knock at the counter, Jack turns around with a satisfied smile. Before he spots me and his face drops entirely.

He strides over sheepishly. "Listen—"

"You never had a reservation, did you?" I accuse, unable to keep the smile from my face.

Jack's shoulders sag in relief. "Can you blame me for wanting to spend more time with you?"

I stand, brushing off my dress as I do. "You could have just asked."

"Would you have said yes?"

I look up at him, suddenly feeling quite vulnerable under the intensity of his gaze. "Yes."

He gives me that heart-wrenching smile again and offers me his arm. I take it carefully and allow myself a moment of indulgence to admire the subtle texture of the muscles beneath his shirt.

Jack leads me to an elevator, and we ride it all the way to the top. It's so high, I can feel my ears pop slightly—but it's worth it as soon as we step out into the restaurant. Every wall is made entirely of glass, forming a huge dome that offers a 360-degree view of the city below. And the view is simply breathtaking.

"You're not scared of heights, are you?" Jack says, leaning in a little too close to be casual.

I simply shake my head, and he takes my hand. He leads me through the restaurant toward the far edge of the room, where a private booth has already been set up for use. Whoever this man is, he clearly wasn't lying about having friends in high places. Quite literally, it seems, in this case.

Jack shows me to my seat, but I bypass him altogether to press my face up against the glass. I've always loved looking at New York like this, the way all the tiny cars move through the streets, watching the lights in the high rises flicker on and off. A city that never sleeps.

It takes me a moment to remember I have company, and I turn around to see Jack looking at me with soft, hazel eyes and that cocky little smile of his.

I clear my throat and straighten up. "I suppose this is where you take all your actresses, then?"

"Only the good ones," he teases back.

We both take a seat just as a waiter appears to take our drink order. I hesitate a little; this doesn't really seem like the place to do two-for-one cocktails, and my paycheck isn't coming through until the end of the month.

Jack, however, seems unperturbed. "Red or white?"

"Erm… white, I guess?" I say a little awkwardly.

Jack nods and reels off a French-sounding name that the waiter disappears to fetch.

"Don't look so concerned," Jack says after glancing back at me. "This will all go on my father's tab."

"Are you sure?"

Jack chuckles a little. "In fact, if you wanted to order some champagne too, I'd encourage it."

I look at him curiously. "Are you and Daddy not seeing eye to eye?"

"Let's call it creative differences."

The waiter returns with our wine and takes our food order. All the while, Jack doesn't break eye contact. I nervously take a sip of wine, and holy crap, it tastes good. I can't remember the last time I drank a wine that wasn't Two Buck Chuck.

Whatever Jack sees on my face makes him smile, and he finally releases me from his gaze to nurse his own glass.

"So…" I say in an attempt to break through the tension. "Did you say the agency was a family business?"

Jack hides his smile with a glass. "Emphasis on family."

"You must represent some important people," I say, glancing around the room. Again, I'm overcome by the magnificence of it all. "Who's the most famous person you've ever met?"

"I would hate to incriminate anyone like that," Jack teases. "What about you? If you're not an actress, what were you doing backstage?"

"I thought I told you I'm the security detail," I joke back. "I keep all the men vying for Roisin's affection at bay."

Despite my subtle deflection, I can see the cogs beginning to turn in Jack's head. "By dating them yourself?"

"It's a new technique that I'm trying."

The real technique is actually trying to be so overly cautious about sharing my personal details that Jack will leave this date knowing less than nothing about me. I don't want another encounter with the mob, and they're probably looking for me as we speak. So, I can't give up any information that might lead them back to me. No matter how attractive Jack looks right now.

Okay, well, maybe until I at least know I can trust him. Old families always have an annoying way of knowing each other, so I can't rule it out just yet… But giving him my number should be fine… right?

"How do you know Roisin?" he asks casually.

"Pretty well," I tell him, equally nonchalant. "I can tell you she's exactly the kind of person you'd want to represent, if that's what you mean."

He narrows his eyes at me. Crap, he's figured out what I'm doing. "Remind me why I should trust your judgment of character?"

"Well, I'm here, aren't I?" I say lightly.

He sits back in his chair with a shake of his head and raises his wine to me. "Touché."

The food arrives at that moment, and it smells incredible. I bask in the aromas for a moment before digging in heartily—not caring that Jack is watching me again.

"Well, if you're not going to tell me about yourself, what shall we talk about?"

"Perhaps a game?" I reply, giving him a sarcastic look.

"Fine," Jack says, looking more than a little bemused. "I'm going to guess something about you, and you have to tell me if it's true or not."

I consider the pros and cons of this, balancing my "no personal details" plan against my intrigue with the man in front of me. "Then I get to guess about you?"

"Why not?"

"All right," I concede. "Hit me."

He examines me a little before replying. "You work in a high-pressure environment, which means sometimes you forget or don't have time to eat."

My surprise must be evident on my face, because Jack begins to chuckle.

"Drink," he instructs.

"So this is a drinking game now?"

"May as well make this interesting."

I take a sip of wine without breaking disgruntled eye contact. "Fine. My turn."

I look him up and down. His leather jacket is thrown carelessly across the back of his chair, revealing a shirt that (on closer inspection) is probably worth more than my rent. His sleeves are rolled up to his elbows, and my eyes hone in on the classic timepiece on his wrist.

"Your family is old money," I conclude.

He grins at me and takes a sip of wine. "Very good."

"You're not that hard to read," I tease.

"You're new to New York," he counters.

I open my mouth to disagree but then remember I'm supposed to be keeping a low profile. I take a sip. "How did you know?"

"You looked like a kid on Christmas when you were looking out that window."

I glance back at it again and sigh a little. "It's a beautiful view."

"Hmm…" Jack replies in agreement. Only when I turn back to him, he's looking straight at me.

I can feel the blush spreading over my cheeks. It's so corny. Logically, I know it is. So why do I feel like my heart is about to burst out of my chest?

"Your turn," Jack reminds me, nudging my leg a little with his hand.

The feeling sends shivers of delight up my spine, and I wrack my brain to try and distract myself. I end up looking directly at his face, really looking at it.

His dark hair sweeps perfectly away from his face, fading down the sides of his head. Clean-shaven, but a shadow forming across his strong jawline that's slightly uneven on one side, making him look like he's smirking even when he's not. And his eyes… Dear God. Framed by thick brows and a scattering of near-invisible scars, they're hypnotic. I could get lost in his hazel eyes for hours.

"I'd say military service, but… something tells me you don't have the discipline."

Jack barks a laugh at that. "I'm disciplined when it counts."

I refuse to let the mischievous sparkle in his eye distract me, but when his hand touches my thigh again, I can't help but falter.

"Um… I was thinking maybe some kind of… sport?" I finish lamely.

Jack strokes my leg encouragingly. "Sport?"

"Like a contact sport."

"Ah," Jack replies, looking far too pleased with himself as he raises his glass to his lips. "You're a clever girl."

His praise does something to me I can't quite explain, but it has me squirming in my seat. I clear my throat. "What do you play?"

"I box," he says easily.

"Like, with the gloves and everything?"

Jack puts his hands out in front of me, revealing his hardened knuckles. "Bare-knuckle.."

Bare-knuckle boxing. I shudder, remembering how one of my first patients back in LA received a nasty slash across his eye from a BKB fight. "Isn't that dangerous?"

Jack seems to consider this. "For the other guy, sure."

I can't help but giggle at his show of unyielding confidence, only to feel his soft hazel eyes on me again.

I scowl at him. "You have to stop staring at me like that."

"Why?"

"It's unnerving."

"But you're so very beautiful."

His eyes go dark as he looks me over hungrily. There's nothing I want more than to reach over and start tracing the scars across his brow. To feel his skin on mine…

I swallow before my imagination gets away from me. That wine has clearly gone straight to my head.

"So, what did you give the receptionist earlier?" I say, trying to change the subject.

Jack looks a little surprised. "You saw that?"

"Mmhmm," I confirm, waiting for him to answer the original question.

Jack smirks and leans in closer. His hand returns to my thigh, stroking up a little higher, and I feel myself gravitating toward him like a magnet. "Just a little incentive not to give away the master suite this evening."

My breath catches, and I let it out shakily. "You're very sure of yourself, aren't you?"

"I'm good at what I do."

The unspoken question hovers in the air between us.

I pick up my glass to disguise the slight shake in my hand. "I have work tomorrow evening."

"Then don't stay until the evening."

I swirl what's left of my wine in my glass, wondering why this feels like such a compelling argument. But as I take the last sip, I figure out why.

My sister's words come back to me.

We're young, free, and single in New York City. We can be whoever we want to be.

Tonight, I want to be the kind of girl that lets herself be seduced by a handsome, rich stranger.

Chapter Seven

Aimee

Jack pulls me through the hotel, pointing out more of the beautiful paintings when he notices me staring at them in passing. The views out of the windows are stunning on every corridor we turn down, and the neon lights cast his features in mysterious darkness.

Finally, we reach the door at the very end. Jack taps something against the handle and opens it.

The lights turn on automatically, illuminating the two floors in a dimmed yellow light. Looking over Jack's shoulder, I swear I can make out floor-to-ceiling windows and an *infinity pool.*

"Is that…"

Jack turns back to me, releasing my hand. "We can go swimming if you'd like."

"You're joking." I don't bother trying to hide how impressed I am. Because, honestly, how could I not be?

As the door closes behind me, I'm suddenly very aware that we're alone in a hotel room. Desire pulses through me as we stare at each other, and I can feel myself breathing heavily. His hazel eyes bore into mine. There's something wild about the way he looks at me that only makes me want him more.

He steps forward once, twice, cornering me again against the door like he did when we first met. Was that only a few hours ago? It feels like we've been playing this game for a lifetime, teasing each other like this. His arm goes above my head, and he leans in. My breathing hitches, mingling with his, and I freeze.

It's only been a few hours.

"Is this what you want?" he whispers as if sensing my hesitation. Giving me space to deny him, deny *this*. This thing between us that's so intense I can barely breathe.

I realize at that moment that I couldn't fight it. That there's no need to fight it.

"Yes," I breathe back.

He pushes me back against the closed door, and his mouth crushes into mine.

The feeling is so electric I almost moan out loud. It's like every bone in my body has been set alight with passion, and I crumble into him, my legs suddenly too weak to hold me up.

But his hand is suddenly there, holding my chin so he can take his time savoring my every response. Soft kisses at first, then longer ones. Ones that beg me to open my lips so he can explore my mouth. Every kiss is seemingly designed to unravel me more and more until I submit to him.

My arms reach out to cling to his neck, bringing him ever closer. I want more. I *need* more of him.

I bite at his bottom lip, and he pulls away with a hiss.

"Sorry," I say quickly, suddenly feeling very exposed without his body so close to mine.

But if his eyes were wild before, they're *feral* now.

"Don't you fucking dare apologize," he growls.

"I–"

He's suddenly close again, only this time, his arms encircle me, and he lifts me from the floor. My legs wrap around his waist as he begins laying filthy kisses against my chest, my neck. I can't get enough of him.

"I don't want to hear how sorry you are that you're with me."

"I'm not," I say, searching desperately for his lips with mine.

"I've been thinking about fucking you all night." He presses his impressive bulge against me, and I gasp.

I finally find his mouth and bite down on his lip again. The effect is instant; I can feel him twitch beneath me as a growl rumbles through his chest.

"I've been waiting for you to fuck me all night," I whisper against his lips, emboldened by the sudden power I seem to have over him.

We're moving, crashing through the room while hungrily devouring each other. His whole body is addictive. Every touch, every kiss makes my skin, my blood, all of me scream out for more. I don't know where his shirt goes or when my dress begins hanging from my waist, but I couldn't be more grateful for it. The feel of his skin against mine is equal parts torment and pleasure.

I claw at him desperately, whimpering, and he seems to know exactly what I want. One moment I'm attached to him; the next, I'm being laid down on a huge bed. His fingers deftly free me from the constraints of my bra and pull down my dress the rest of the way.

Jack sits back and just seems to admire me for a moment. All laid out and ready for him to consume.

"Close your eyes," he demands, and I obey.

I feel his tongue first. Then his hands. Trailing their way up my bare legs. Nothing has ever felt so tantalizing and frustrating in all my life. Just imagining his face there, between my legs…

I risk a peek at him, and the sensation immediately stops.

"Aimee."

My eyes close again. There's nothing I can do but lie there and let him explore me, tease me. The wetness between my legs is becoming excruciating to bear without any kind of friction.

So I touch myself. I massage my tits, and I groan a stupid, sexy sound I've only ever heard in porn.

The sensation stops again.

Suddenly, Jack is on top of me, and my eyes flash open. He's completely naked—his hard cock pressed into my stomach.

"Don't do that again unless I *make* you. Are we clear?"

I stare up at him in challenge and let the throaty sound escape my lips again.

His fingers slip beneath my underwear, and the sounds I make when my back arches into his touch are genuine and *loud*. When he stops, I'm gasping for air.

"What did I tell you?" He smirks at me arrogantly.

"Please," I beg, reaching up for his lips again.

There's a tear and a slight wonderful sting as my panties are ripped from my body, and Jack's fingers work me again. All conscious thoughts leave me when he speeds up his rhythm, kissing my neck as I groan over and over and over until I'm spilling out onto his hand.

"Good," he says gruffly in my ear as I quiver beneath him.

"Fuck."

Jack smirks again. "Turn over."

My eyes go wide as his strong hands maneuver me onto my front and raise my ass into the air. He presses his cock against me, and I tremble a little and reach out, grabbing onto a pillow.

But his arm is suddenly there, stopping me.

"No, I want to hear you make that sound again."

It's the only warning I get before he slides into me to the hilt.

I see stars. The scream I let out is more than I ever could have imitated. The sheer *size* of him inside of me makes me wonder how he didn't just split me in two. When he withdraws again, I only have a moment to gather myself before he enters me again.

But this time, I'm ready for him. This time I lean into him, pushing him impossibly further. He lets out a hiss in my ear, and suddenly his hand is right there, around my neck, tilting me up to him.

He kisses me so sweetly I lose all the breath inside my lungs.

"I'm going to fuck you now. And you're going to take it, aren't you?"

"Yes," I breathe against his lips.

"I want to hear you scream."

"Yes!" I say louder.

Jack withdraws and grabs hold of my waist, "That's my girl."

This time when he enters me, he withdraws quickly and then slams straight back in. Over and over and over and over and… Oh my God.

My fingers grip desperately at the sheets, trying to find any kind of purchase against the relentless force behind me. But when I come again, there's so little strength left in my body I can barely hold myself up. No one has ever made me feel this way. So desperate for release and yet so weak to it. When Jack lifts my hips higher, I submit to him entirely.

The only thing that matters is the feeling of him inside of me again and again and again. The sounds of him coming undone. Every groan, every breath sends shivers of delight down my spine.

Suddenly he grabs my neck again and pulls me in closer. His mouth crashes against mine as he shivers and finds his own release.

I reach up and hang onto his neck, holding him there. We pant together in harmony, and I *feel* an ungodly tension leave his body.

Slowly, wordlessly, we collapse into the bed.

The last thing I remember before sleep captures me are his muscular arms pulling me into his chest.

Chapter Eight

Aimee

Last night was a dream; it had to be. When I open my eyes, I just know I'm going to be back in my tiny apartment, alone and *very* frustrated.

Only when I do…

It's to see unfamiliar bed sheets drawn across my bare chest.

Holy crap.

The room I'm in is *huge*. Completely open plan with a kitchen on one side and a fully stocked bar on the other. But the pièce de résistance is the infinity pool. It starts only a few meters away from the bed, looping around the room and then out onto the glass balcony. I've only ever seen rooms like this on those insane travel blogs.

The only thing that would make this whole situation even more unreal is if Jack had actually stuck around.

Glancing at the empty space next to me, I can't help but feel like a fool for even getting my hopes up.

Last night was… unforgettable. Spontaneous. Two things I'm not known for in the real world and doubt I'll ever get comfortable with. No, a one-night stand is probably for the best. Being around Jack makes me lose my head, which could be really dangerous for us right now.

I sit up and run my fingers through my tangled hair. All I need to do now is somehow convince myself that I'm not feeling the sting of rejection. Maybe a quick swim will help…

"Your hair has a little red in it."

"Jack!" I squeak, pulling the sheets up to cover myself automatically.

The man himself stands at the door, fully dressed with a carton of coffee cups. My heart suddenly pounds a thousand beats a minute. He's here. He came back.

He noticed my hair.

I furiously pull it up on top of my head. "Does it?"

"Must be the New York sunlight." He looks at me a little oddly before waltzing over and placing down the two cups of fresh coffee on the table beside the bed.

"There's sunlight in New York?" I tease as he turns and places an arm on either side of me.

When he bends down to kiss me, I accept it happily. God, that feels nice.

"Good morning," he whispers against my lips.

"Mmm…" I reply.

I feel the corners of his mouth turn up in a smile. "Coherent."

I push him away playfully and glance at the table. "Did you bring me coffee?"

"I didn't know what you liked, but—"

He cuts himself off when he realizes I've already made a grab for the cup and begun drinking it enthusiastically.

"This is perfect," I say in between gulps.

"I brought milk and sugar if you'd like?" he tries again.

I shake my head. "Black is fine. I never usually have time to find milk when I'm working, so it kinda became a habit."

"And where would work be, exactly?" Jack presses.

The coffee cup crumples a little in my hand, and I place it as casually as I can back on the table.

"That's kind of a second date sort of question," I reply lightly, hoping he'll just drop it.

"Aimee."

"What?"

He clasps his hands together, taking in a deep breath. "I need to know."

I freeze. "Need to know what?"

"If you're… you know…" Jack suddenly looks serious.

If I wasn't so terrified that I'd somehow given myself away and Jack was about to sell me out to my enemy—or worse, my *family*—I might have thought the look on his face was incredibly cute.

"I'm what?" I reply calmly.

"I don't know! Like an escort or something."

I blink at him. Then again. Taking in his nervous body language, the way he's grabbing at his clasped hands.

He's being deadly serious.

"You think I'm a *what?*"

I leap up from the bed, and he staggers back a step or two, throwing his hands in the air in surrender.

"I'm sorry, okay? You were just being so elusive, I thought—"

"Do I look like a sex worker to you?" My voice rises in disbelief.

Jack goes white as a sheet, taking another few steps back. "No! I mean, you're beautiful and, quite frankly, incredible in bed—"

I push him for that. My hands connect with his rock-hard abs, and he has the decency to stagger back a little, even though I'm fairly certain he didn't feel it at all.

"I completely respect sex work as a viable profession. It's just that I had an amazing night, and I wanted to make sure—"

I square up to him. "Choose your next words very. *Very*. Carefully."

For all his confidence, Jack finally seems to be at a loss.

"I wanted to make sure I was the best you'd ever had?"

I push him again. Hard.

… And he falls into the pool with an almighty splash.

When he resurfaces, the look of pure shock, outrage, and confusion on his face immediately has me doubling over in laughter. His shirt balloons around his ears, and he tries to remove it with little success, only making me laugh even harder. I have to dab away the tears that formed in my eyes by the time he finally removes it.

"Guess I deserved that," he mutters, and when I look up at him again, his expression has lost some of its bite.

I go to sit on the edge of the pool, only to be rewarded with a shake of Jack's hair.

"Hey!" I whine half-heartedly as the splatter of droplets hits me.

He simply wades over, encircling me with his arms, and I lean into the embrace happily. For all my shouting, I wasn't all that offended—not really. Besides, it's not like I gave him anything else to work with.

"Can you forgive me?" he says softly.

I offer him a sweet smile. "Yes."

"Can you tell me just a little about yourself?"

I kiss him, letting my lips linger there a moment before resting my forehead against his. "I'm a very private person."

"I figured that much," Jack replies quietly.

There's this stupid, irrational part of me that wants to lay myself bare before this man and let him see every single thing I've ever done, ever been through. It's such a shocking revelation that the impact knocks the breath out of me. The Aimee from a month ago—hell, the Aimee from *yesterday*— would wring my neck for thinking something like that.

But there's just something about Jack. The way he's so gentle and yet so firm with me, the way his desires are written all over his face, makes me want to trust him. He's exactly the kind of man I could let fall in love with me because I can see a world where I fall head over heels for him too.

But to do any of that, you need to be able to let the other person in. And right now, I know I can't do that. I can't risk Roisin's safety or my sanity.

The problem is, I *want* to trust him. Desperately. Despite how reckless that would be.

"I…" I begin, then pause. "Things are kinda complicated for me right now."

I can feel him emotionally withdraw as the words leave my mouth.

"No, wait. I'm not saying this right." I lay a hand on his chest. "I wasn't expecting *this* to happen."

Jack's hand tilts my chin up, and my eyes meet with him. "For what it's worth, me neither."

"And I really like… *this*," I whisper.

"Then keep liking it."

I smile at his sincerity. "I'd like to trust you. Very much."

"You don't trust me?" he replies with mock outrage.

"I wouldn't take it personally," I say, rolling my eyes. "I don't trust anyone."

He nods at this. "I suppose I can accept that. We did meet yesterday."

"Exactly."

Jack leans in and kisses me again. "I'm not asking for your life story. I just want to know something real about you so that when you disappear, I can find a way to make *this* make sense."

His words pierce my icy heart like a knife.

"Who the fuck do you think are you, Jack?" I whisper against his lips before kissing him again. "Coming into my life and saying stuff like that to me."

He kisses me back vigorously. "I can be romantic when I need to be."

We stay like that for a moment. Our tongues dance together as the pool ripples around us. My bare chest pressed up against his, his hands tangling themselves in my hair.

When he pulls away, I'm entirely breathless, and my lips feel swollen.

"Come on," Jack says, pulling me fully into the water. "I want to show you this view."

We swim over to the sheet that separates the room from the balcony, and Jack opens it wide for me to wade through.

The brisk morning air bites at my cheeks as I swim out to the edge of the infinity pool. We're not as high as the restaurant—a fact I'm insanely grateful for, considering there's no glass in the way to stop me from falling off the edge. But the view is magnificent all the same.

I can see the little dots of people making their morning commutes to work or heading to the grocery store, or even heading home after a long night. I wonder absently if Roisin is okay. She went out with all the other cast and crew members after the show last night and, knowing her, she might be one of those stragglers carrying their heels at seven AM.

"You like it?" Jack says from behind me.

I look back at him over my shoulder. "I'm a little cold."

He takes the hint immediately and wraps his strong arms around me, and pulls me into his chest. His body heat instantly relaxes me, and we stand there for a moment, watching the lives of busy people down below.

"I always wanted to live in an apartment above the city," I say, finally finding something to be honest about.

Jack kisses me on the back of the head as if to say: *Keep going.*

"We used to live in this big old house; it was practically falling apart by the time we left. But when I look at cities like this, I always knew I wanted more."

"Where do you live now?"

I turn around to face him. "In an apartment, about halfway up."

"I'd say you're making progress then," Jack says with a cocky smile. "Come on, let's go back in; I don't want you catching a cold."

I shake my head. "I'm more likely to catch a cold on the subway on my way home."

"All the same," Jack insists. "I'd rather not fuck you again with the whole world watching."

I can feel my face filling with color, but I allow him to lift me up and carry me back inside. He doesn't waste much time, his mouth crashes into mine, and his arms tighten around my waist, my ass.

I grunt in frustration when I realize he's still wearing pants. Pants that will no doubt be more difficult to remove than his shirt.

Jack chuckles at me. "Are you really that desperate for me again?"

"If I say 'yes,' will you undress quicker?" I quip back.

The next kiss is so hard and passionate that it makes my head spin. It promises me everything, adoration, satisfaction... It makes me long for his touch even though we are already so tightly wrapped together.

An intense chirp from the hotel phone goes off, cutting harshly through our moment.

Jack withdraws, resting his head against mine. "I'm sorry," he says quietly.

"Do you really need to take that?"

He grimaces. "I think my father may have seen the bill we left him last night."

He kisses me softly before pulling away completely. I watch as he effortlessly swims to the side of the pool and pulls himself out. Water drips tantalizingly down his back as he rises.

He keeps his back to me as he picks up the phone, and he mutters quietly into the receiver. Without glancing my way, he heads back into the bathroom.

"Is everything okay?" I call out to him.

When he returns a moment later, a towel replaces his sodden pants, and there's another in his hand as he dries himself off. "It will be."

"You're leaving?"

Jack doesn't reply as he strides over to the walk-in closet and pulls out some fresh clothes. I swim closer to the side of the pool, a sinking feeling in my stomach.

"Stay as long as you like," he says finally, now fully dressed. "Make yourself at home."

"Will I…" I swallow down the sudden nerves. "Will I see you again?"

He finally turns to look at me. There's a hunger in his eyes I recognize from last night. Now, as he looks at my soaking wet, naked body, it makes me flush.

"You will call me when you get home safe," he replies.

"I don't have your number," I counter.

He smirks, grabbing a pen from the side and scribbling something down on a napkin. "You do now."

"Okay. But…"

Jack strides over and crouches down by the poolside. I have to stand on my toes to kiss him goodbye.

"Don't worry, Aimee. We'll see each other again."

***

Despite his reassurances, when Jack leaves, I can't help but feel completely out of my depth. It's like a drowning sensation in my throat as if I'm watching him walk away forever, and I'm helpless to stop it.

It's pathetic, and I tell myself as much as I get out of the pool and head for the bathroom to shower. There's no reason for me to feel this intensely about someone I only met yesterday. It doesn't matter how good the sex is.

In the shower, I come face-to-face with one of the most complicated systems to turn on a stream of water that I have ever seen. After attempting to wash my hair in something called 'violet steam' and accidentally setting off what felt like jet washers on my feet, I finally find a setting that seems relatively normal. Only to face my next problem: which of the thousands of bath products lined up should I even be using?

By the time I leave the bathroom again, it's almost midday. The products I didn't use up go straight into my bag to stock up my own bathroom back home. Jack did say to make myself at home, after all. Freebies are freebies.

Besides, if, for some reason, Roisin isn't sound asleep when I get home, I can definitely use them to bribe her. I do feel a little guilty about not texting her where I was or who I was with. She could be sitting at home right now worrying about me. But that means she'd have to notice I wasn't back already, which, considering how late she stays out usually, isn't hugely likely. At least, that's what I tell myself as I make my way home.

I scramble as quietly as I can to find my apartment keys and slot them in carefully. The old door gives out a comically loud 'squeak' as I open it, and I wince before stepping through.

I immediately glance at Roisin's door. Closed. Good, that means she's probably still in bed. If she's in a deep enough sleep, the door probably won't have woken her up…

"Good morning!"

Shit.

I turn to see Roisin leaning against the kitchen counter, coffee in hand. I don't bother correcting her that it's past midday; by the looks of things, she's only just woken up herself.

"Morning," I mumble.

"Good night?"

I nod sheepishly. "Yes, the musical was fantastic, Roshe. Congratulations."

"It sucked, and you know it." She looks me up and down, no doubt taking in the crumpled dress I wore the night before. "I thought you were heading home?"

"I… got a little sidetracked?" I reply tentatively.

Luckily, on the spectrum of concern and amusement, Roisin seems to be leaning toward the latter. "Was it the sound technician?"

I gag a little. "No, it wasn't the sound technician, Jesus."

"Then who?"

I hesitate a moment. There's no way she'd believe me even if I told her. But if I don't give her all the details now, she'll get the story out of me one way or another.

"There was an agent who came by looking for you," I concede.

Roisin's eyes go wide. "For me? Oh my god, was it Chris from *talentZ*? Douglas said he might show up, but I didn't think he'd actually come. Oh my God, did he say anything about me?"

I shake my head. "It was someone called Jack? I didn't get a surname, but his family owns a hotel downtown, so I think maybe it was a bigger agency."

"Jack?" Roisin frowns. "Did he say who he represented?"

"Nope, sorry."

"Leave a card or anything?"

I dig out the napkin from my bag and show it to her. "I have his number?"

"Aimee!" Roisin practically squeals. "You slept with my future agent?"

"I didn't mean to! He was just... very persuasive."

Roisin grins at me wildly and grabs onto my hand. "You need to tell me everything. Now."

By the time I finish the full story, Roisin's jaw is on the floor, and we've migrated to the couch.

"Wow."

"I know."

"I'm so proud of you."

I give her an incredulous look. "For hooking up with a bazillionaire?"

"For getting yourself out there! Doing something spontaneous for once," she replies earnestly.

She's right, of course; it's been a long time since I've actually been able to let loose like that. There's just something about Jack that made me lose my inhibitions and take that chance.

"Do you think you'll see him again?" Roisin presses excitedly.

Don't worry, Aimee. We'll see each other again.

At the moment, I didn't doubt it for a second, but the moment he left…. "I think you'll see him first; he said he was going to the show again tonight."

Roisin deflates. "Ah… yeah, about that."

"What?" My attention snaps to her immediately.

"Well… last night got a bit wild for me too…."

Shit. "Roisin—"

"I promise I didn't do anything, okay? Just alcohol," she insists.

I give her a look

"Okay, maybe a bit too much alcohol," she concedes. "But it was a party, and there's just this whole drinking culture after a big show and–"

"It's okay, Roshe, I trust you," I say before she can work herself up too much. "I just want you to be safe."

She sighs. "I know. I am."

"So what happened?"

Roisin readjusts her sitting position before she launches in. "The director got into a fight with the lead actor over something super stupid. Apparently, his vision wasn't to make the show a musical at all, but the casting director had hired a professional singer for the lead, so it had been like a waste not to use him, you know?"

I shake my head. "Sure."

"To be honest, this whole time, the director has been a bit of an asshole. So, we all decided to strike," Roisin finally concludes.

"You're striking a musical? I thought you weren't getting paid anyway?"

"This is about working conditions, Aimee," Roisin replies. "Also, there's a party at Coney Island tonight, and we all really wanted to go."

I hold my head in my hands. "I can't believe you."

"You should come!"

"I have work," I point out. The "some of us have to" is implied by my tone.

Ever oblivious, Roisin counters, "You don't; Dr. Lous called and said your lanyard has been delayed again."

"Again? Those sloths in admin, I swear to God." I've already been off work for two days. What am I supposed to do with myself now?

Roisin leans back on the couch and closes her eyes. "I don't see why you're so adamant about changing your name anyway."

"It's just a precaution, Roshe. You know me."

"I do; that's why I just want to make sure you're being rational."

"I'm fine." I look down at my hands. "I was thinking, though, maybe you should start going by a stage name?"

She cracks an eye open to look at me. "That doesn't sound very rational."

"I just… With Juilliard and Jack showing up… What happens when you get famous, Roshe?"

"We buy a better apartment."

"I'm being serious."

Roisin sits up again, anger beginning to show on her tight lips. "What's wrong with Roisin Maguire?"

I sigh.

There's only one way she might listen to me, and as much as I don't want to play this card, I know it will be for the best in the long run.

"Roisin Maguire spent two and a half months in rehab."

Roisin recoils slightly, and I instantly regret being so harsh. "I just mean, I don't want people to find out the wrong way and then hurt you because of it."

"Are you ashamed of me?"

"No!"

"Because I'm not!" She jumps up and starts pacing across the floor. "If people find out, they find out. I'm not hiding from my past."

"I'm just trying to—"

"Drop it, okay? This isn't something you need to protect me from."

When I don't reply, she storms away to her room—only to hesitate at the door. I watch as her shoulders rise and fall, and she takes back control of her breathing.

I take the opportunity to say quietly, "I don't want to be in a fight."

When she turns back to look at me, she looks completely exhausted. "Look… I'll consider it, okay?"

"That's all I ask."

"But please don't… push me on it again."

"I won't."

"Aimee?"

"Hmm?"

She looks torn about something, so I wait patiently for her to find the right words. But then, finally, she simply sighs and says, "I prefer you as a redhead."

"I'll keep that in mind."

She turns away from me with a tentative smile and heads back into her room, closing the door behind her.

Chapter Nine

Jack

I'm surprised to see Kate waiting for me when I make it down to the hotel foyer. When the receptionist called, he made it sound like Padraic himself had come to carry me home.

Although, to the guy's credit, I'm not sure which of them is more intimidating.

"Please tell me you didn't escape house arrest just to come to Padraic's *hotel?*" she snaps at me as soon as I'm in earshot.

I shrug. "I'm working."

"That's not what Padraic thinks," Kate hisses. "He thinks you came here to rub it in."

"Then he's wrong, isn't he?"

"So you're telling me if I go upstairs right now, I won't find a doe-eyed brunette in the master suite?"

I try my best not to smile a little at the mention of Aimee. The way I left her up there, naked in the pool… Dear God, I don't think I've ever seen anything as beautiful. It makes me more than a little pissed at Kate for forcing me away from her. Especially when she seemed so keen to relive last night's… pleasantries.

But who am I kidding? The sex was amazing, but the whole evening was just otherworldly. It was like I was in an entirely different universe, where I could just spend hours talking and flirting with the most stunning woman I'd ever seen. One where the family business was nothing but a faded memory, and the grief of Graham's death could be kept at bay.

I'm no fool; I know that people like that don't just come into your world without a reason. But whatever I did to deserve her, even for this small respite, I will always be grateful.

Kate taps her foot impatiently, so I shrug again. "Like I said, I've been working."

"Well, could you 'work' a little closer to home next time?" Kate snaps back before storming past me and out the door. She doesn't bother looking back as she calls out, "Walk with me."

I offer the ashen-faced receptionist a sarcastic salute in goodbye before jogging to catch up.

"Do you have any idea what kind of damage control I had to do with him this morning?" Kate scolds me like a child. "You must have realized somewhere in that thick skull of yours that this was a god-awful idea."

We exit the hotel, and I see a parked car with shaded windows waiting for us. Kate's driver nods at us respectfully as we walk toward it.

"Well, let's just say I owe you one for dealing with a temper tantrum and leave it at that," I say as Kate approaches the door.

"This isn't just a tantrum. He's pissed."

I can't help rolling my eyes at how dramatic Kate is. "If he was really that pissed, he wouldn't have sent you."

Kate simply opens the car door. Revealing none other than Padraic himself.

Perhaps Kate wasn't being dramatic.

Because the way Padraic looks at me right now is more than a little pissed.

He's goddamn furious.

I exchange a glance with Kate before sliding into the back seat. Her expression screams, "I told you so" so loud I can almost hear the words.

"Jack," Padraic says stiffly.

Kate sits beside me and begins examining her nails, a picture of indifference. Seems she's done her part and is more than happy to sit back and watch whatever is about to happen unfold. Some ally she is.

The driver hits the gas, and we pull away from the hotel and into the city. All the while, Padraic stares at me as if waiting for me to make the first move. Undoubtedly, he can counter it with whatever punishment he has locked and loaded in his verbal arsenal.

I sigh. "Do you even want to hear my explanation?"

"I don't want to hear another word come out of your goddamn mouth," Padraic replies gruffly. "You made a fool of me coming here, and I will not tolerate this kind of disrespect again. Do you hear me?"

"Yes, sir," I say obediently.

His face colors red. "What did I just say?!"

I almost respond but think better of it. There's no arguing with him when he's like this.

Padraic looks out the window, and I watch as he regains control of his anger before he bothers looking at me again, "I clearly can't trust my men to keep you in, so this is how it's going to go. I'm assigning Morris to you twenty-four seven."

Fucking *Morris*.

The guy I've had to bail out on more than one occasion because he fucked up and started a fight with the wrong person. The guy who's been *banned* from dealing with hostages because of his sadistic tendency to kill them before Padraic can even get an offer on the table.

The same thing must cross Kate's mind as she looks up from her nails with a frown. "Morris is barely a grunt."

"So is he." Padraic thrusts a thumb at me.

I can't maintain my silence a second longer. "You're kidding me."

"Shut up!" Padraic yells, losing his cool. "You will report to him every morning and every goddamn evening. Do I make myself clear?"

"I'm not a child!" I say, matching his anger.

"Yes, you goddamn are." Padraic's eyes are twin flames of pure rage. His anger is barely contained within his shaking frame, and I thank the gods Kate is next to me at that moment. With her here, he won't release his control in case she gets caught in the crossfire. Still, I'm not willing to test that theory.

Instead, I sink back into my chair and lower my head in submission. My pride tastes bitter in my mouth, but I know this isn't a battle I can win right now.

Padraic seems to relax at my display. "You try this again, and the next girl you bring up to one of my hotels will never come out."

***

"Jacky!" Morris greets me with a wicked grin on his face as I approach the apartment complex. One look at the delight in his eyes tells me all I need to know. He's going to make this hell for me.

"Morris," I reply stiffly, walking past him toward the door.

He picks himself up from leaning against the wall and follows me inside. "First day back on the ground, hm?"

God, his voice is already grating on my nerves. "I've worked the ground all my life."

"Aye, but this is the real shit. The roughing up, getting your hands dirty," he says as we climb the stairs up to the second floor. "There's really nothing like the sweet smell of fear up close and personal."

I ignore him, mentally begging him to shut the hell up, and walk ahead down the corridor.

But Morris doesn't seem to take the hint. "No more sitting up in your high tower, boy. Now you're working for *me;* we're going to have a grand old time."

I try not to bristle as I knock on the door. "I don't work for you."

"Sure you do; you're not Padraic's left hand anymore."

"Padraic's left hand" had always been a backhanded compliment, even when I had that seat on the table. Graham was always his right hand from the moment he could hold a gun and count higher than ten. But the seat at Padraic's side was something a bastard like me had to *earn*. I jumped through every hoop he sent my way, making myself invaluable to the family.

But even if Graham was half the man he was, I couldn't have resented him for it. Leadership came so naturally to him, and he helped me more than anyone to get to my position. A position I apparently just lost.

"He assigned you to *me*," Morris continues, leaning up against the doorframe as we wait. "So, if I say hit that guy in there, you hit that guy."

Over my dead body.

"If I say wipe my arse, you wipe my arse."

I move without thinking. Morris is a head shorter than me, so pinning him to the wall is child's play.

The slimy little man grunts in surprise, clawing desperately at the arm I'm resting firmly against his neck.

"You keep pushing this, Morris, and next time you get your ass beaten to a pulp, I'll be there to deliver the final blow. Are we clear?"

He gasps for breath. "Yes, sir."

"Now act like a goddamn professional," I spit before releasing him.

Just as the door opens.

The kid standing there must be fresh out of high school. Behind him, the apartment is dirty in the way people who have no clue how to look after themselves tend to leave their homes. Take-out boxes litter the floor. A pile of dishes spills out of the sink, ready to be washed.

"You know who we are?" I ask calmly, taking little satisfaction at how pale he suddenly becomes.

"Y-yes."

"Can we come in?"

He nods, moving to the side and gesturing for us to enter.

I stride in, Morris close on my heels. "Let's make this quick."

He closes the door behind us and shuffles closer. "Listen… I-I–"

Morris strides forward and strikes the kid across the face. "He said, make it quick."

My jaw tightens; this is not how it's supposed to go.

Nonetheless, the kid scrambles away from Morris and into a nearby room, reappearing a moment later with a plastic bag filled with cash. He empties it onto the coffee table in front of us, brushing the garbage and litter away first.

He looks up at us expectantly.

"Count it," I say, already bored.

The kid nods and begins his task, shuffling the notes into piles of ten. "One… Two… Three…"

Morris groans. "Hurry up."

"Four… Five…"

"You've got to be joking," Morris whines again. "We'll be here forever."

"Six—"

Morris slams his fist on the table, and I restrain myself from putting my head in my hands. The kid practically jumps out of his skin.

"S-s-s-six—"

"Can't you count, boy? You already said 'six,' you thick bastard," Morris yells at him. "How long are you going to take?"

"Perhaps if you stopped interrupting?"

For a split second, I thought I'd spoken my mind aloud.

Only to flinch when I turn and see a tall man standing next to me. Every hair on the back of my neck stands to attention. How the hell…?

"Who the fuck are you?" I snap, entirely unnerved, and pull out my gun.

This guy snuck up on me as silently as the grave, and that's not a feat anyone has been able to accomplish in a long time. Whoever this guy is, he's dangerous.

The man tuts and moves past me toward the window, seemingly unperturbed by the fact my gun is locked on his every move as I stalk him there. Morris looks about as dumbstruck as I feel as I pass by him.

"Pity. Connor said you might be smart enough to figure it out, Jack."

I cock my gun. "Give me one good reason why I shouldn't unload this into your skull."

He turns from the window to look at me and merely nods toward my shirt. I grit my teeth, already knowing what I'm going to see as I look down.

Sure enough, a red dot has appeared over my chest. Fuck.

Still, I keep my gun trained on him. "The Maguires are so poor they want a fight over a few grand, is that it?"

"You're on their turf," he replies simply. "Surely you, of all people, know how important it is to maintain a perimeter."

Morris finally speaks up. "This hasn't been Maguire turf for—"

"Twenty years?" the man finishes for him. "Yes, well. Not sure if you heard, but the Maguires have had a recent change in management."

"This is a declaration of war," I hiss through my teeth.

The man lets out a dry laugh. "Was the bullet through Graham Duffy's heart not obvious enough for you? Christ, you really are a disappointment, Jack."

"You want to move away from the window and say that again?" I growl.

The man smirks. "When you're all caught up and want to have a civilized conversation, give me a call, will you? I'm sure we have a few things to discuss."

"Go to hell."

"There are five men on the roof of this building. Ten more on the ground," the man says matter-of-factly. "You're not going to be able to shoot your way out of this one."

"I've survived worse odds."

"Are the Duffys so stubborn they're willing to fight over a couple grand?" He parrots my own words back to me. "If you were a smart man, which we have already established you are not, you'd retreat now while you still have the chance."

***

Retreating from a fight never feels good. Morris was sure to make that clear on our way back to the mansion compound.

I console myself with the fact the trip wasn't a total failure. We now know more about Connor's MO, and we know that his next move is to reclaim the territory his father lost to us decades ago.

"What did he look like?" Andy asks.

I stand in the conference room once more to present my report to a smaller group of Padraic's more trusted advisers.

"Dark hair, slimmer build. Stealthy as all hell."

Kate furrows her brow. "How stealthy are we talking?"

"Snuck up on me," I admit, albeit bitterly.

Kate nods in understanding, considering she's the only person who's been able to do that before. "Sounds a bit like Arnold Knight."

"Arnie?" Buzz pipes up. "He's a hit man, not a mobster."

"Aye, but his uncle was Tony Nova," Padraic mutters. "Kate. Set me up a call with the Italians. I want to know what's left of the Novas."

"I thought they'd all been hunted down," I say, wracking my brain for the details of their recent demise at the hands of the Lucas.

"Clearly, not all of them," Padraic snaps at me without bothering to look my way.

Kate seems to sense the tension and steps in. "But even if the Novas are aligning themselves with the Maguires… that can't pose much of a threat. The state both their families are in…"

"Families are always at their most hair-triggered when they've got nothing left to lose," Andy says slowly before turning to address Padraic directly. "Both the Novas and the Maguires will be fighting for their lives on the ground. It would be wise not to underestimate them."

"Complacency is what got Graham killed, after all," Buzz says with a pointed look at me.

I try not to seethe on the spot. "May I suggest leading a search party for this Arnie person? He seemed interested in making contact with me specifically; I think I could draw him out."

"You are dismissed, Jack," Padraic cuts across me like a knife.

I blink. "But I can help—"

"You are dismissed."

I look at Padraic in disbelief. Surely he knows I have a tactical advantage in this situation? He's never sacrificed the success of the family to take it out on someone like this before. Hell, he even found a use for *Morris* in his ranks.

But as I search for an ally among my father's closest ranks, I find nothing but unreadable reservation—or, in Buzz's case, delight.

"Fine," I say through my teeth and turn on my heel.

As I leave the conference room, I check my phone. Hoping that perhaps Aimee had a chance to call. Hoping she might, at the very least, provide a distraction for the pounding anger currently reverberating in my skull.

Instead, I see a message from Raymond.

RAY: *I heard you got yourself caught at Padraic's hotel.*

JACK: *I didn't snitch on you, if that's what you're worried about.*

RAY: *Will you be trying again?*

JACK: *Why?*

RAY: *Our friend just checked into Coney Island Amusement Park.*

Chapter Ten

Jack

If anyone asks, I invited Aimee to Coney Island because Ray pointed out I'd stick out like a sore thumb if I went on my own. Big Irish guy stalking the attractions and stalls on his own? Creepy as fuck. Big Irish guy taking a girl on a date to one of the most popular places this side of the East River, on the other hand? The way I see it, this is a two-birds-one-stone operation.

I watch her from a distance, leaning casually against a low wall and scrolling through her phone. She arrived almost ten minutes ago, looking even more stunning than when I left her naked in the pool this morning—a feat I wasn't sure anyone would ever be able to accomplish.

She's also completely oblivious to the fact that I've been watching her. Obviously, I didn't want to seem like I arrived too early. For one, it would make me look a bit desperate, and two, I needed to climb a fire escape to survey the area *before* we met. It isn't really "agent" behavior.

Lying to Aimee leaves a bad taste on my tongue, and I dislike both the fact and the realization. But it's not like she's the most forthcoming with her own truths, either.

She looks up from her phone and glances around, looking for someone. Looking for *me,* I realize with a start. Looks like my cue. I jump down from my perch and straighten out my shirt. Whatever happens today, my number one priority has to be to find Roisin. Aimee being here is just a cover; it doesn't matter how great her legs look in slim jeans.

The pressure was tangible back at the compound. I may not have been in the room, but Padraic's orders to search for Arnie Knight trickled down to me eventually. By which point, Morris was already on the warpath. Slipping out without him or anyone else noticing was almost too easy.

With everyone distracted, now would be the perfect time to show up with Roisin. All I have to do is focus…

Aimee's smile is bright and warm when she spots me walking over to her.

"You came!"

"It would be poor form if I didn't, considering I invited you." I place a hand on the small of her back, unable to deny myself a kiss a moment longer.

She hums happily against my lips before pulling away. "How was your day?"

There is something so natural and easy about the way she asks me this, as if we've been doing this routine far longer than we have. "Not as good as my morning."

"Was everything okay with your dad?"

I try not to flinch at that before shrugging off the question. "He threw a fit and now he's threatening to take his toys and go home, but I daresay he has more pressing things on his mind now. How are you? I thought you said you were working tonight?"

"There was a change of plans," she replies. I wait for her to elaborate further, but she doesn't.

I shake my head with a smile. "Elusive as ever. Well, you won't catch me complaining that I have you all to myself." The wink I give her makes a beautiful blush spread across her heart-shaped face.

She coughs a little in embarrassment before nodding toward the boardwalk. "Shall we get going?"

I offer her my arm, and she takes it readily. "Have you been here yet?"

"No."

"Then allow me to show you around."

Like any other mild evening of the year, Coney Island has a steady trickle of tourists and locals wandering up and down the beach looking at the various attractions the boardwalk has to offer. I'd only ever come here offseason like this, it's too easy to get stuck in the crowds when the sun is out, and the lines are much more manageable now.

We pass the Ferris wheel, and I tug her toward it. "The view won't be as good as the hotel, but…"

Aimee merely grins in return.

***

I thought maybe by getting a bird's-eye view, I'd have a better chance of spotting a stray redhead in the crowds. But by the time we get back down from the Ferris wheel, I'm no closer to finding Roisin.

Not that I can concentrate on my search. There is just such an overwhelming lightness to being in Aimee's company. She makes the world seem manageable, like no matter what you're going through, there's a solution to it. The weight in my chest entirely evaporates whenever she's around.

I glance down at her as we continue down the boardwalk, only to find her scanning the faces of the people we pass.

"You okay?" I ask, concern lacing my voice.

Aimee looks up, her eyes flickering with a mix of curiosity and worry.

She offers me a reassuring smile. "Yeah, sorry," she replies. "I just thought I saw someone I knew."

I raise an eyebrow, intrigued by her sudden shift in demeanor.

"New York is a big city," I remark. "It's hard to run into people."

Aimee's gaze lingers on the crowd, her expression pensive.

"You'd be surprised," she says softly, her voice filled with a hint of mystery.

She turns to me, a mischievous glint in her eyes.

"Do you shoot?" she asks excitedly, changing the subject.

I chuckle at her enthusiasm, enjoying the way her energy effortlessly pulls me away from my worries.

"A little," I confess.

Aimee's smile widens, her excitement contagious.

"We should play!" she suggests, already pulling me over to a stall brandishing targets and a few BB guns. Before I even have a chance to think about it, she's handing over cash to the attendant and picking up the gun to hand to me.

"Show me how it's done?" she says earnestly, and I can feel the tug of modesty as it wars with my pride.

I handle the gun carefully as if I haven't been shooting these things from the moment I could hold up their weight. I take aim and let my instincts take over. The first two shots are off-target on purpose, but the final, I make sure goes right through the bull's-eye. It earns me a hug and a kiss on the cheek from Aimee.

"That's eighty-eight points! Congratulations, that's the highest score of the day," the attendant says as he retrieves my paper target. "Want to try it yourself, ma'am?"

Aimee looks a little nervous as she takes a gun from him. "I'm not sure…"

"Don't tell me you're scared?"

She raises an eyebrow at me. "Why would I be scared?"

Aimee turns back to face her target and hauls the firearm up to her chest, experimenting with her grip.

"I don't know; it looks kinda heavy for you."

"Oh, I see," she says, closing one eye, then the other, staring down the barrel.

"See what?"

"You're worried I might beat your score."

I laugh at her, standing there with her shoulders relaxed, her feet square on without any regard for recoil. "I know you won't beat my score."

"Wanna bet?"

I can feel my smile stretch across my face. Little does she know just how much of a betting man I am.

"What are you offering?"

"What do you want?"

I look her up and down as if it's obvious.

"What do *you* want?"

She pretends to think about it. "I want to know how many girls you've ever taken up to the king suite of your father's hotel."

Oh. This can't end well.

"What makes you think I've done it before?" I inquire cautiously, trying to gauge her reaction.

"Your face just now."

"Fine. If you win, you will get your answer." I lean in closer. "But, if I win, I get to do whatever I want to you tonight."

Aimee narrows her eyes at me playfully. "What makes you think there's even going to be a 'tonight'?"

"Your face just now."

Bang.

Bang.

Bang.

Without even taking her eyes off me, Aimee lets off three consecutive shots in quick succession. Each one hits the target dead center.

My jaw drops.

Who is this woman?

She smiles happily at the result and hands the gun back to an equally gobsmacked attendant. "D-do you want a prize?" he asks.

Aimee turns back to me with a mischievous grin. "No, I'm good. This one already promised me a prize."

I scowl at her before letting out a sigh, no longer able to hide the truth.

"Fine, a few," I admit reluctantly.

Aimee raises an eyebrow, her intrigue evident. "A few?" she echoes.

"Three or four," I confess, bracing myself for her reaction.

"Wow…" She trails off, seemingly taken aback.

"But you're the only one I ever called again after," I quickly add.

Aimee's expression softens, a mix of skepticism and curiosity lingering in her eyes. "Is that supposed to make me feel special?"

"It's supposed to let you know I know a good thing when I see it."

She rolls her eyes at me, but I can see how my words affect her in the way she bites at her lip.

"My legs are feeling a little tired," she announces a little too casually.

"Yeah?" I respond, catching her hint.

"All this walking…" she trails off, her gaze flickering toward the distance we've covered.

I don't need to point out we barely walked a half mile down the boardwalk.

"Of course," I agree earnestly.

"I just live in Brooklyn," she adds.

"In an apartment halfway up the building?"

Aimee's face lights up with delight, a mixture of surprise and joy dancing in her eyes that I remembered, and I'm entirely captivated by her reaction.

"You should come to see it," she suggests. The way she looks up at me with those chocolate doe eyes has me practically drooling over her proposition. There's nothing I want more than to let her whisk me away. The things I want to do to her right now aren't suitable for a place as public as this.

An annoying voice at the back of my mind reminds me I have a job to do. That my priority here isn't getting laid, it's finding Roisin.

But Jesus Christ, I want this.

No, I think I need it.

She makes everything feel a thousand times better.

I might need her right now more than I need to find Roisin.

"Lead the way."

***

Aimee seems nervous as she opens the door to her apartment as if expecting me to comment on her home. In truth, it may not be as large as the mansion or my own apartment or have a pool in the middle of it like Padraic's hotel, but there's a warmth to the space that I've never experienced in my own home.

I see it in the well-worn couch, the mismatched kitchen chairs. The sticky notes on the fridge, covered in hand-drawn hearts, and the novelty mugs that hang from the cup stand. There are so many tiny details that tell a story about the woman standing before me.

"This is me," Aimee says lightly, but her eyes betray that she's waiting for a reaction.

I merely smirk and stride toward her, enveloping her in my arms. "You have a beautiful home."

"We can always go to a hotel or—"

I crush her lips with mine to cut her off.

She relaxes into me instantly, deepening the kiss with her tongue, and I pull her in tighter. Closer, yet not close enough.

The frustration builds quickly, and without warning, I lift her up.

She squeals playfully as she wraps her legs around me. "Jack! Put me down!"

"I'd rather not," I reply, capturing her lips again.

The kiss becomes more desperate, almost feral. Aimee moves herself against my hips, trying to find some kind of friction.

Not close enough.

I take one step, then another. Never breaking the kiss but entirely focused on getting us to the couch. When we reach it, I throw her down unceremoniously, her legs hooking over the arms.

"I suppose that's on me for not specifying that I wanted to be put down gently," she huffs as I grin down at her. Appreciating the way she looks, lying there all flustered and *wanting.*

I reach out and grip her calves, pulling her flush against the sofa arm. "You want me to be gentle with you?"

I'm rewarded with a beautiful blush that colors her face. She bites her lip nervously, and from her expression alone, I know exactly how gentle she wants me to be.

But first, she needs to be wearing far fewer clothes. I remove her trousers deftly as she stares at me with her wide, doe-like eyes. Irresistible. I lift her leg up, gently kissing my way down. Every inch of skin my lips touch sends shocks of pure desire through my veins, and I can already feel my hardening cock push uncomfortably against my pants.

When I reach her inner thigh, it draws a soft gasp from her lips. Good, I want her to enjoy this as much as I know I will.

I yank her forward again, encouraging her to fold her legs over my shoulders as I hold her hips up. Allowing my hands to wander down to her perfect ass.

"Please, Jack… I–"

But I'm too impatient to listen to her beg. I'm too desperate to taste her. I push her panties to one side and begin my feast.

The effect on her is instant. Her back arches against the couch arm, and her legs tighten around my neck. Her body shudders with a wave of overwhelming delight.

I bury myself into her, lapping up her juices feverishly. I'm sure my fingers will leave bruises on her ass the way I'm gripping onto her to hold her in place.

A cry bursts out of her, and her eyes roll back as I suck harder, deeper into her core.

Her hands finally find purchase on my hair, and she clings to me desperately, pulling me closer still. As if I'm the only anchor to her building orgasm.

"That's it," I growl in between worshiping her with my tongue. "Good girl. Are you going to cum for me?"

"Oh, fuck," she cries, tugging me harder, closer. Her hips move in tandem with my tongue, and I can feel her quivering against me as her orgasm builds and builds.

I change tactics, suddenly moving to her most sensitive spot and sucking on it gently at first, then allowing my tongue to play.

When Aimee comes undone, I'm there to match her as the ripples of pleasure cascade through her body.

Her panting is deep and breathless, and I leave her there lying on the couch to recover as I remove my own shirt and pants. My cock visibly pushes against the fabric of my boxers, so I reach down to stroke myself once, twice…

"What are you doing?"

I look up to see Aimee sitting up on the couch arm and staring at me hungrily. Her own shirt is discarded on the floor, leaving her dressed in only her pretty little bra that leaves very little to the imagination.

"You want this?" I say, holding myself in my hand.

She nods eagerly.

I stalk over to her, and she reaches for me automatically as I pick her up again.

"Where's the bedroom?" I say between feverish kisses.

Aimee merely points toward the door closest to us, and I make my way over with us both.

"This time, I'm not going to fuck you from behind," I say as I lower her to the bed. "This time, I want to see your face when you cum again."

Aimee stares up at me, biting at her beautifully swollen lips.

"Don't do that," I demand as I lie down on top of her, tugging her lips away from her teeth with my own. "I don't want you to hold back. Do you understand?"

I finally put the weight of my crotch against hers, and she gasps deliciously.

"Aimee?"

She seems to struggle to focus on my question. "Mmmhmm?"

"You're going to scream for me, aren't you?"

As I guide my cock to her entrance, I make sure it rubs against her clit.

"Yes! Oh God, yes!"

The anticipation of being inside of her has me shaking as I spread her legs. I feel like I've been starved of this, even though I only had her yesterday. She's like an addiction; the sheer *need* I feel as I hover over her is intoxicating. Nothing in the world exists except the two of us and the burning core of our desire.

She raises her hips impatiently, and it shatters every ounce of my restraint. I plunge into her, bringing our bodies so close you couldn't fit a molecule between us.

Not close enough.

I grunt in frustration and attack her mouth again, swallowing her gasps as I begin to move in and out, in and out.

The feeling of being inside her is unparalleled. It takes everything within me not to come undone within the first few strokes.

"Pull on my hair," I demand, and her small hands obediently tug at my roots. The sharp pain provides a wonderful distraction, and I can concentrate on my goal.

Closer.

I cling to her, feeling every moan released from her lips in my own body as if I were the one making the noises. I pound harder, our bodies moving in tandem. Both chasing the pleasure of release desperately.

I feel Aimee tense first, and her core tightens around me.

Yes. This is it.

This is how close I need us to be.

Her scream barely reaches my ears before I come too, and we collapse as we orgasm in harmony.

Chapter Eleven

Aimee

I could definitely get used to waking up next to Jack. He sleeps so soundly, the morning sun bouncing through his dark hair and splaying across his muscled back.

I'm immediately jealous of my past self, watching those muscles work as he pleasured me over and over...

I contemplate waking him up to see if he'd be willing to do it again. But one look at his peaceful face has me reconsidering.

When I saw him yesterday, walking over to me by the boardwalk, it looked as if the weight of the world was on his shoulders. It took me most of the evening to get him to relax and be comfortable around me again.

Whatever he's going through with work, or this argument with his father, is clearly taking its toll.

Instead, I slip out of my bedroom and head for the shower. The hot water soothes the aches I didn't know I had from last night's activities. I make a mental note to sign up for the gym again. Maybe enroll in a few self-defense classes for good measure.

By the time I leave the bathroom and pull on an old pair of sweats, there's a familiar mop of red hair hunched over the kitchen table.

"Morning!" I say.

"Ugh, how are you so chirpy?" Roisin groans.

I bite my tongue before I blurt out the fact there's a man in my room. "It's nine AM. I thought you'd be out already. Or are you protesting again today?"

Roisin goes a little green. "Definitely protesting. I only got in a few hours ago."

"How was Coney Island?" I ask, trying not to let it show how curious I am. I realized the moment I arrived that going there was a mistake. Even with the excuse of being on a date with Jack, it wasn't cool of me to tail Roisin like that. Even so, I can't help worrying about my sister and this new crowd she's begun partying with.

"Tacky as always," she replies dismissively. "Do you remember going when we were little?"

"Yeah, a bit," I answer, reminiscing briefly. We'd only ever gone with my mother when she was still alive. Roisin couldn't have been older than ten at the time.

"Hasn't changed at all. They still have that shooting game you always beat me at," Roisin complains, a hint of playful resentment in her voice.

"That's because you never practiced," I retort teasingly.

"It was way too noisy in the shooting range," she defends herself.

I smile at the memory before trying to steer the conversation back on track. "You had fun though?"

"It was fine," Roisin replies, her tone somewhat guarded as she realizes what I'm really asking. "The director ended up showing up and having a blue fit that we were striking. Kind of ruined the vibe."

I press on regardless. "Where did you go after that?"

Roisin's expression tightens, a sign that she's not in the mood for further questioning. "I don't know, here and there. Why?"

"Just…" I look at the challenge in her eyes and know this isn't the right time to push it. We had this discussion yesterday already, and despite the fact we've made up now, things are clearly still a bit tense between us. "Never mind."

Roisin relaxes a little and continues nursing her coffee. I turn away to make my own.

"Your hair. It's going back to normal."

"Is it?"

"You've almost washed all the brown out," she remarks.

"I'll have to get some more then."

Roisin's eyes sparkle mischievously. "Why? Does your new 'friend' not like gingers?"

"I—" Caught off guard, I instinctively glance at my bedroom door, a knee-jerk reaction.

One Roisin does not miss. Her eyes go wide as she mouths, "Is he here?"

Well, there's no use denying it now.

I nod.

Roisin covers her mouth as she squeals in glee.

"Shh!" I say, mentally begging her to shut up. "He's still asleep."

She shakes her head in disbelief. "You bought a guy home? Into our actual apartment?"

I glance at the door again before hissing, "Roisin!"

"I'm so proud of you!" she mock-whispers. "Can I meet him?"

I look her up and down. "You're hungover as all hell. So, no, you cannot meet him."

Roisin pouts. "Why?"

"He wants to sign you, remember?" I pull the fact out of thin air. But honestly, I just know the two of them meeting will end in disaster when she's like this.

"I can't believe you slept with my future agent. Brownie points go to Aimee Maguire," Roisin teases.

I snort. "It was hardly a hardship."

"Yeah?" Roisin gives me a naughty look, wiggling her eyebrows up and down.

"He's very *charming*," I emphasize as I hit her in the arm playfully. "And excellent company."

"Was he excellent *company* last night, then?"

I roll my eyes at her. "I'm not having this conversation with you."

"Oh, please!"

"No."

Roisin pouts again. "Come on, let me live vicariously through your sex life."

"I want you nowhere *near* my sex life, thank you very much."

When Roisin doesn't reply, I look up at her to see her staring over my shoulder. Her jaw is practically scraping the floor.

Huh, I didn't even hear him come in.

I turn to Jack brightly. "Morning!"

But he's not looking at me; he's looking straight at Roisin. His face is completely unreadable. "Sorry… I didn't know we were expecting company."

"You must be Jack!" Roisin says. "I'd get up, but the hangover might make me puke on you. I've heard… great things."

She gives me a look that makes me blush. "Jack, this is-"

"Roisin Maguire," he finishes for me, staring at her blankly again.

"The one and only." Roisin bows her head a little. "I promise, I'm not usually such a mess."

I stand up to make Jack a coffee. "Sure you're not."

"Come on," Roisin whines at me. "Give me some credit; you're making me look bad."

I pour out a cup and hesitate by the counter. "You make yourself look bad. Do you want any sugar, Jack?"

"How…" Jack's voice cracks, and he clears his throat, ignoring my question. "You two are pretty close, huh?"

"Two peas," Roisin replies, crossing her figures to show how tight we are. "So don't hurt her or whatever."

"Thanks, Roshe," I say sarcastically. "Jack? Sugar?"

Again, he ignores me to address Roisin. "And how long have you…"

"Lived together? Oh, at least like five years, right, Aimee?" Roisin looks over to me for confirmation. "We only just moved back to New York, but before that, we were in LA."

Jack's face is set in perfectly blank lines.. "Right."

I give up on the coffee. Clearly, something is very wrong.

"Sorry I didn't mention it before," I say cautiously. "Sometimes guys get a bit weird when I say I live with my sister."

"I need to go."

Jack swerves around me and beelines toward the door.

I blink in confusion. "What?"

"Yeah… um. Work just called so…" he replies without even a glance over his shoulder.

"Oh, right. Sure," I say, hating the way rejection seems to blossom so quickly in my stomach. "I made you a coffee. Do you want it for the road?"

"No!" Jack replies a little too loudly before correcting his tone. "No."

He opens the front door and hesitates a moment, and Roisin glances at me in confusion.

"Okay, well," I try again, my voice tinged with disappointment. "I'll see you around?"

Jack lets out a frustrated sigh and walks through the door, slamming it behind him.

The sound reverberates through the room, leaving me standing there, completely dumbstruck.

"Was it something I said?" Roisin says quietly behind me.

My head spins, trying to make sense of the sudden turn of events.

We had a great time last night and the night before. There was nothing that made him react like that; there was no logical reason he would just…

Except that he discovered I was lying to him.

Or at least withholding information about Roisin from him.

I'm walking toward the front door before my brain catches up with me.

When I look down the corridor of the apartment complex, Jack is still there, anxiously waiting by the elevator. He doesn't turn to me as I approach.

"Hey!" I shout out to him, but he ignores me.

Every step I take makes me more and more frustrated about the situation.

"Jack?" I call out again, this time more urgently.

He finally tears his gaze away from the elevator door and meets my eyes. The torment in his eyes is undeniable.

"I'm sorry I didn't tell you earlier that Roisin was my sister," I begin, my voice filled with a mixture of regret and confusion.

"Aimee…" Jack starts to speak, but his words hang in the air, caught between us.

"But why are you acting like this?" I continue.

"Like what?" Jack's voice is tinged with frustration, mirroring my own.

I'm surprised by how much his indifference hurts. "Like you're running out on me!"

"I told you, I have work."

"I thought *this* was different." My voice cracks with emotion.

"It is; it's just…" Jack's voice trails off, struggling to find the right words.

"Just what?"

His face forms an uncomfortable grimace, and he turns away, clearly exasperated. "Jesus Christ, Aimee, stop it."

"Stop what?" I retort, my own frustration boiling over.

"You lied to me," Jack states bluntly as if that's enough of an explanation.

"Yeah… but…"

Jack looks at me again with pleading eyes. "Please, I need to go."

I can see there's no winning this conversation. Whatever I've done, whatever lying like this means to Jack, I'm not going to find out today.

"Right," I respond, my voice barely above a whisper, the weight of the situation settling heavily on my shoulders.

Despite the tension, the harshness, and the way he looks at me like something he will always regret, he closes the distance between us and kisses me on the forehead firmly.

He lingers for only a moment before turning away.

"Goodbye, Aimee Maguire."

With those words, he walks away, leaving me standing there, feeling the sting of his departure.

Chapter Twelve

Jack

New Yorkers don't look at each other on the sidewalks. But the snarl I try to repress has even the most jaded of commuters giving me a wide berth.

Aimee Maguire.

Aimee *fucking* Maguire.

A fucking Maguire.

All this time, I was looking for Roisin, and the older sister was under my nose the whole time. I could have delivered her to Padraic at any point over the last few days. She would have come with me so willingly, eagerly even. No idea that my intentions were anything less than pure.

But… why did it have to be Aimee?

My Aimee.

The woman who landed so perfectly into my life, lighting up every part of me.

What we have is just so *easy*. It feels like neither of us has been shy about our feelings; neither of us is playing any games about it. I feel like I've known her for years, like she sees a part of me that I've never been able to understand myself. God and she's funny. Whether she knows it or not, she's quick, clever, and can make me howl in laughter in ways no one has ever been able to before. The way her eyes glisten when she's being earnest, or her eyebrow shoots up with unspoken questions. Everything about her is so beautiful.

It would be so easy to fall in love with her.

I would be so *happy* to fall in love with her.

No, I can't let her cloud my mind.

I stride through Brooklyn at a breakneck pace, finally flagging down a taxi a few blocks away from their apartment. I might not know what to do yet, but I'm sure as hell not leading the whole of Hell's Kitchen to their doorstep by calling my driver.

I slam the taxi door behind me and the car starts putting some distance between me and the two women who will likely be my undoing. The blare of horns and the sputtering engines around me give me something else to focus on, and my head begins to clear.

Aimee and Roisin likely had nothing to do with Graham's death. From the little Aimee has told me about her life before New York and what Roisin said this morning, it's clear they were either still in LA or in the process of moving when it happened. If that fact isn't enough, I don't believe… No. *Can't* believe that someone like Aimee would stand by her brother on this.

That being said, the Maguires and the Duffys have a long and tormented history of despising one another. Who's to say Aimee or her sister haven't ever harmed a Duffy or a Dead Eye for the sake of family pride before? You don't become as good a shot as Aimee is by practicing at the funfair.

A few things click into place—her uncanny ability to eavesdrop, her elusiveness when it comes to anything about her past, even her work. Did she know someone identified her at the hospital? I know for a fact she hasn't been back the last few days, while my father's goons have been searching high and low for her.

Yes, Aimee Maguire knows who she is and who her family are. Hatred for the Duffys was probably ingrained in her as much as my hatred for her family.

Despite everything, we're each other's natural enemies. When she discovers the truth, she'll likely be as hostile to me as I should be to her.

Should be. Have to be. I let down my guard and remember Graham. The way he looked as he died in my arms, the hatred that filled me for Connor Maguire. I swore on that day that I would seek revenge for his death, whatever it took.

If the thing that stands between me and that justice is Aimee… I can't let my personal feelings stop me. I have to do what's right for my family. It's the only way to redeem myself in Padraic's eyes and the only way I'll have a fighting chance at being the one to take down Connor Maguire once and for all.

Aimee makes my heart soar. But my heart's not as important as my family.

I need to come up with a plan.

***

The taxi drops me off a street down from the mansion compound, and I walk through the front gates with a wave to the doorman. The dogs he has on a chain calm the moment they recognize me, and I pause to give them a gentle scratch behind the ears.

"I thought you weren't allowed out?" the doorman says with a bemused huff.

"I won't tell if you won't," I reply with a slight smirk.

"Morris has been looking for you," he informs me.

I grimace at the news. "Great."

His gaze shifts toward the mansion. "He's up there getting ready with the others." the doorman continues.

"Ready for what?"

"They didn't tell you?" he asks, surprise evident in his voice.

I clench my fist to keep the anger at bay. "Care to fill me in?" My tone was tinged with a mix of anticipation and apprehension.

"Someone found the Maguire girl."

His words hit me like a punch to the gut. My blood runs cold, a wave of panic washing over me.

"What?"

"I don't know the full story, but…" the doorman begins, but I can't bear to hear more.

Without bothering to say goodbye, I hastily leave, my mind racing. I sprint down the stairs from the foyer, trying not to panic about the amount of movement I can already make out. People are buzzing in the equipment room beneath the main floor—trusted men with heavy guns. Whatever they've found out, Padraic's taking it damn seriously.

In the chaos, Kate isn't easy to spot. But when I do, I find her checking through her equipment methodically.

"Kate," I call out, relieved to see her.

She glances up at me for a moment before continuing her work. "Oh, good, you're here."

"What's going on?"

Kate gives me the brief. "Buzz finally managed to pull the admin records from Lenox Hill ER. Seems they had someone on file called 'Aimee' who recently requested a name change."

"There must be a hundred thousand 'Amys' in New York City," I point out, slurring the name in an attempt to downplay the significance.

"Aye. Not many changing their name from Maguire, though," she counters.

Shit, I curse internally. "So we're going to the hospital?"

"No, we have her home address," Kate reveals, unaware that the news is crushing me.

My heart pounds in my chest. "Where?"

"Brooklyn."

In a small apartment about halfway up the building. Soft, pale curtains and bedsheets. A well-used coffee machine. A couch that's seen better days. They're going to find her because that's exactly where I was this morning.

"You okay?" Kate's voice breaks through my thoughts, concern etched on her face.

"What's the plan?" I redirect, trying to buy time to regain my focus.

Kate narrows her eyes at me but replies anyway, "Three men have gone to scout ahead. Then we'll approach together. See if we can't lure her out without violence."

"And if we can't?" I press, my voice betraying a mix of worry and doubt.

Kate nods toward where Morris and Buzz are loading up a four-by-four with an obscene amount of hardware.

I swallow hard, the weight of the situation settling heavily on my shoulders. "She's just one woman."

"So am I," Kate points out, her tone resolute. "But Buzz said she listed someone called 'Roisin Maguire' as her next of kin. Do you remember seeing the Maguire kids when we were younger? There were two sisters."

"You think they're both in New York?" I ask, mentally cursing Buzz to high hell.

"I never saw one without the other," Kate says, landing on the same conclusion I did only a few days ago.

"That was almost twenty years ago, Kate," I say to try and throw her off. "Things change."

"Maybe. But after what happened last time, Padraic doesn't want to take any risks." Her words carry the weight of what she left unsaid. Padraic doesn't want another Graham.

I watch Kate for a moment, her focused demeanor and unwavering determination, and I can't help but feel a pang of admiration amidst my turmoil. As much as it has often pained me to admit, she's always impressed me with her unwavering loyalty to the family and her fierce dedication. It's still strange to discover that we share a bond forged through our grief and a deep understanding of the dangerous world we inhabit. That we share a common goal, to get justice for Graham's death, whatever it takes.

But now, as she sets out to find Aimee… I feel my resolve wavering.

The mere thought of Aimee falling into the clutches of the mob… I can't help but imagine the horrors that could happen to her if she is caught.

I know that Morris would have no qualms about subjecting Aimee to interrogation tactics that go far beyond mere questioning. I've seen firsthand the way he thrives on the power he holds over others, reveling in their anguish. The thought of him intimidating her, using his sadistic methods to extract information or force compliance, fuels the anger growing inside of me.

But it's not just Morris I fear. The entire family poses a threat to Aimee's safety if she is caught. Padraic's mind is clouded by his own fury, and if he's willing to let Buzz and Morris use brute force to get her to cooperate, I don't want to think about what he might do if he perceives her as a liability.

For the first time, I find myself questioning the morality of it all. Does Aimee truly pose a threat to the family, or is she merely caught up in circumstances beyond her control? I can't believe that she was in any way involved with Graham's murder. What could capturing her do other than antagonize Connor even further?

"Jack?" Kate says, snapping me out of my spiral. I turn to face her, seeing genuine concern in the way her brow furrows.

I remind myself that we're allies now, that this shouldn't be so surprising. But it doesn't shake the novelty of my childhood rival becoming a friend. I silently appreciate the change in our dynamic.

But we're not close enough for me to tell her the truth. Not yet.

"I'm thinking I should go ahead," I suggest, my mind still racing with the potential dangers awaiting Aimee.

"Why?" Kate replies, clearly curious about my sudden decision.

"If this turns out like it did last time," I explain, "the scouts may need backup."

"They're not meant to engage," she reminds me, her voice carrying a firmness that signals her authority.

But I won't back down. "How many Dead Eyes do you think wouldn't jump at the chance to bring in a Maguire themselves?" I challenge. "Do you really trust them not to engage if the opportunity presents itself?"

Kate takes a moment to consider my words, weighing the risks and implications.

Finally, she relents, understanding the gravity of the situation. "Fine, take a bike. Do not engage until I get there."

"What if it's self-defense?" I push back cheekily.

"Did I stutter?" Kate snaps back sharply.

There's the Kate I'm used to.

I can't help but smirk at her response, appreciating her unwavering commitment to the plan.

"Aye, aye, captain."

Chapter Thirteen

Aimee

Jack's words still ring in my ears as I return to the apartment.

"You lied *to me."*

He looked so hurt, so betrayed... I had no idea lying to him about this would cause such an intense reaction.

I could kick myself.

Of *course* he's upset.

I didn't tell him Roisin was my sister.

He's the agent trying to sign her to his family business. I can't say I know a whole lot about that industry, but I imagine sleeping with your prospective client's sister isn't considered hugely professional.

Still, I can't blame myself for hoping it would be something we could work through. I mean, aside from this little hiccup, things have been almost frighteningly good between us. The date to Coney Island was one thing, but last night... No one has ever made me feel like that. Like I was safe and wanted and *worshipped* by someone.

Surely when he said "goodbye," it wasn't goodbye for good... right?

I'm not sure if I could take a blow like that. Not after the way we connected. I feel crazy just thinking about it because, logically, I know I've only known him for a few days. But I don't want it to end, and aside from this, he's not given me any indication that he'd want it to end, either.

"Is everything okay?" Roisin asks as I walk back into the kitchen.

I contemplate telling her that my head is spinning so hard it feels like it might fall off, but think better of it. "Yeah, he just has work."

Roisin doesn't look entirely convinced, but she seems too preoccupied to press it any further.

I offer her a gentle rub on the back as I sit down next to her. "Still feeling rough?"

"I don't want to talk about it," she replies, placing her forehead on the table.

"Go back to bed," I suggest. "I'll make you some soup—"

Suddenly, Roisin's fist slams dramatically down on the table, making me jump. "Dear God, Aimee," she exclaims. "Are you really going to sit there and ignore the fact that the guy you're sleeping with is insanely attractive?"

Confused and surprised by her outburst, I stammer, "What?"

"He's like famous-person-hot," she continues, emphasizing her point.

I nod, trying to comprehend her astonishment. "I did tell you he was hot, remember?"

"Yes, but there is regular-person-hot, and then there's straight-off-the-runway-hot," she says as if she's not spouting absolute nonsense. "And somehow, that man is more attractive than even that."

Realizing her point, I ask, "Are you saying I'm punching above my weight class?"

"I'm saying," she declares with certainty. "Jesus Christ, Aimee. People don't look like that in real life."

"So I'm outmatched."

She looks up at me from the table with exasperation. "Listen to me; you could never be outmatched. You're gorgeous, and there's no man on this earth who could ever deserve you."

"Thank you," I reply, oddly moved by her words.

"But that man comes pretty close," she adds in hindsight.

I roll my eyes. "You met him for like twenty seconds."

"I'm a great judge of character," she defends herself.

"Right, that's enough," I say, formulating a plan to divert the conversation away from my love life. "Go back to bed, you party animal."

Roisin pouts but proceeds to get up anyway with a groan. "Are you heading out today? We're out of ibuprofen."

I walk over to the medical cabinet to double-check and grimace a little when I discover she's correct. I pull out some aspirin and throw it to her. "Take this for now. I think I'm going to go for a walk to the hospital—I haven't heard anything from Dr. Lous yet. I'll grab you some ibuprofen while I'm there."

"You're a saint."

***

As I walk through the bustling streets of New York, a wave of nostalgia washes over me. The city, with its vibrant energy and ceaseless movement, it hasn't changed at all since I was last here.

But I have.

I remind myself of that as I pass by shop window after window advertising the latest fashions. There was a time when I would have fought and screamed with my father for even a moment longer to stare at the displays. Now I walk by, barely noticing them in my peripheral vision.

All I wanted as a child was everything we didn't have. I didn't understand that there were more important things and that the people around me were hurting.

My father was hurting because he lost my mother. It made him drunk and miserable, and he took it out on every one of us, even if I didn't recognize it at the time.

I didn't realize how far Roisin had slipped into her own pain before it was almost too late. She was barely seventeen when I found her, dying of an overdose and addicted to the drugs my father let her take. I knew then that we couldn't stay in New York, that I would have to put away my dreams of nice things and a penthouse apartment to keep her safe.

Walking these streets again fills me with such a conflicting storm of emotions. That's before I even consider everything that just happened with Jack.

The sounds of traffic and the rhythm of footsteps blend with my turmoil. I can almost feel his presence beside me, his deep voice resonating in my ears, his warm breath against my skin. It's as if the city itself is conspiring to keep the thoughts of him fresh in my mind. The laughter we shared at Coney Island, the way his hand felt intertwined with mine, the electric spark that ignited between us—it all feels like a dream that I'm subconsciously, desperately trying to hold on to.

It wars with my logical brain. *He* said goodbye.

Shouldn't I be doubting that our connection was as real as it felt?

Yet, despite the uncertainty, I can't deny the ache within me. I miss his infectious smile, his unwavering charm, and the way he made me feel like the most cherished person in his world. I find myself torn between the desire to reach out to him, to lay bare my feelings and seek a way back to what we had, and the fear of rejection and further heartache. It's a delicate dance, navigating the labyrinth of emotions that roil within me.

As I continue my solitary journey through the city that never sleeps, I hold onto the flickering hope that our paths will cross again. Maybe fate will intervene, nudging us back together when the time is right. Or maybe I'm just pinning my hopes on a fantasy.

About three blocks away from the hospital, I pause at a traffic light and use the time to take in my surroundings. That's usually a habit for me, clocking the passersby, noting any repeating faces. However, with everything on my mind, I realize this is the first time I've bothered since I left the apartment.

It's not until I make it across to the other side that I notice a flicker out of the corner of my eyes. My eyes immediately home in on the movement, catching only the back of a man's head as he darts into a nearby alley.

It could be nothing, but I pick up my pace a little, throwing glances over my shoulder every few seconds to see if the man reappears.

I'm so distracted by what's behind me I don't notice the man in front of me at first. Perhaps a few hundred yards away, a man stands stock still in the middle of New York's ever-moving crowds.

Staring straight at me.

My blood runs cold. With one last glance behind me, I dart to my left and quickly speed down a new street. Enough left turns, and I will reappear at my original location while shaking off anyone attempting to follow.

"What's the rush, sugar?"

I almost jump out of my skin when I hear a voice call out to me from my left. I don't glance his way, but I know from the direction of his voice that he's blocking off my exit.

I turn right instead and instantly regret it.

The alleyway is tight and littered with trash, and in my hurry, I don't realize that there's a dead end until the wire is practically digging into my face.

I swear under my breath. The fence is almost ten feet tall. Not impossible to scale, but it would leave me vulnerable to attacks if my pursuers were to reach me before I made it to the other side.

"What's your hurry?" another voice coos from behind me.

I stiffen at the sound of three more sets of footsteps.

"You need to stay the hell away from me," I say without turning around. If they're just some creepy assholes looking to intimidate me, they picked the wrong woman.

"Why?" another voice says. "You going to set your brother on us?"

My skin turns to ice. These aren't just creepy assholes. These are Dead Eyes.

Dead Eyes who know exactly who I am.

I pull my gun out of my purse and turn around in one swift movement, leveling them all with the biggest sneer I can muster. "I don't need my brother to defend myself."

As I stare them down, I commit their faces to memory. The three men look relatively smart and wear their suits like they were born in them. Annoying, as it makes it near impossible to tell how well-armed they are.

"You're just one girl," the third man croons. "You don't have it in you, and there's no one here that will hear you scream when we take you."

"I have backup," I lie easily.

The third man laughs. "No, you don't."

"We've been watching you, Aimee," the second clarifies. "You really think you could come back to New York without anyone noticing?"

"I'm not going anywhere with you. You'll have to kill me."

The men look to the first man—clearly the leader, judging by his posture and the way the other two seem to be waiting on his cues.

Finally, the leader answers for the three of them. "I'm okay with that."

Fuck. I'll defend myself, but I've only ever shot another person once, and it was non-lethal. If I'm going to escape this alley with my life, I'm going to have to kill all three of them.

I take a deep breath, trying to steady the trembling in my hands. The weight of the situation presses down on me, and the reality of what I may have to do in order to survive fills my mind.

How many bullet wounds have I cleaned? How many people will I have to save to make up for the three lives here? I've witnessed the pain and suffering caused by violence, and I've dedicated myself to undoing that damage. As a doctor, my purpose has always been to heal, to save lives, and to bring hope to those in need. Yet, here I am, faced with the brutal reality of doing the exact opposite.

The weight of their lives hangs heavily on my conscience. But amidst the turmoil, a flicker of determination ignites within me. I must find strength in the knowledge that my actions, however difficult and harrowing they may be, are driven by the primal instinct to survive. And I need to survive. For Roisin.

With every ounce of resolve, I push aside my doubts and embrace the survival instinct coursing through my veins. These men have cornered me, threatening my life, my family, and I will not become a helpless victim.

As I think this, another figure enters the alleyway. A hoodie covers his face from view, but the way the other men acknowledge him tells me everything I need to know. It's four against one, and my odds are looking worse by the second.

"Kate told you not to engage," the new man says gruffly.

The leader lets out a grunt. "So?"

"Stand down," he barks. The order seems to echo in the alleyway, bouncing off the walls. There's something familiar about the sound that I can't quite place.

"You know what?" the leader says, turning on me with a dark look in his eye. "I don't think I will."

I turn to aim my gun at him as he begins to stalk toward me. With every step, his mouth spreads into a crude smile. The kind that promises that whatever terrible things he has planned for me, he's going to *enjoy* it.

I take off the safety and breathe. Slowly. In and out. A clean shot through the heart at this distance will kill him instantly. It would take me only a few seconds more to hit the others in the same spot. There's a possibility that one of them might have a faster draw, so I mentally size them up and determine which order I need to fire. The calculations sharpen my mind and help me detach as I begin to pull the trigger—

Thump.

The leader approaching me suddenly falls to the floor.

Behind him, the man in the hoodie quickly withdraws his hand before kicking the guy next to him in the chest. The second guy goes flying to the floor.

"The fuck!" the third man yells in surprise, withdrawing a knife from his jacket and turning away from me to face his new opponent.

My savior stalks closer to him, effortlessly dodging the haphazard swings of the Dead Eyes' knife. In a flash, the knife is knocked to the floor, and the Dead Eye takes a fist straight to the face with a sickening crunch. He buckles at the impact, and I watch his eyes roll back as he hits the ground, out like a light.

Under different circumstances, I might even be impressed. But just as I think it, the other Dead Eye recovers from the kick to the stomach and approaches the other man from behind, locking his arms around his neck.

The two scramble for a moment, the Dead Eye pulling down the other man's hood so I can finally see who it is.

At first, it's just a crop of dark hair, but then I see the hard lines of his forehead, his jaw. His hazel eyes, gleaming in anger.

My world starts spinning.

Relief hits me first.

If he's here, that means I'm okay, right? He's here to rescue me and make sure these men can't hurt me anymore.

But they knew him. The Dead Eyes knew him.

He knows who I am.

I watch in horror as he flattens the Dead Eye to the floor and begins kicking him mercilessly. Each blow has the man on the floor jolting into angles that shouldn't be possible for the human body to attain.

It's relentless. Every hit has my mind spiraling further and further into madness.

I hear myself gasp, the name tumbling out of my mouth a moment later.

"J-Jack?"

Chapter Fourteen

Jack

"J-Jack?"

I breathe heavily, staring down at the man on the floor. I don't know what came over me. As soon as I saw them advancing on Aimee, the betting man I am vanished and something else took his place. All I could see, all I could hear was the roar in my mind.

Stay away from her.

The poor fucker at my feet got it the worst. He's bloodied up good, but there's no way he won't rat on me the minute he wakes up.

But right now, there are more pressing concerns.

I turn to Aimee, ready to find a quivering mess of the woman I left only a few hours ago...

...Only to find her standing there with her gun trained on my chest.

She looks torn between horror and relief.

"Aimee..." I say

"Who are you?"

Her grip on the gun tightens, her gaze locked onto me. The tension in the air is palpable as silence hangs between us.

"We can't stay here," I urge, my eyes darting to the unconscious man on the floor. Time is slipping away, and if we don't get out of here soon, things are going to get messier than they already are.

Aimee's expression contorts with a mix of disbelief, confusion, and anger.

"Who are you?" she demands again, her voice quivering with a hint of betrayal.

I take a deep breath, searching for the right words to convince her. "The Duffys are coming for you, Aimee. All of them. You think you can take them on your own?"

Her eyes flicker with conflicting emotions, torn between trusting me and doubting my intentions. I can sense her vulnerability, her fear for her own safety.

"You stay here, you're dead too," I assert firmly, my voice laced with urgency. "I know you don't trust me, but right now, we need to focus on getting out of here alive."

"How did they know where I was?"

"I don't have time for this." I grab my phone out of my pocket and hit Kate's number.

She picks up at the second ring. "Talk to me."

"Withdraw. Your three scouts were unconscious when I arrived."

"Copy that," she says, hanging up. The text comes through a second later.

KATE: *wtf is going on*

I ignore it for now, shoving the phone deep into my pocket as I approach Aimee. She still has her gun trained on me and doesn't waver, even as I come so close that I can feel the cold metal of her gun pressed against my chest. Despite the tension and the danger, I remain steady, meeting her unwavering gaze.

"If you were going to shoot me, you would have done it already," I say calmly.

She hesitates for a moment, her finger poised near the trigger. Then, with a defiant click, she switches off the safety. The intensity in her eyes doesn't waver.

"Aimee," I speak her name softly, hoping to break through her anger and mistrust.

"Give me one goddamn reason I shouldn't shoot you for selling me out to the Duffys," she whispers, her voice laced with frustration and betrayal.

"Because I didn't."

Her gaze narrows, searching for the truth in my words. I hold my breath, waiting for her decision, hoping that she'll see the sincerity in my eyes. The weight of the situation hangs heavily between us.

"Then who?" she finally asks.

"We can have this conversation in a more secure location," I reply. "But right now, I need you to lower the gun and come with me."

I half expect her to deny me, but after a moment, something in her breaks, and I watch in relief as she puts her gun down. I open a hand to her and she hands it over reluctantly.

"I have a bike just around the corner," I say, tucking the gun in my jacket and setting off down the alley.

Aimee is at my side a split second later, glancing around us, more alert than I've ever seen her. "A bike?"

I lead her to my Harley—which is currently leaning against the wall of a boarded-up shop. I wouldn't usually leave her out in the open like this, but thankfully off the main street, there are not as many people around. The black paint glistens like new, and I know when I start up the engine, she'll purr like she's just been wheeled off the showroom floor.

Usually, people are at least a little impressed when they see her. Aimee, however, looks entirely disenchanted with the idea.

"You can wear the helmet if you don't trust my driving skills," I say, offering it to her.

She mutters something under her breath about "safety" and "road traffic accidents" before taking the helmet from me and fastening it under her chin.

I shake my head. All the things to be worried about, and she's fixating on traffic hazards?

Jumping onto the bike, I go through my usual checks. Thank God, the fuel is looking good; we're going to need it. I rev the engine once, twice, before realizing Aimee hasn't got on yet.

"Aimee…"

Through the windshield of the helmet, I can see her biting her lip. No doubt weighing up her options if the glance behind her is anything to go by.

"I'm the devil you know," I say firmly, hoping it's enough to sway her. "Promise I'm better than the devil you don't."

If we hang around much longer, someone will discover the bodies.

She seems to realize this too and, without a word, jumps on the back of the bike. Her arms hesitate before wrapping themselves around me.

I try not to think too hard about her warm body pressed against mine as I kick off the sidewalk and take us back to the main street.

**

The only place secure from Padraic is my apartment on the upper east side. It's not as extravagant as the Duffys' usual taste in properties, but it's sturdy. Most importantly, it's off the books for whenever I need to lie low. Especially from my family.

The moment we step into the industrial-style apartment, I'm hit with the familiar wave of raw urban charm. The spacious loft, with its open floor plan and high ceilings, finds a balance between ruggedness and sophistication.

The walls, all exposed bricks and weathered concrete, whisper stories of the building's industrial past. Large windows stretch from floor to ceiling, flooding the space with an abundance of natural light.

A mix of vintage and contemporary furnishings fills the room. A plush leather sofa, an heirloom from my grandfather, sits next to a sleek glass coffee table. In one corner, an industrial metal bookshelf displays a curated collection of some of my favorite books, and a vintage record player perches on a reclaimed wood console, ready to fill the air with the warm melodies of vinyl.

It's been a while since I've ever had need of it, but there have been countless times where I've had to lay low here. Usually, it rankled to be unable to do anything but sit on that couch, listening to the dulcet tones of 70s R&B, but if I could, I'd take Aimee and pull this place in around us for a few months.

When I walk into the living room, it takes me a moment to realize Aimee hasn't budged an inch from the door.

I sigh. "You can come in, you know."

"Who are you?"

Her expression is filled with determination, and I know getting through this particular conversation is going to take more than a little work. I'm quickly discovering that you'd be hard-pressed to meet a woman as stubborn as Aimee Maguire.

I wrack my brain for a simple answer. "It's complicated."

"Just answer the goddamn question, Jack. It's not that complicated."

"My name is Jack Duffy, and yours is Aimee Maguire. There is nothing about *this* that isn't complicated."

I see the realization dawn on her. It's like it's happening in slow motion, watching her mentally piece together all the information. She staggers forward, and the door slams shut behind her, making her flinch.

"I'm sorry," I say unnecessarily.

What am I apologizing for, the door? The deception? The decades of rivalry our families have had?

Aimee takes another step; her eyes are now glazed over entirely. Suddenly, she springs forward to strike me, and I catch her arm a fraction of a second before she's able to land the blow. Only for her to maneuver herself expertly and attack me with her other hand. It hits me square on the neck, and I gasp out on impact.

"You're a fucking Duffy?" she hisses at me as she tries to shake my hand from her arm.

Despite the fact I feel like I'm choking, I hold it firm. "You're a fucking *Maguire*."

"This whole time?" Aimee tries to hit me again, but I grab her other hand and take out her legs from under her. She collapses, and I hold her arms above her head.

"Don't make me tie you up," I threaten her.

She sneers at me and kicks out at my crotch, and I barely dodge out of the way in time. Aimee shrieks in frustration.

"Aimee."

"Fuck you."

"Aimee."

"You lied to me!" she cries out.

"You lied to *me*."

Aimee collapses to the floor, her whole body shaking.

"But I wasn't cruel about it." She lets out a heart-wrenching sob. "You flirted with me. You had *sex* with me, Jack. You… you won me stupid prizes on the boardwalk. You made me think you might actually like me."

Slowly, I let go of her hands. Her pain affects me more than I would ever admit to anyone.

I did this to her.

I caused this.

Whatever happens next, I don't think I will ever be able to forgive myself for this moment.

I kneel down next to her, watching helplessly as her body shakes with her sobs.

"Please… Aimee…" I say softly. "I didn't know. You have to believe me."

She looks up at me skeptically. "How could you not know?"

"I was looking for Roisin, not—"

She suddenly lurches forward to try and hit me again. "Stay away from my sister. She has nothing to do with this!"

Again, she narrowly misses my face with her swipe, and I grab hold of her wrists in my hand.

"Okay, okay. I know that now," I say, trying to calm her down. "I'm not going to hurt Roisin, and I'm not going to hurt you."

Aimee stares at me before asking quietly, "She's safe?"

I grimace. "From me."

"What's that supposed to mean?" Aimee glowers at me.

I run a hand through my hair. "Padraic is looking for you both."

Aimee's eyes widen with disbelief, her voice trembling. "What have we ever done? Why would he be looking for both of us?"

"Because your brother killed mine," I say quietly, my tone heavy with the weight of the truth.

Aimee's face contorts. "Connor… He… No, he wouldn't."

"I was there."

"You're lying," Aimee accuses, her voice laced with bitterness.

I try to keep my frustration at bay. "Why would I lie about this?"

"You've been lying to me since the moment we met!" Aimee raises her quivering voice. "How can you stand there and ask me to believe you?"

"Because I just put everything on the line to get you out of there," I roar. "They were coming for you with the full strength of the Dead Eye forces. If anyone finds out what I've done here today, I have as much to lose as you do."

I instantly regret losing my temper. A flicker of alarm crosses Aimee's face as she backs away from me, straining against my grip. I close my eyes and try to regain some composure.

"You expect me to say 'thank you'?" Aimee says once there's space between us again. "It's your fault they came after us in the first place."

I breathe in and out. "I didn't tell them anything, I swear. Someone found out you worked at the hospital and pulled your records."

The mood immediately shifts. Where there was once anger and resentment, Aimee's doe-like eyes are now filled with fear. "They... they know where we live?" Her voice is barely a whisper.

"Yes."

"Roisin. Roisin is still in the apartment."

My heart sinks. I failed to consider Roisin's safety in the chaos.

"Jack," Aimee pleads, struggling against my grip. "Jack, please. Let me go. I need to go get her. I need to make sure she's safe."

I shake my head. "You can't leave this apartment."

Aimee's eyes blaze with defiance. "You can't keep me here."

"I can and I will," I assert, my grip tightening. "You don't know what's out there waiting for you."

She changes her tactic and begins to beg. "Please. Leave her out of this. I'll do anything. You can take me to Padraic, even. I won't resist."

Aimee's pleading eyes pierce through my resolve, but I know deep down that leaving her behind is the only way to keep her safe.

"I'm sorry."

Aimee's anger flares, her voice trembling. "You think you can make decisions for me? You think you know what's best?"

"I'm doing this because I care about you," I reply, hating the fact that I'm only admitting this aloud for the first time during *this* conversation. But it seems to soften Aimee's hardness. "I will find Roisin and make sure she's safe. It's too dangerous for you out there right now."

I let go of Aimee's wrists, and she slumps to the floor. "What about you? You just took out three of your own men."

"I'll be fine," I say as I stand up.

This is entirely the wrong thing to say. "So, I'm not allowed to leave because I'm not a big, scary man, is that it?"

I watch as Aimee tries to stand up again, only her legs keep shaking so hard they give out from under her. She's such a force to be reckoned with; even when she's too weak to inflict physical damage, her tongue will lash out like a holdout gun. Despite everything, there's a deep fondness beginning to take root in my chest that I can't shake.

"You're not leaving because I'm not ready to lose you."

"You... selfish bastard! This is my sister we're talking about!"

Without looking back, I step out of the apartment, leaving Aimee behind.

I can still hear her cursing me out as I close the door behind me.

Chapter Fifteen

Jack

I look down at my phone and reread the text.

KATE: *wtf is going on*

It can't have been more than an hour since she sent it, but I can practically feel her impatience for my reply. It's not that I distrust my cousin (okay, maybe a little), but this isn't exactly something I want to drag her into.

My thumbs hover over the keyboard for a moment before I shoot over my response.

JACK: *I've taken care of it.*

Her reply comes seconds later, as if she is staring at her phone.

KATE: *That's not an answer.*

I mentally weigh up the pros and cons of telling her. Knowing Kate, keeping things from her will lead to disaster. She has a tendency to stick her nose into places it doesn't belong, and I can't gauge how far she'd be willing to go to get her answers. But telling her could put both myself and Aimee at risk.

I just need to give her enough information so she'll back off.

JACK: *There's an asset at the apartment.*

KATE: *Ok.*

JACK: *Did you withdraw?*

KATE: *3 still missing; everyone else is back.*

I put my phone away with a sigh; at least I've managed to solve one of my problems today. I still finish walking the perimeter of Aimee's apartment, just in case. But it seems Kate came through—there's no sign of anyone lingering in Brooklyn this afternoon.

There's a tiny cafe on the street opposite Aimee's apartment that I slowly make my way over to. Maybe coffee will help my dismal outlook on life.

How the hell did things go wrong so quickly? It was only a couple days ago we were walking the boardwalk at Coney Island. Dating Aimee was meant to be simple, a respite from the rest of my life. Perhaps it was foolish of me to believe that I could have something like that without consequences. Lord knows He doesn't usually let me catch a break.

I order a coffee at the bar and take it to the wobbly wooden table outside. It's not entirely practical, but the vantage point of the entrance to Aimee and Roisin's apartment complex is perfect.

It was a complete oversight on my part, not thinking about Roisin. When Kate told me that they were closing in on Brooklyn, the only thing I was focused on was getting Aimee out of there. But the truth is, Roisin is in just as much danger as Aimee.

Their apartment is now compromised, so ideally, I want to move her out as quickly as I can. But I can't guarantee that she'd follow me if I approached her directly, and it seems like a disaster waiting to happen to take her back to my apartment. Both sisters in one place would mean double the reward for Padraic when he finds us.

And it is a question of *when.* Sure, only Kate and I know about the apartment. But it wouldn't take them long to find out, especially if Ray starts looking into my online history.

So the question remains, where do I take her, and how do I get her to come with me?

From our brief interaction, I could tell Roisin was definitely the younger sibling—unguarded and audacious in a way her sister certainly isn't. Looking back, it makes me wonder just how much Roisin is aware of the underworld sniffing at her doorstep.

I take a sip of my coffee as I scan the cars passing by. No familiar license plates.

Aimee has already proven she is willing to do anything to keep her sister safe, even at the cost of her own life and well-being. I wouldn't put it past her to try and shield her from their past.

I mentally do the math—Roisin would have been about sixteen when they left for LA. Old enough to remember, then. Odd. Although, she is training to be an actor. Maybe she's just better than the rest of us at pretending it isn't real.

Actor.

She's at Julliard.

The idea is still forming in my brain as I hit the call button on my phone.

"Jack Duffy, how the devil are you, my boy?" Douglas Jones' booming British accent sounds down the receiver only a few moments later.

"I thought you might be too famous to answer my calls these days," I immediately quip back.

"Did you not hear my Oscar's speech? You got name-checked."

"Aye," I reply, unable to keep the smirk off my face at the memory. "It was kind of you to mention me before your wife and all."

"Ex-wife now, I'm afraid."

"Pity. She was flirting with me, you know."

Douglas lets out a low chortle. "I've missed you, my boy. What can I do for you?"

I get straight to the point. "Are you still lecturing at Julliard?"

"When I can," he replies, the question of why evident in his voice.

"I need one of your students in witness protection."

There's a moment of silence as Douglas processes this. I'm not the kind of person who cashes in favors like this, and Douglas knows that as well as anyone. If it were anyone else making the request, I imagine he'd deny them. His integrity as a scholar and artist is absolutely paramount to his success.

"When?" His voice finally comes through the receiver, and I let out a sigh.

"Now."

Another pause; this time, my heart begins to race.

"Consider it done, my boy," Douglas assures me.

I feel a sense of relief washing over me. "Thank you."

"Campus security is tighter than Fort Knox these days, and there's plenty of accommodation," Douglas replies as if thinking aloud his plan of action.

"Perfect," I reply sincerely.

"May I ask who?" Douglas's voice holds a hint of curiosity.

I freeze.

I knew I would have to tell him, but the more people that know, the greater the risk to all of us.

"I'm going to need your absolute discretion," I emphasize.

"You think so little of me?" Douglas responds playfully.

"Padraic *cannot* hear a word of this," I insist, needing him to understand the gravity of the situation.

Douglas' tone becomes more serious. "Understood."

"Her name is Roisin Maguire."

"Roisin? Dear God… I thought the hair was just a coincidence…" Douglas' surprise is palpable.

"Your discretion, Douglas," I remind him firmly.

"Of course, of course. I will have someone call her now and make sure preparations have been made by the time she arrives."

I glance over to the apartment doors again, but there's still no one in sight. But for how long?

"This is time-sensitive."

"Then I will make the call myself. You have my word," Douglas promises.

I don't doubt that Douglas will handle the matter with utmost care and secrecy. The only issue now is making sure Roisin reaches her destination in one piece.

I thank Douglas, hang up my phone, and settle into my chair. Knowing the state Roisin was in this morning, it may take a while for her to surface, so I begin nursing my coffee slowly.

Once Roisin is safe, the next thing on my ever-growing damage-control list is her sister.

My reaction in the alleyway might have been motivated by anger, but I stand by it. Those men should never have approached her like that.

Would I have done anything differently if Padraic's plan had worked out as intended?

Would I have beaten Kate to a pulp if she tried to take Aimee away?

I'd like to think not. I'd like to think I have at least a shred of respect left for my family or, at the very least, Kate. But really, what difference would it have made?

In both scenarios, Padraic would eventually have had Aimee in his clutches.

I grimace, knowing exactly what Padraic would do. At best, she would be used as bait to draw Connor out into the open. At worst... I don't want to think about it.

Saving an innocent woman from that fate has to be the right thing to do. Even if the family resents me for it.

But for how long will I be able to save her?

Padraic will get her one way or another. Whether I keep her in my apartment or let her go, or hand her over myself.

I need to find a way to protect her. If I could somehow prove Aimee's innocence or persuade Padraic that she's not worth the effort...

If I could use the turmoil over the Dead Eyes' line of succession to my advantage, make a play for the position of heir that undeniably supports my claim to even Padraic… Maybe I could find a way to make it clear that she's under my jurisdiction.

Graham used to have that kind of power—no one would defy his decisions, not even Padraic. The respect given to the heir to the Duffy line is, historically speaking, unparalleled. We were always looking forward to the future, which is why we denied the British during the famine.

All I need now is to figure out how I can make that play…

My thoughts are interrupted by a redhead emerging from the apartment complex, weighed down by an oversized suitcase and several large bags. Whatever Douglas told Roisin, she clearly intends to be away for a while. That, or she's slightly more high-maintenance than her sister.

She doesn't notice me watching her intently as she stands on the curb of the sidewalk and waits patiently for a taxi to pass by.

I finish my coffee quickly and hurry back to my bike parked up around the corner. By the time I ride by the apartment, Roisin is throwing her last bag into the back of a yellow cab and sliding into the passenger seat.

I watch in my rear-view as the cab pulls out and begins its journey to Manhattan.

It's easy enough to stay within line of sight of the cab. The New York traffic never fails to disappoint when it comes to snail-paced speeds. Every now and again, I spy a flash of red hair in the back window, and I'm reminded of the redhead I have back home.

I hope Aimee is holding up all right on her own. At least I had the advantage of figuring this all out this morning; I imagine she's still reeling from the information.

Because seriously, what are the odds of something like this happening? The whiplash of feelings would be enough to blindside anyone, and Lord knows I have no idea where I stand with her anymore.

Yet a selfish part of me is comforted by the fact I don't have to deal with this alone anymore. At least now, whatever happens, we'll both be on the same page.

If she never wants to see me again after this, then I will have to deal with that. But for now, it's in both our self-interests to work together. And that provides me with no shortage of comfort, even under the circumstances.

Finally, Roisin's taxi pulls into West 65th Street, and I'm forced to abandon my bike and continue my mission on foot.

There are kids of all different artistic persuasions lingering by the entrance, and I can only pray that I blend in on some level. Maybe I look like a drummer or something, I don't know.

I keep a keen eye on Roisin as she exits the cab when finally, another figure catches my attention.

The last time I saw Douglas, it was on TV, and the camera certainly did him a favor or two. Nonetheless, he approaches Roisin warmly and offers to take one of her bags. As she unloads her suitcase, Douglas glances around cautiously until his eyes meet mine.

He offers me a friendly smile, and I nod in return.

Roisin is safe. My duty here is done.

I don't linger a moment longer and disappear into the crowds of New York City.

Chapter Sixteen

Aimee

I think I must have screamed myself hoarse, cursing out Jack Duffy. *Jack fucking Duffy.*

All this time, I'd been doing everything I possibly could to stay away from the Irish families. Then, not only did I lead them straight to us, but I went and slept with Padraic Duffy's bastard son.

I wrack my brain, trying to place him in the memories I spent so long trying to repress. I remember once seeing him from a distance at a gala. Back then, he was nothing more than skin, bones, and a mop of dark hair that Connor told me to stay away from. I couldn't have been more than eight or nine.

How was I supposed to know that my Jack, or at least the guy I had been kinda dating, was that same boy?

A shiver runs down my spine when I think about what Connor might say now. His vendetta against the Duffy boys was always at the forefront of his mind. But for him to actually kill one, in cold blood...

What happened to my brother in the years we were away?

The last time I saw him, I'd been begging for his help. Begging for him to come with us to LA. But Connor's place has always been in New York. It didn't matter how bad things got with my father, how many awful things

Caleb Maguire did to his family, to Roisin… Connor was never going to give that up.

He'd been making plans for the Maguires well before my father died, and I was an idiot to think that he might have let the family waste away. That without my father here, Roisin and I would be safe to come back to New York.

The last I heard from him was the invitation to my father's funeral. I don't know how he got our address, but I will never forget the day that small envelope arrived through our door. Roisin celebrated, of course—but her only memories were of the man who would encourage her to take the drugs he was supposed to sell.

But I still remember what he was like when my mother was still alive. It doesn't make everything he did afterward okay, nor is my mother's death a valid excuse for his behavior. Logically I know that. Which is why it surprised me so much that I truly grieved for his loss.

Grief. That's the emotion I'm feeling right now too. Grief for my sister, who doesn't know what the hell we've walked into by coming here. Grief that if she's caught, her life will be snatched away from her again after we spent so long trying to rebuild.

Grief that I couldn't have just one nice *normal* thing. That after everything, the universe still doesn't believe I deserve it.

Fuck this.

I've played it safe; I've kept my cool. I did everything I could to protect my sister—now, whether or not Jack makes good on his promise to keep her safe, I need to protect myself.

I stalk over to the kitchen and start pulling out drawers. This is the home of a mobster; if there aren't any concealed weapons somewhere, I'd be very surprised. However, after a few minutes of searching, all I can find is a serrated cooking knife that at least looks sharp enough to do some damage.

My next stop is the bedroom. I don't know why I'm so surprised to discover this apartment only has one bedroom, but I suppose Jack doesn't really strike me as the kind of guy to entertain.

I can't say I love the industrial look as a design choice in usual circumstances, but Jack's room has a certain charm that couldn't be pulled off without the exposed-brick walls or the iron beams supporting the ceiling. His bed is built into the foundation of the room, and there are a dozen built-in lights that cast a warm glow.

I beeline for the bed, turning over all the pillows and sheets. It's not until I lift up the mattress that I find it. A short pistol. East to conceal, fully loaded. Bingo. I tuck it into the back of my pants and do my best to reset the bed.

When Jack took my gun off me, I knew I'd come to regret it. Now, with the reassuring weight pressed into my back, I begin to relax a little.

Yes, this might be the worst situation I've ever been in, but I've gotten myself out of sticky situations before. The one thing I lack right now is information. What is Padraic's plan if he catches me? How long will Jack be willing to keep me here before he relents and hands me over? How could I get a message to Connor to tell him I'm alright?

I'm drawn out of my musings by the sound of the front door opening, and I'm immediately on high alert.

Slowly, I creep out of the bedroom, my knife tucked in close to my body. If it's an enemy, I need the element of surprise to have even the slightest hope of bringing them down. If it's Jack... well... that's too bad.

I step out into the living room quietly, taking cover behind one of the steel pillars before peering around to look at the front door.

But there's no one there.

I frown; I swear I heard the door open...

"I take it you're not expecting any visitors today?"

I spin instantly to find a stunning blonde leaning casually on the couch behind me. *Behind me.* How did I not hear her?

Lowering the knife slightly, I take a step toward her cautiously. "You usually break into people's homes, do you?"

The blonde fixes me with a dazzling smile. "As a matter of fact, yes. But in this instance, I didn't really break in. I used to live here."

Shit, a Duffy then. "'Used to' being the operative words there."

"Touché," she concedes. "I admit it; I'm only here to make sure Jack hasn't burned it down yet."

Despite her elegant features and perfect mask of indifference, I can tell she's sizing me up. Seeing how I'll react to the mention of Jack's name.

We stare at each other for a moment, sizing each other up until she finally breaks and shakes her head. "What a fucking mess."

I cringe at her assessment. "Who are you?"

"Kate St. Michael," she replies without hesitation.

The name rings a bell. "He spoke to you on the phone before?"

"Yes," Kate replies, tilting her head. "May I ask who you are?"

"He didn't tell you?"

She smirks and looks down at her hands. "I can guess."

I hold the knife in my own hand more securely. "He knows you're here?"

"Said you might be staying here a while," she replies, holding up a plastic bag and chucking it to me.

I catch it awkwardly and quickly scan the contents. It's just clothing; however, the sizes and styles don't particularly give away that she knew a woman would be wearing them.

With nothing to lose, I take a stab in the dark. "You didn't know who you'd find here, did you?"

Kate's eyes light up. "Oh, you're a smart one, aren't you! Wonderful."

"Does Jack actually know you're here?" I press.

"He will soon," she says with a mischievous smile. "Can I ask you something?" she says casually, changing the subject.

"I feel like you will anyway," I reply as I take another few steps into the living room and take a seat opposite her.

"Why is he protecting you?"

She's watching me so closely; I can imagine she can see how my pupils dilate and contract.

"I don't know."

She makes a thoughtful noise. "You're an excellent liar, I'll give you that much. But Jack always has his reasons, and I suspect you know them."

Do I really, though? He told me he cared about me, but it was in the heat of an argument, and he's done nothing but lie to me since the moment I met him.

I simply shrug. "Maybe he just wants to take me to Padraic himself."

"No, he would have done that already. Why go to all the trouble of hiding you and asking me to help?" Her mouth quirks thoughtfully. "Did you sleep with him?"

I don't respond.

I watch as Kate's eyes go wide in disbelief before regaining her composure. "Yikes, this really is a mess."

For some reason, I feel the need to defend myself to this woman. "I didn't know who he was."

Kate's face breaks into another gorgeous smile as she nods. "Sounds like you've had a rough day."

We both bask in the truth of that statement. Jesus, this morning I was worrying about normal things like Roisin and when I'd be allowed to go back to work. Now I'm worrying about my *life*. Kate, at least, seems to understand some of this. Whatever the reason, she's here.

"St. Michael…" I say after a moment. "You're not a Duffy?"

"Aunty Eliza was married to Padraic, I'm afraid," Kate confesses, throwing her hands up in defense.

I let out a humorless laugh. "So you hate me too?"

She sits back and thinks about that for a moment. "I hate your brother. I hate your family for what they've done to ours for generations, as I suspect you hate mine. But you? I don't know you. I can hate that I don't know you or that I barely remembered you existed until fairly recently. But the rest remains to be seen."

I nod at this. It seems we have a very similar understanding.

"What about you?" Kate asks in return.

"I put that part of my life behind me a long time ago," I reply.

Kate nods toward my hand. "Yet, you're the one still holding the knife."

I glance down at the weapon in my hand and adjust my grip. "Old habits. Padraic killed my mother."

"Connor killed my cousin," Kate counters. "Both acts, I daresay, were done without either of our consent."

The most annoying thing about Kate, I realize, is that she's right.

Padraic killed my mother eleven years ago with a car bomb intended for my father. How old must Kate have been then? Barely a teenager. She had no part in it, as I had none in Connor's murder of the Duffy heir. The only difference that matters now is that her grief probably still keeps her up at night, whereas I haven't dreamed of my mother in years.

"Yet here we are," I say with a hint of irony. But I adjust my tone to something much more sincere when I say. "I'm sorry for your loss."

She waves me off flippantly, but I catch a brief moment of sadness in her eyes. "Are you going to drop the knife now?"

"No."

She furrows her brow. "Seriously?"

"I need it to stab Jack when he gets back."

Kate barks a laugh. "By all means. You're not the only one he's been keeping in the dark."

"He used me."

Kate's eyes turn sad at this. "Whatever you think Jack is going through right now, I can tell you you're wrong. If he pursued you, he would have had his reasons. I know him; he wouldn't stoop that low out of mere revenge."

"He wants to kill my brother," I say as a fact, although somewhere I hope Kate will deny it.

She simply sighs and replies, "I wouldn't put it past him, no."

"You understand why I can't just accept that. Why do I have to hate him?"

"Sure," she says earnestly. "Doesn't make the situation any less shit, though, does it?"

I fall back into the couch. "I suppose you're right."

"Usually am," Kate remarks cheekily. "But Jack? He's an asshole, sure. But he's not as bad as you think."

I scoff. "He's bad enough."

At that moment, the telltale creak of the front door opening fills the space between us, and I'm instantly on my feet. Knife ready to strike at a moment's notice.

When the door opens, and Jack steps through, I falter.

He looks furious.

Chapter Seventeen

Jack

Aimee's words pierce through me as I listen to their conversation through the door.

What the hell is Kate even doing here?

I only told her I had an asset secured at my apartment. A courtesy, more than anything, considering the apartment used to be hers.

I should have known our newly formed "alliance" would only get us so far.

"He's not as bad as you think."

I hear Aimee scoff. "He's bad enough."

Something churns in my stomach. I can't listen to any more of this. I don't bother trying to be quiet as I open the front door and walk into the living room.

Aimee immediately schools her expression into something so cold, she looks almost unrecognizable, a kitchen knife clutched in her hand. Kate, on the other hand, seems entirely unperturbed. When she glances over at me, she doesn't even have the decency to look sheepish.

"Oh, you're back," Kate says, picking herself up from the couch. "I was wondering what was taking so long."

"Kate?" I say evenly.

She throws me an unconcerned look. "Hmm?"

"Outside. Now."

Kate shrugs nonchalantly and does as I ask. She throws a quick glance toward Aimee as she reaches the door. "See you later, Maguire."

My blood boils. Unable to look Aimee in the eye, I simply follow my cousin outside.

She's already standing down the hallway examining her nails—a picture of casual grace.

"The fuck are you doing?" I say quietly.

Kate snorts. "Shouldn't I be asking you that?"

"What are you planning? If you're going to sell me out to Padraic–"

"I'm not going to sell you out to Padraic," Kate cuts me off firmly. "Or any of the other Dead Eyes."

I feel somewhat thrown. "Then why bother coming here?"

"Because you were keeping something from me, and I wanted to know what it was," she snaps. "I thought we were supposed to be on the same side."

"You're annoyed at me because I didn't drag you into this mess?" I say in disbelief.

Kate lets out a tight laugh. "You wouldn't be *in* this mess if you'd told me what was going on before all this happened."

I stare at her. "It's not any of your concern."

"Don't be stubborn about this, Jack," Kate says with an exasperated sigh. "Or maybe I will tell Padraic after all."

"Why do you care?"

She shrugs again. "I like to know things. You hurt my feelings."

Helpful.

I don't have time for this. I simply turn on my heel and walk back toward the apartment door.

"Oh, and Jack?" Kate calls out.

I turn my attention to her, annoyance seeping into my tone. "What now?"

"There's an update on the Arnie Knight situation," she informs me.

"Time and place, Kate. I don't care about that skinny prick right now."

She hesitates for a moment as if gauging my reaction, then continues. "You might in a moment."

Impatience rises within me. "Just spit it out already, Kate."

"The alliance between the Maguires and the Novas has been confirmed," she says slowly.

"We knew that already."

Her eyes narrow, a hint of a smile playing on her lips. "Yes, but rumor has it, Connor is marrying off his sister to secure the deal."

I feel a chill crawl up my spine as the significance of her words sinks in. It makes sense; a marriage alliance would benefit both the Maguires and the Novas. It's not the first time the head of a family has married off their siblings or children to secure loyalty.

But if he intends to marry Aimee…

That sneaky bastard putting his hands on her, making love to her, and drawing out those delicious sounds I know she can make? The wave of jealousy hits me harder than a punch to the face. My own fists tighten in response, begging me to let them hit something until they're bruised and bloodied.

If only Arnie was here right now.

Kate looks at me curiously. "You good?"

I simply nod, not trusting my voice.

"I don't need to tell you that *that*–"She points over my shoulder toward the door. "--is a powder keg just begging you to let it explode."

I turn my gaze toward the door, my jaw tightening. "I know."

Her eyes narrow, a flicker of concern crossing her face. "You are going to have to be careful."

I crack my neck and take a moment to let the tension seep out of my body. "Always am."

Kate just snorts. But then her voice lowers. "I can only cover for you for so long. Padraic is already impatient, and when those scouts report back…"

I take a look at the concern flooding her expression and smirk. "Careful, Kate, it's starting to sound like you're worried about me."

She exhales sharply, her voice tinged with frustration. "I'm worried about the family, Jack. Your house arrest or whatever punishment Padraic is putting you through now has been divisive enough as it is."

Curiosity tugs at me. "What do you mean?"

Her gaze meets mine, filled with a mix of warning and concern. "Padraic is still putting off choosing a new heir. Everyone's on edge with the Maguires crawling out of the woodwork. So if it comes down to it…"

I lean in closer, our voices reduced to a mere whisper. "Are you saying people would back me in a coup?"

"I'm saying," she hisses, coming closer so that she's barely breathing the words, "that this is political, Jack. And that girl in there will not improve your standing."

Another smirk forms on my lips. "Are you my campaign manager now?"

She leans back, her gaze unwavering. "No. I'm your right hand."

It's not something we've ever discussed, but there's something in her eyes that tells me I'll have a fight on my hands if I deny her. But really, why would I? She's the only person I trusted enough to tell about Aimee, the only person who truly feels the way I do about Graham. Despite our differences, our childhood rivalry, I look back on growing up with the two of them now so fucking fondly.

"If only Graham could see us now," I comment.

The hard lines on Kate's face melt into a sad smile. "Then let's do him proud."

I nod at her as she turns away down the corridor.

Throughout the whole exchange, I can practically feel Aimee's eyes burning through the door. For a moment, I wonder how much she heard, but I put it to the back of my mind. There are more important things.

Like a shower.

I can feel a tension headache coming on, and it only gets worse every time I think of the name Arnie fucking Knight.

When I enter the apartment again, it doesn't look like Aimee has moved at all. She just stares at me as I close the door behind me and walk toward the bathroom.

"You going to stand there all day?" I ask.

She doesn't respond, and a glance over my shoulder tells me that she has no intention of engaging in conversation that doesn't involve that knife at my throat.

Shower it is.

Closing the bathroom door behind me, I immediately stick the shower on to let it run. I lean against the sink as the steam begins to fill the room.

The anxiety finally breaks through my carefully built walls.

What the hell am I doing? I can't keep Aimee here against her will, but I can't sit by and let Padraic take her and use her in one of his games.

I can't let her marry Arnie Knight.

I growl at myself.

No. What Aimee does or doesn't do when this is all over is none of my concern right now. I have an entire mob looking for her, and it's only a matter of time before they catch up with me and punish me for betraying the family.

I had a plan before. It could still work, but…

I can't let her marry Arnie Knight.

God, I need to get myself back in the ring. I need to hit something hard.

Instead, I get in the shower and let the firm pressure work out some of the knots in my back. By the time I get out and look in the mirror at my exhausted face, the solution emerges from the chaos. Crystal clear.

Fuck. Aimee is not going to like it.

I dry off quickly and throw on some sweatpants before I step out of the bathroom, a towel hanging from my bare shoulder. Unsurprisingly, I find Aimee's eyes trailing me from the living room. Hawk eyes now, not doe eyes.

"Where is Roisin?" she demands.

I towel off my hair with one hand as I respond, "Safe."

"Where?"

"Julliard," I admit with a sigh. "I have a friend who will keep her on campus until it's safe for her to leave."

The cold look on Aimee's face doesn't warm one bit. "How can I trust this 'friend' of yours?"

I shrug. "You can't. You probably can't trust me, either. What you can trust is the fact that the Dead Eyes won't be able to touch her in school."

She remains stock-still, but I see a little tension leave her shoulders.

I nod toward the knife in her hand. "That for me?"

"Do you want it to be?" she counters bitterly.

I smirk a little, wander over to the bar, and grab a couple glasses. Aimee watches but doesn't leave her sentry post. "What are you doing?"

"Well," I say, dropping two tumblers onto the counter. "I'm about to tell you my plan, and I imagine you'll take it better with alcohol."

I pour us two generous shots of whiskey and push her glass over to the bar stool, indicating for her to sit. Still, she doesn't move.

Sighing, I pick up my glass and throw it down in one. "We have only a few hours before one of those men from the alley report to Padraic. Then, if we're lucky, another day until they find this place."

Aimee absorbs every word but doesn't respond.

"We need to get ahead of this if we both want to survive. Padraic may still be sympathetic if I bring you in now, but I can't guarantee your safety. There are men in that house who will kill you if they get the chance, simply because of your name."

Aimee flinches. "Why do you even care what your goons do to me?"

I reach over and grab the other glass of whiskey and drink it quickly. "It may have escaped your notice, but up until about twenty-four hours ago, I'd come to care about you quite a bit."

She laughs bitterly. "Is this where you tell me you love me and you'll do anything to protect me?"

"This is where you grasp the seriousness of your situation," I hiss, hating the way her words twist painfully through my chest. "On some level I think you know how bad this is, or else you would have left already."

Aimee frowns. "You didn't lock the door?"

"You didn't even *try* to open it?"

She looks away, hiding her embarrassment. "I'm assuming your plan involves working together."

I pour another whiskey. "A bit more than that."

"What more could you possibly want from me?" Aimee says with a humorless laugh. "You've already dragged me kicking and screaming from the life I built for myself, already humiliated me, already put my sister at risk. What more do I have to give you?"

The third shot of whiskey stings as it hits the back of my throat.

"Marry me."

Chapter Eighteen

Aimee

I'm completely frozen in place.

Of all the things that have happened in the last few hours, this is the thing that somehow dumbfounds me the most. Threats to my life, sure. Racing through the streets on a Harley? Whatever. But did he just *propose* to me?

"What?" I reply, suddenly regretting not taking him up on the whiskey.

As if reading my mind, Jack goes to pour us both another glass.

"I appreciate," he begins, not looking me in the eye, "that this might not be the most romantic proposal you could have hoped for."

"It's not romantic at all, Jack," I reply, the bubbling hysteria seeping into my tone despite my best efforts.

"But," he carries on through his clenched teeth, "it's the only way I know to protect you from Padraic."

I take the glass the second he finishes pouring. "What, with a ring on my finger, he's not going to hold me for ransom?"

The alcohol doesn't go down as smoothly as I hoped. It's been a while since I've drunk hard liquor, and Jack doesn't miss my quiet cough when I put my empty glass back down.

The bastard doesn't flinch as he downs yet another shot. "There's a code of respect. If I declare publicly that you're mine, the Duffys won't touch you. That I can promise."

"But there are other ways they can hurt me," I point out.

"Yes," Jack says, finally looking at me with his fierce, hazel eyes. "But they might think twice about it if they think I'm invested in keeping you safe."

The way his eyes pierce through me almost makes me want to believe him. But how many times has this man lied to me now with that same expression on his face? "Forgive me for not feeling remotely reassured by that."

He looks away, but not before I see the anger that flashes across his face. "You have any better ideas?"

"I call my brother right now. He picks me up. You blame him for the attack on those three scouts. We go our separate ways."

He blinks at me as if he wasn't expecting me to have thought it through. "There's a few holes in that plan," Jack reasons.

"Worse than walking into the lion's den with you?" I counter.

"The scouts know I was there, that I attacked them."

I'm shaking my head before he even finishes his sentence. "They got hit over the head! They could be confused."

"One of them, maybe," Jack says, starting to sound exasperated. "But there were three witnesses. And my word doesn't carry the same weight it used to."

"Why?" I demand.

He looks at me for a moment, then pours me another drink. I watch as his hand shakes a little, and the liquor splashes onto the bar. "Padraic… He blames me for Graham's death. He's been punishing me ever since."

I stare at the wasted alcohol, trying to piece together his reaction. Can Jack really be scared of Padraic? Or is there more to it?

"So what, you thought hunting down Roisin would get you back in his good books?" I deduce slowly.

Jack grimaces. "Something like that."

We down our drinks in unison. This time, the alcohol pleasantly warms the twisting sensation in my stomach.

"God," I say after a beat. "I really fucking hate the underworld."

"For what it's worth, I'm sorry I dragged you back into it," Jack replies.

"No, you're not." I laugh bitterly. "I know how this works. It might be a shitty situation, but the fact that you have me here gives you some kind of advantage."

"That's not why—"

I cut him off, uninterested in any more of his excuses. "It's true, though, isn't it? I'm a valuable asset. Whether you hand me over to Padraic or let me go or do something insane like *marry me,* I give you power."

"You owe me nothing," Jack replies cooly.

"Yet you'll have it anyway." I sigh and take another drink. "When my mother died, I swore revenge on the lot of you. Especially Padraic. If Connor asked me to jump, I'd say, 'How high?'"

Jack seems to double-take. "You were on the ground?"

"I was more of a spy… bar work, mostly," I admit. No point hiding it now, I suppose. It was a long time ago now, but I still remember those dark nights like they were yesterday. "But I was so wrapped up in grabbing hold of every morsel of information that would give me the power to take you down, I didn't notice that Roisin…"

I trail off, cursing the alcohol for loosening my tongue so much. Still, it's not like this situation could get any worse.

Jack seems to notice my hesitation. A moment later, he softly asks, "What happened?"

I hesitate, not because I think Jack knowing will change anything, but because it isn't my story to tell. "She got… sick. My father got into some dodgy dealings with the cartel, and Roisin was caught in the middle. She was barely sixteen the night I found her, already going into cardiac arrest."

Jack fills up my glass wordlessly.

"I gave her CPR for so long." I swallow, remembering the fear racing through my veins, the burn of my muscles as I pushed, breathed, pushed. "I still have no idea how she pulled through."

Jack huffs out in amusement, "Maguires are stubborn; I'll give you that."

He's not wrong. I take the shot to prove it. "After she was stable, I packed our bags, and we left."

"That fast?"

I nod. "I begged Connor to come with us, but… he was so consumed by this world. Achieving power and glory and vengeance for our mother's death. Even as he watched me half-carry my sister to the car, he couldn't understand that there was anything more important than this life… even his family."

Apparently Connor had chosen Family—the power, the danger, the responsibility—over *family*, the two girls he was lucky enough to have as sisters. In his position, I might have made the same choice. Didn't make it any less stupid. A tale as old as time, really.

I can practically see the thoughts swimming through Jack's head as I put my glass down on the bar and stand up. "It's all just a game of power, really. Doesn't matter who it is or why they do it—hell, even how much time has passed. It's always the same."

Jack says nothing. He simply watches me like I'm some kind of predator as I turn on him, stepping around the bar to approach him head-on.

"I know what you think you have to do in this situation. But let me tell you, there is always a choice. You can let me go, and I will never come back here. I can live my life. This doesn't have to be a power play."

"He'll keep looking for you," Jack says with a shake of his head.

"Then I'll keep running.'"

"That's not living," he replies, his voice gravelly as I draw nearer. "That's surviving."

I stand before him and stick out my chin defiantly. "I'm not going to marry you, Jack."

"Aimee..." Jack's irritation—and something more—is evident as he reaches out to touch me, but I back away.

"It's too much," I say as my back presses up against a wall.

Jack stalks closer. "I know what this would mean to you."

I laugh bitterly. "I tell you one sob story, and suddenly you think you know me? You have no *idea* what this means."

"You think I'm not affected by this too? You think I haven't had my share of sob stories?" Jack hisses. "I'm sorry. I truly am. But Jesus, Aimee. I'm talking about life and death here."

I shake my head. "You can't make me."

"It's the only way to keep you safe!" His voice booms through the apartment with finality, and I can feel the bottled rage radiating from him as he breathes rapidly in and out.

So, I raise my voice too. "You keep saying that, but why do you even care?"

His hands are suddenly yanking me forward, and his lips crash into mine. It feels like I've been electrocuted, the way my entire body reacts to his touch. I curl into him instantly, instinctively, submitting myself to him.

It would be so easy to lose myself like this...

I pull away abruptly, "For God's sake, Jack. No! You can't just kiss me and expect this to be okay."

He ignores me and kisses me again. His mouth greedily consumes mine, biting at my lip as he tugs my hair, pulling my face toward him.

"Stop it." I feel angry tears welling up in my eyes as his arms envelop me, my body betraying every word that comes out my mouth.

"Marry me," he whispers against my lips.

I shake my head as he kisses me again and again.

"Aimee… please."

Something inside my chest begins to crack. But I ignore it and grab onto his shirt to push him away. "You can't make me."

I barely gain a few inches of space between us. My hands rest on his chest, stopping him from getting any closer, but he rests his forehead against mine.

"You've spent far too long looking after everyone around you," he whispers. "Let me protect you for a change."

"Don't you dare." My voice cracks, and I have to swallow back more tears.

"Then how do I convince you? What will it take, *chroí*?" His voice is laced with desperation, and I can feel my resolve crumbling. He seems to sense it, scooping me up by the knees and carrying me through the apartment.

I could resist this. I *should* resist this.

But the feeling of his fingers digging into my back… His frustrated breaths against my neck as he kisses me there…

"You want a goddamn ring? You want me to fuck you so hard you can't see straight?" he growls as he drops me onto the bed unceremoniously. "What will it take for you to believe that we're on the same side here?"

Jack towers over me, his body shaking, a promise that he will make good on at least one of his threats.

"You're Padraic Duffy's son," I say firmly, refusing to let myself be intimidated by him. "How could I ever trust you?"

Something feral crosses Jack's eyes, and whatever confidence I had a moment before falls away.

"I am not my father."

He pushes me into the mattress, dragging my hands above my head and wrapping them around the bed frame. His breaths come out in gruff pants as he lowers himself on top of me.

Jack leans across me to bite at my shoulder, my neck, my ear. It's torture staying still as his breath caresses my body, so I lower my hands to run them through his hair.

"No," he growls, grabbing my hands and putting them back on the bed frame. "Let me worship you like you deserve."

"You're not going to change my mind by—oh!"

He lifts his knee to press into my core. I don't even register that I'm mindlessly grinding against him until he whispers in my ear. "That's it. Good girl."

I stiffen, and Jack chuckles.

"Why stop now?" he asks, pulling away to slowly unbutton my blouse. He stops with every button to plant a filthy kiss on my lips.

I shake my head as he frees me from my clothes, my bra falling away at the swipe of his hands. Before I have a chance to protest, his mouth is on my chest. His tongue circles my hardening nipple, and my back arches in pleasure.

But then he's gone again. Undressing me more while I try to recover from the sensation of his mouth caressing almost every inch of my body as he kisses a trail up my bare legs. Only stopping when he reaches my throbbing core.

"What will it take for you to marry me?" he asks again, hovering dangerously close to my center.

All I can do is shake my head and pray I can cling on to my resolve.

He accepts the challenge readily, stroking my bare stomach with one hand while his finger dips lazily into my wetness.

"Jack," I breathe.

Not sure if I should be begging him to stop or keep going.

Jack makes the decision for me. He pushes his finger into me. I feel his knuckles push past my entrance, sending blissful sensations of friction through my body. When he withdraws, I instantly crave more.

I moan pathetically, arching up to him encouragingly.

"You like that?" he says, his voice laced with desire.

I can barely whimper my response as he plunges in again.

"We could do this all the time, you know." Jack works me harder, faster. There's nothing else that matters in this world except the way his fingers feel inside of me. "You could have me any time you wanted."

I bite into a pillow to muffle my scream when my climax hits, dampening the bed around me.

Jack growls again. "I told you I want to hear you when I make you cum."

"Fuck you," I say on a rush of air, suddenly very aware of how close I was to giving in to his seduction.

"What will it take?" he asks again, ignoring the venom in my tone.

My patience snaps.

I jerk up quickly, catching him off guard. He falls back onto the bed, and I maneuver to straddle him before he has a chance to manhandle me off. I pin his hands to the mattress, enjoying the wild surprise in his eyes.

"There is nothing you can do to convince me," I reply, reaching for the hardening bulge beneath his pants.

Now it's Jack's turn to stiffen. His muscles go taut beneath as I slowly work his bulge free.

"You think you can offer me your cock, and I will just give in to your every whim?" I say, poising myself over it, coating the tip in my juices. "When I want your cock, I will take it for myself."

I'm so distracted by the fire in his hazel eyes that I almost lose my balance when he stands up.

I yelp, wrapping my legs around him as he backs me into a wall.

"Yes. You. Will," Jack grunts as he presses himself against my stomach. "You see what you're doing to me? You see how much better we are together?"

I scramble to hold onto him, to cling to anything that will give me any kind of momentum. I need him inside me right now, or I think I might explode. But I'm completely restrained by the weight of his body, pressing me harder and harder against the wall.

"Answer me!" he says desperately against my chest, or is it my hair? His hands, his mouth, they're everywhere, consuming me inch by inch.

"Tell me why," I gasp out. Just as my fingers finally find purchase and my nails scrape down the hard muscles of his back. The groan of pleasure it draws from Jack is nothing short of delightful. I do it again.

Whatever restraint was holding him back completely crumbles.

Jack lifts me up, his lips never leaving mine, as he thrusts into me. He swallows my gasp of pleasure as he lowers me down onto a dresser. Bottles and canisters go tumbling to the ground as he begins fucking me, over and over and over.

"I want to protect you," he says gruffly, his rhythm never faltering.

It takes everything within me not to give in to that answer. I begin wriggling away, ignoring his grunts of frustration as I sit up and try to cling to him.

"I don't need your protection!"

Jack grabs my hands again and pins them above my head, moving us against the wall again. The momentum drives him deeper within me, and I scream in pleasure.

His mouth is suddenly by my ear. "Yes. You. Do."

"*Why?*" I breathe, almost too far gone, to remember why I need to know so badly.

But Jack finally breaks. He pulls at my hair, drawing out foreheads together as he pants heavily.

"Because I want you. For fuck's sakes, Aimee. I *crave* you. Even now. This isn't enough. I need to be closer."

I can feel myself tighten around his cock at his words. Jack groans in agony. "Every minute we're apart, you're all I can goddamn think about. You think I want you in the hands of those assholes? You're *mine*."

It's enough to tip me over the edge. All I can do is submit to this pleasure as Jack claims me as his own. My cries fill the apartment as my orgasm shudders through me. Every nerve in my body feels as if it's on fire and my mind goes entirely blank.

All that exists is my ecstasy and sound of the steady, thump, thump, thump of our skin colliding in perfect rhythm. Every second stretches out before us endlessly.

I don't realize I'm sinking slowly to the floor until Jack is picking me up again. He never breaks his delicious movements as he kisses me deeply, licking lazily around my mouth as if tasting my pleasure for himself.

"Mine," he growls against my lips and I feel the vibration of the sound all the way to my throbbing core.

"Yes," I reply breathlessly as Jack lowers us to the bed.

My knees shake as I straddle him, but his hands are suddenly there, supporting me. Helping me lower myself further on to him, and he into me. The feeling of his cock pressing into me so deeply has my back arching in pleasure.

"Say it," Jack says gruffly as his hands ghost over my hips, my chest.

The feeling of him inside me is the most intoxicating ache. I can't help but move myself up and down his shaft to try and find satisfaction as the end of my orgasm threatens to chase it away.

I'm so distracted, I don't realize that Jack's hands stay on my hips until he holds me there, firmly.

"Say it!"he repeats. This time, his tone conveys such a desperate vulnerability, I cave instantly.

"I'm yours," I whisper.

He pushes my hips down. Hard.

"Yours!" I scream. Over and over again.

Water leaks from my eyes as I take him once, twice, three times more before Jack reaches his own climax. His body reaches for mine, and I his.

Wet, panting kisses pepper my face as I cling to him desperately.

Nothing has ever felt like this. No one has ever cared for me, cherished me, *fucked me* like this. There is no one that will ever compare.

"I'll do it," I take a quivering breath in and out. "I'll marry you."

Chapter Nineteen

Aimee

The headache hits first. Then the annoying feeling of my paper-dry tongue against the roof of my mouth.

Perhaps I had a little too much whiskey last night…

… But not enough to forget what I agreed to.

Somehow, that feels worse than the hangover.

The only consolation is that I wake up resting on a hard, warm body. Jack's hand gently strokes up and down my back, sending delightful shivers down my spine. His breath tickles my forehead, where his lips barely graze my skin.

In another life, this would be the perfect way to wake up.

But when I open my eyes and see the face of the man I'm supposed to marry, the cold reality begins to sink in.

In another life, I wouldn't be falling for the son of my greatest enemy.

Jack seems to be lost in his own thoughts too. He doesn't notice my gaze until a moment later.

"Good morning," he says softly.

"You're still here?"

He presses his lips firmly to my forehead. "Where else would I be?"

"A million miles away if you were smart."

Jack smirks at that. "What kind of husband would that make me?"

I grimace. "Too soon."

His smile fades. "I meant it, you know. What I said last night, *chroí*."

I let out a deep sigh as I sit up. "I know."

"If there was any justice in the world, we could have done this properly," he says earnestly. "I could have courted you, taken you for dinner… Some place nice."

"You did do those things," I remind him.

"Once hardly seems enough," Jack remarks before turning to gaze out the window. "If… Aimee, if we get through this… You don't have to stay with me. As long as we're able to convince Padraic and he moves on to the next big thing—"

"You mean after he's killed my brother?"

Jack throws me a weary glance. "That's not what I meant."

"It's true, though, isn't it?" I say, suddenly feeling completely exhausted. "You might be able to protect me with this marriage, but the rest of my family are still fair game."

Not just Connor, but Roisin too…. Sure, Jack may have helped get her somewhere safe. But how long will that stop Padraic from finding her? How long will it take before Roisin suspects something is amiss? Or wanders into trouble by accident?

There has to be a better way to keep her out of this.

Jack watches me carefully. "I don't expect you to stand by while your brother is targeted."

"Good."

"Which is why…" Jack takes a long breath in. "…I'm offering you an out."

I stare at him for a moment to try and discern what he means. "So, when the time comes for Padraic to make his move on Connor…"

"You can leave me," he replies simply.

"Aren't you worried I'll go straight to my brother as soon as I leave? Warn him that you're coming for him?" I say in disbelief. Surely he can't be so trusting of me.

But Jack doesn't waver. "I can only hope that you don't. For your own sake."

My blood runs cold—I know a threat when I hear one. "You'd kill me if we were on opposite sides of the battlefield?" I say bitterly.

"No," he says firmly. "No. But I wouldn't want you to see the person I become when the fighting starts."

I exhale hard. I understand; I'm not sure he'd like the person I would become, either.

"This situation is so fucked," I say after a moment, running my hands through my hair to try and detangle the mess it has become during the night.

Jack offers me a fond smile. "Perhaps we should just focus on one thing at a time?"

Right. First things first: somehow, we need to convince Padraic that we're happily engaged and that I'm not a threat to the Duffys.

A wave of nausea comes over me and Jack places a reassuring hand on my thigh. "It's going to be okay, *chroí.*"

I bite back a response along the lines of "There's no way you can know that" and instead place my hand on top of his and give it a reassuring squeeze. "You keep calling me that…?"

"What, your father never made you learn Gaelic?" Jack says in bemusement.

"*Dia duit,*" I say confidently.

"*A bheil thu gam thuigsinn?*"

I blink. "*Dia… duit?*"

Jack merely grins and kisses me gently. "If we make it through this week, I'll tell you what it means, *chroí.*"

***

Jack's bathroom is blissfully well stocked, and I get the feeling I probably have Kate to thank, judging by all the products tailored to maintaining platinum blonde hair.

It's almost funny how much better I feel after a warm shower and wrapping myself in one of Jack's super soft bathrobes. I step back into the living area of the apartment in a cloud of steam—okay, perhaps I was a little indulgent with the hot water, but it's not like Jack can't afford it.

When I can't find him on the couch or in the kitchen, I return to the bedroom to see him fully clothed and perched on the side of the bed, turning something small over and over in his hands.

"What is that?" I say curiously, and Jack's eyes snap to mine.

"See for yourself," Jack replies, throwing it to me.

I catch the box with one hand and try not to feel too smug about my reflexes. Jack must see it on my face anyway as he sighs dramatically. "Yes, I get it. You're not some helpless damsel in distress. Can you just open it already?"

In an act of total maturity, I stick out my tongue before glancing down at the open box in my hand. I freeze in place.

Resting on a worn, velvet cushion is a dainty platinum ring woven together with tiny rubies and diamonds. It's as if it were made from the branches of a magical, silver rose bush. Though there's not one main stone, the beautiful craftsmanship makes me think I'm holding something priceless.

"It's not exactly an engagement ring, but…" Jack says a little nervously from the bed. "It's the only thing I have of my mother's."

I stare at the way the gems sparkle in the morning light. "It's beautiful."

It's not until he's standing before me that I realize Jack has gotten up.

"I'm glad you like it," he says, offering a hand out for the box.

After another moment, I reluctantly hand it over to him. "Do you remember her at all?"

"My mother?" Jack says, taking a look at the ring himself. "I don't even know who she is. Padraic never spoke of her. Story goes, she left me on Padraic's doorstep with the ring, a fifty-dollar bill, and a note saying the fifty should cover my vaccinations."

I blink a little in surprise. I don't know why I assumed Jack's mother was some kind of ongoing side piece—perhaps because when it comes to Padraic Duffy, I usually assume the worst. But for Jack not to know his own mother...

"What about Padraic's wife?"

Jack snorts. "Eliza was a spiteful witch. In her eyes, I was no more Padraic's son than I was hers." He pauses to lift the ring out of the box. "Even if she had known who my mother was, she would never have told me."

"She died?" I ask, unable to take my eyes off the platinum band.

"Aye, a couple of years ago now."

Jack reaches out to take my hand and my breath catches. With agonizing gentleness, he puts the beautiful ring onto my finger.

We both stare at it wordlessly. The tension between us becomes so thick it's almost tangible.

"It fits perfectly," I whisper, not trusting my voice to speak any louder.

Everything around us seems to drop from existence as if we are in our own little sanctuary. All that matters is the sound of his breathing, how his fingers linger on mine as we watch the ring sparkle on my hand. It's a moment I've only ever dreamt about, but it's happening. Right here and now.

And I can't help the pure joy that fills me from the inside. The anxious, tentative hope that someone might adore me enough to put this ring on my finger. A man who wants me, a man who wants to protect me. A man who *needs* to claim me as his own.

In another life, there would be a thousand fluttering things I'd tell that man right now.

But just as quickly as this feeling envelops us, it breaks away.

Jack suddenly jerks back, clearing his throat. "Make sure Padraic sees it. It might help convince him we're serious."

I gulp back my disappointment and look away, chastising myself.

But dear God, for a moment, I was ready to leap headfirst into that abyss.

Chapter Twenty

Jack

There are about ten thousand things that could go wrong. Every scenario, and every possible outcome to that scenario, plays out in my mind as I take Aimee down to the garage.

Last night everything felt so simple. I was so sure this plan would work, that we'd be able to playact our way out of this.

But waking up with Aimee in my arms... just reminded me of everything I have to lose if this goes wrong. I never meant to start falling for her. But I've never met anyone as fierce, smart, and compassionate as the woman who holds my hand so trustingly now. If anything were to happen to her, I know I couldn't forgive myself.

"Which one's yours?" Aimee asks absently as we walk through the cool basement parking lot.

I cringe a little. But I suppose she'd find out eventually.

"All of them."

"*All* of them?"

"There's parking out back for the other residents," I say by way of explanation.

Aimee stops in her tracks and looks around, her eyes wide as she takes in the numerous sports cars, four-by-fours, and a couple self-indulgent motorbikes I've been meaning to tune up.

"It's like the Batcave down here," she mutters. "How do you afford all this? I thought you said Padraic cut you off."

"Aye, but I was never going to inherit Padraic's fortune, even before all this. Not really the hotel type," I grin at her. "Graham and I, we took over the boxing rings across town. Split them in half, did them all up."

"And they do well, do they?"

I smirk. "Mine does. Although Padraic likes to think the success of Luckies is all his doing."

This makes her smile too. I want to hate the way the curve of her lips pulls at my heartstrings like this, but she just looks so breathtaking. With everything hanging over us, with all this new information out in the open, a part of me had hoped that these feelings would stop.

I have to look away. I pretend to search for the sleek, black BMW I already know we'll be traveling in. It was a gift from Graham after my fighter beat his at the annuals last year. A fact that might at least get us at least through the mansion gates if Padraic is feeling sentimental.

It's not until we reach the car that Aimee asks her next question.

"What happened to Graham's properties after…" She trails off as if anticipating the subject might still be sore.

I offer her a reassuring smile. "Kate has been looking after them, but I know it's not really her thing."

We both slip into the car, which purrs to life at my command.

"Shouldn't you take them on?" Aimee says curiously.

I look over my shoulder to reverse out of the garage. "Hmm?"

"Your brother's fight clubs," she clarifies, her distaste evident in her tone.

"In case you haven't noticed, I've been a bit busy," I say a little defensively. "And they aren't 'fight clubs.'"

Aimee throws up her arms in surrender. "I'm just saying if half the properties are making you *this* much money… Why not break away from the Duffys altogether and start your own legitimate business?"

I raise an eyebrow at her.

Aimee deflates. "It's not a legitimate business, is it?"

"Underground fighting isn't strictly illegal," I say, turning out of the garage and onto the familiar road back to the mansion. "But Bare Knuckle is… frowned upon by most authorities."

"Okay, now it really sounds like 'Fight Club'."

I gasp as if insulted. "Of course not. We actually make money."

"How?"

"Bookies."

"Naturally," she replies, sarcastically.

I bite my cheek to suppress a smile. "You don't approve?"

"Of gambling? No," she says with distaste. "It's a miracle you make any money at all."

"I may have said this before, but I am actually good at what I do," I reply cheekily, which earns me a push on my shoulder.

It feels nice to be like this with her, to joke around and be a normal couple before everything hits the fan. It makes me think about what it might be like… if circumstances were different… to have an ex-mobster as smart as Aimee by my side.

"How would you do it, *chroi*?" I say suddenly, curiosity getting the better of me.

"Do what?"

I gesture outside the car. "Expand my 'fight club' empire?"

She thinks about this for a moment. "Probably by not calling it a fight club."

"You started it," I reply with a laugh.

"You must be quite impressionable, then, for it to have caught on so quickly."

"That's because you're a bad influence."

"Probably more trouble than I'm worth," she jibes back, only to go immediately quiet.

I don't push her, focusing on the road ahead. We're almost halfway there now, and sooner or later, this little bubble we've created for ourselves is going to burst.

"It's going to be okay... isn't it?" Aimee says quietly after a few minutes of stewing in her own thoughts.

Despite my own apprehensions, my gut instinct is to comfort her. To reassure her. But I don't want to lie to her either.

"As long as we work together," I say, finally landing on an appropriate response.

She nods, getting a faraway look in her deep, chocolate eyes. "Copy that."

I have to remind myself to focus on the road. "And stay close."

"Sure," she says a little too quickly.

"I mean it, Aimee. I don't want you wandering around on your own."

She snorts. "Worried I might find something incriminating in a house full of criminals?"

"No, I'm worried those 'criminals' will take their chances with you," I reply, taking a corner a little too aggressively.

"I thought you said they wouldn't touch me if they knew I was your fiancé?"

"Well, no one has ever had a fiancé that looked like you," I say honestly. Theoretically, the lieutenants should discipline their men if they step out of line. But when they're thinking with their cocks... there's no way of knowing what lengths they might go to.

At least Aimee seems unperturbed. "Is that meant to be flattering?"

"Yes," I say, a smile tugging on my lips, knowing exactly how much my response will wind her up.

"It's going to be a long few days, isn't it?" she groans to herself.

I don't bother correcting her. There *is* a possibility that all of this will be over in a few days. A very tiny possibility, but it's still there.

174

Unfortunately, knowing Padraic, his revenge on me will probably drag on longer than needed. All I can do is pray he keeps Aimee out of it.

"Remember," I say, shaking off the thought. "We're deeply in love. You don't know anything about your brother because you've been out of town these last few years…."

"I *don't* know anything about my brother," Aimee points out.

"Then that part will be easy for you." I leave the 'deeply in love part' dangling between us.

Aimee coughs. "How did we meet?"

That makes me pause… I hadn't thought of that. "Hospital?"

"No," Aimee replies determinedly. "I'd rather keep them out of this."

"Okay, so what?"

We finally reach the road leading up to the mansion, and I slow down. The cameras have probably already identified the car, so we may as well give Padraic more time to cool off.

"We met at a bar," Aimee says, drawing me back to our conversation.

"Which one?"

"A nice one; I don't remember the name."

"How long ago?"

"A month."

I nod; that fits the timeline, at least. "Isn't that a short time to be getting engaged?"

"Love is love, right?"

I glance at Aimee. Her face is carefully schooled into a neutral expression. There was no malice in her voice, no resentment. But I can't help but feel a twinge of pain at her words, the deadness of her tone.

Looking back at the road, I realize we're approaching the front gates. Perhaps that's why Aimee has gone so still.

I bring us to a stop next to the intercom but pause before opening the window.

"You ready, *chroí*?" I say quietly.

When she doesn't reply, I look at her again to find her sitting with her eyes closed. The lines of her brow are deeply furrowed, her lips pulled into a thin, displeased frown. She's worn this face in one form or another since the moment I found her in the alleyway. Even in sleep, there was a tenseness to her jaw that wouldn't ease.

Yet, as I watch her, it all begins to melt away.

Her mouth breaks into a pleasant smile, and her eyes open again. It's like she's become a whole new person, a happy, carefree version of herself—and a caricature of the woman I first met. And here she said Roisin was the actor.

"Yes," Aimee finally says with a soft tilt of her head. "I'm ready."

***

The mansion is thankfully quiet as we arrive. But perhaps that's because, according to the doorman, Padraic has been on the warpath ever since I left.

There's no avoiding the pure opulence of the place. It's all tall ceilings and regal architecture—even the corridors are adorned with paintings that make the place feel more like a gallery. For all the distaste the Irish hold for the English, I've often thought the King of England wouldn't seem amiss walking these halls.

Whatever shock Aimee might feel, she seems to have pushed it away. She walks confidently by my side as I take her through each room, barely glancing at the original Monet as we pass by the great lounge.

When we finally reach the doors of my father's office, the guards stationed there barely acknowledge us.

"Is he in?" I ask, taking a casual step in front of Aimee to block her from a thorough inspection.

The men merely nod at me, and I half turn to Aimee, not trusting the guards enough to take my eyes off them. "Perhaps you should let me go in first?"

"I'll be right behind you," she replies quietly.

The guards open the doors for me. I give myself a second, a breath, before striding in purposefully.

Padraic isn't at his desk as he usually is. Instead, he resides in his armchair with a glass of liquor in his hand. He's staring blankly into the flames of the fireplace until he hears me enter and looks up.

His face is a storm of incensed rage. "If it isn't my traitorous bastard."

"Father," I greet curtly.

"Care to explain why you beat up three of my scouts and then disappeared off the face of the earth?"

I bite my tongue. "It's a beguiling tale, I assure you."

"Where the hell have you been?" Padraic snaps, standing from his chair to approach me.

"Busy."

"You evaded Morris."

"Aye."

"Betrayed my order, my final warning."

"Aye."

He gets right up into my face, threateningly staring me right in the eye. "Give me one good reason I shouldn't throw you into the Hudson."

I do not flinch.

"May I introduce you to my fiancé?"

Aimee takes her cue to emerge from the shadows. Her rich red hair flows behind her. Her dark clothes accentuate her hips, her chest, intimidating and yet entirely suggestive. In the time that I've known her, she's never looked quite like this. A vision of pure power.

As she strides toward my father, there's no denying who she is. The power in her walk, the fierce look on her face. She's a Maguire through and through, and a dangerous one at that.

"Dear God," Padraic whispers, the shock evident in his features.

Aimee smiles at him, sickly sweet. "Actually, my name is Roisin. Roisin Maguire."

Chapter Twenty-One

Aimee

I stare at Padraic Maguire without allowing myself to blink.

I've not seen his crooked face in years, and yet he looks exactly the same. The face I've seen in my nightmares, the face my brother swore every vengeance against.

In my peripheral vision, I see Jack staring at me with urgency, but I ignore him.

With me here posing as Roisin, there's no longer a reason for Padraic to go out looking for her. As much as I might want to trust Jack's ability to keep her safe, it's not like he hasn't lied to me before. And when it comes to my sister, it's not a risk I'm willing to take.

To my satisfaction, Padraic lowers his gaze first to look at his son. "Are you going to explain the meaning of this madness?"

"My *Roisin* here," Jack says a little bitterly, "and I got engaged a few days ago, and your men came after her. So, I defended her."

"That's a fucking Maguire."

"We're aware," I say calmly.

"Traitor was too soft a word for you, boy." Padraic sneers. "You are a disgrace to the Duffy name!"

"We knew things would get complicated," Jack replies evenly. "But I assure you *Roisin* poses no threat; she knows nothing of her brother's actions."

Padraic looks ready to strangle Jack, "And you believe her?"

"I only returned to New York a month ago," I say quickly, trying to move to get in between the two of them. "I didn't know what Connor had done until Jack told me."

But Jack refuses to let me pass into Padraic's line of fire, and Padraic simply ignores me, channeling his rage at his son.

"You bring a goddamn Maguire spy into my house? Are you a traitor, or just fucking stupid?"

"Padraic–"

Before I have time to react, Padraic hits Jack across the face.

The smack reverberates throughout the room, and I can't help but cringe at the pure strength needed to make it. But Jack stands impressively firm. It takes me a moment to remember Jack showing me his hardened knuckles at a beautiful restaurant. Boxing, he'd said. It feels like a lifetime ago.

But perhaps there were a few things he wasn't lying about.

"Please!" I surge forward, taking advantage of the shock to push in front of Jack. "I've not spoken to my family in five years. I didn't even go to my own father's funeral," I say firmly, hoping he might have at least gotten the facts to confirm my story. "Do you really think I'd spy for the people that ruined my life?"

Padraic finally pays me some regard, the sneer on his face almost as disgusted as the venom in his eyes. "Your brother shot my son in cold blood. I don't believe a thing that comes out of your bitch mouth, Maguire."

"That's my fiancé you're talking about, Padraic," Jack growls quietly.

Padraic lets out a cool laugh, not taking his eyes off me. "Oh, she's got you wrapped around her whorish fingers, hasn't she."

"You will treat her with some goddamn respect!" Jack roars, and Padraic actually flinches back.

I feel Jack place a warm, solid hand on the small of my back and glance up at him. The strong line of his jaw is taunt with anger, his wild eyes almost unrecognizable.

"I don't care if you hate her; I don't care if you approve. This woman is going to be my *wife*," Jack hisses. "You aren't going to say another word against her."

Padraic looks between the two of us and, for the first time, seems to register that there is *something* going on between us. Or at least that we're presenting a united front against him. Something seems to shift in his eyes.

He takes another, more calculated step back. "We've been looking for her and her sister for weeks, and you had this one the whole time?"

"Aimee went back to LA after one of your men scared the crap out of her at the hospital," I say, trying to mimic Roisin's impertinent attitude the best I can. He may never have met Roisin before, but if there's a chance anyone has encountered her, I want the stories to be authentic. And Lord knows she wouldn't put up with Padraic's shit. "Congrats, you already lost the first sister."

"So, you're not the doctor then?" Padraic says evenly. "Pity, you might have had some use to me after all."

"To you?" I say with a haughty laugh and show him the stunning ruby ring on my left hand. "I think this one goes to Jack, don't you think?"

Jack has gone rigid behind me. The hand on my back grips hold of my waist in warning. But I don't care.

Padraic begins to circle us. "Who knows of this?"

Kate's face flashes before my eyes.

"Only the people in this room," I reply quickly.

Lie. He can't suspect we have allies.

"Where are you staying?"

"An apartment in Brooklyn."

Truth. He knows this already.

"And that's where Jack has been sneaking off too?"

"Yes."

Lie. He can't know about Jack's apartment.

"Why have you agreed to marry him?"

"Because I love him."

The words taste bitter on my tongue. A filthy, terrible lie for a filthy, terrible man.

If Jack was tense before, he's rigid now. I have to fight the urge to turn around and remind him that this is all just a game. Of course, I don't love him, really; there's nothing for him to get so stressed about. I'm just playing the part of his fiancé.

The way my body is so acutely aware of his presence, how it leans into him instinctively. It's not real love; it's just rushed emotions and a high-stakes situation.

Truth?

Then why do I wish so badly that I didn't say it in front of Padraic?

Padraic seems to sense my hesitation and shakes his head, circling back around to his desk. A desk that could hold any number of things that could ruin us. Ruin *me*.

This isn't going well; we aren't getting anywhere. We never should have come here; there's no way we'll be able to get out of this alive or, at the very least, with our sanity still intact. I've heard the stories about the kind of monster Padraic becomes in the interrogation room.

I reach down for the knife tucked into my shoe, but Jack grabs hold of my arm.

Instead of answering my questioning expression, he turns to his father. "Can I speak with you?"

"We're already speaking," Padraic replies, sitting down at his desk.

Without looking at me, Jack says, "A-*Roisin,* could you excuse us for a moment?"

I contemplate putting my foot down and insisting he can say whatever he needs to say in front of me. But even I can admit my presence doesn't seem to be helping our cause.

"Of course, *chroí,*" I say a little bitterly.

Nonetheless, Padraic's eyes widen at my words, and he turns on his son expectantly. I don't want to lose the opportunity, so I back away, giving Jack's lingering hand a squeeze before making my retreat.

As I open the door into the corridor, I find myself gasping for breath, and I have to close my eyes while the rise and fall of my chest slowly begin to slow down. God. It felt like Padraic had sucked all the air out of the room.

It takes me a moment to realize the guards from earlier have disappeared. Odd, Padraic doesn't strike me as the type to go lax on those who abandon their posts.

Unless they heard about Jack's engagement and have gone to spread the news. Shit.

But... that must mean they were able to listen in on the conversation.

I turn around to face the door I just came through and lean against it casually. If anyone were to walk by, it wouldn't seem like I was doing anything suspicious.

However, with my ear closer to the crack, I can clearly make out Padraic's gruff tones. "... fuck are you playing at? She was our biggest asset against the Maguires. Why the hell are you throwing away our advantage to get your dick wet?"

I can just about make out Jack's softer voice as he replies, "Didn't you hear?"

"Hear what?"

"The Nova-Maguire alliance is built on the promise that Connor Maguire will marry his sister off to Arnie Knight."

What. *What?*

Every scrap of my casual pose goes out the window as I press my face against the door.

Since when was Arnold Knight in this equation? When was *marrying* him ever a part of our plan?

"Where did you get that information?"

"Kate."

What had Kate said that day? *"Yikes, this really is a mess."*

Oh my God.

Unaware of my impending breakdown, Jack carries on. "And lovely little *Roisin* out there can't marry Arnie if she's already married to me, can she?"

No. No. No, no, no, no.

"Connor will lose his ally," Padraic replies thoughtfully.

"And in the meantime, the Maguires and Novas won't attack if they think Roisin is here by choice."

"You can't know that."

"I know they wouldn't want her to get caught in the crossfire. I know that it's easier to rescue someone who's willing than kidnap someone who's not."

What the fuck.

Something inside of me starts to break. He's thought about this. This is his real plan.

How could I be so fucking stupid? I even gave him that whole speech about how all the Families ever do is make plays for power, and that's *exactly* what he was doing to me.

"You think you can keep her sweet long enough for you to walk down the aisle?"

"Of course," Jack replies without missing a goddamn beat. That arrogant bastard.

"Fine. But listen to me, boy. If you drop something like this on me again without consulting me–"

"How was I supposed to consult you? You barred me from your meetings."

"You know damn well how this makes me look, and still, you seem to take joy in disrespecting me anyway."

"I assure you, that wasn't my intention."

"No," Padraic's voice starts getting louder. "Your intention was to seek all the glory for yourself. Like you did that day, thinking you could take the Maguires on alone with Graham."

"I was trying to win back your favor."

"By leaving me in the dark!" Padraic roars.

There's a moment of silence. The shock of everything I've overheard has kept me paralyzed—but now I barely trust myself to breathe in case they realize I'm still here.

Luckily, Padraic lets out a deep sigh, and I can sink to the floor. "There's no use arguing about it now. These are the cards you've laid out for me, and now I have to play them. I want both of you on display tonight at *Luckies*, then again at the gala next week."

"Of course," Jack replies for the both of us.

"You will socialize, delight, and charm as many of our allies as you can. But most importantly, that girl needs to appear as if she's in love with you. I don't care how you do it. But, if even a sliver of doubt gets back to the Maguires, I will personally see to her interrogation and hoist whatever is left of her up on the mansion walls for Connor to collect. Are we clear?"

"Yes, sir."

So this is how it's going to be. Jack and Padraic are going to dress me up and flaunt me around to get under Connor's skin. And I let this happen.

"You care for this girl, don't you?"

"I care for this family more."

I can't linger a moment longer. The ache in my chest threatens to explode out of me, and I can't cry here. *Roisin* wouldn't cry here.

Roisin would pick her head up and keep moving.

So, I do.

I make it almost five steps down the corridor when I hear someone call out behind me.

"Hey, you! Stop."

Shit. I turn around slowly to see two men approaching me. Neither looks like the guards we saw earlier, but both hold themselves like they would know how to do the job. The taller one with a buzzcut addresses me first.

"What's a pretty thing like you doing down here?"

"Looking for Jack," I say as if their interruption is merely an inconvenience.

But the buzz cut man booms a laugh and hits his sour-faced companion in the shoulder. "Aren't we all, love."

"Can I help you?" I try again.

This time the other man asks the question, "What's your name?"

"Roisin…"

"Roisin what?"

A shiver of dread goes down my spine as he examines me head to toe. I've met men like this before. Cruel men who use the family as an excuse to do things no sane man would ever do. This man is a *predator*.

"Roisin! I've been looking for you everywhere!"

I turn to see a familiar face and almost sob in relief.

Kate strides over to us in thigh-high boots and an expression that screams, "Don't fuck with me."

She greets me with a side hug. "Are these guys giving you trouble?"

The first man bows his head. "None at all, Miss St. Michael. We were just on our way."

Unfortunately, as he goes to leave, the predator lingers. "If you find Jack, tell him he's a dead man."

"Stop being so dramatic, Morris," Kate replies for me flippantly. "Jack escaped because of *your* incompetence; get over yourself."

With that, Kate begins dragging me away down the corridor. Every stride away from those men eases the tension that has gripped my heart.

"Barely recognized you without that knife in your hand," the blonde says with a devilish smile when we're finally alone.

"Kate, I need to get out of here."

Chapter Twenty-Two

Jack

If my father didn't hate me before, he surely loathes me now.

For a moment back then, I thought Padraic was going to strangle Aimee with his bare hands. The sudden, even calm, circling us like his prey. I've seen him like this before, like an animal preparing his perfect strike.

And he always strikes.

Either Aimee didn't understand the danger she was in or chose to ignore it, but her ability to press every single one of Padraic's buttons clearly felt intentional to him. Perhaps we should have gone with a quieter, less abrasive strategy, but the thought of asking Aimee not to speak is laughable.

But, knowing what she went through with Padraic and her parents... I'm not sure I could even look at Connor without it coming to blows, much less have a conversation. For that, I can only admire her.

If only the thing that makes me admire her so much wasn't the thing that could get her killed.

"Are we clear?" Padraic says, and I nod slowly. Thankfully, with Aimee no longer in the room, he's become more manageable.

"Yes, sir."

Causing a rift between the Maguires and the Novas was a thinly-veiled cover-up for my own selfishness. Padraic may have conceded that there is a tactical advantage in marrying Aimee or, rather, *Roisin*. Still, I do no doubt that he saw right through me.

I can see it as he regards me now, with a calculated look. As if trying to decipher why I would risk everything for this girl. Bringing her here was a gamble, and we both know it. Even if I was just doing it to get under Padraic's skin, I would have been aware of the dangers it would put Aimee in.

"You care for this girl, don't you?"

The question seems to reverberate around the room.

A part of me wants to say it, to claim Aimee right here and now in front of my father. To show him how fiercely I'd be willing to defend her if he even thought about harming her. To give up this stupid act.

But looking at the glint in Padraic's eye… he already knows. He's just goading me into a confession, hoping I'll make the wrong move. If the family knew, if our enemies knew I harbored true feelings for Aimee— there would be an uproar loud enough to drown out any claim I had as heir. Freeing Padraic from the pressure to appoint me as such.

Aimee's words come back to me.

It's all just a game of power, really.

"I care for this family more," I reply, matching Padraic's stare firmly.

Padraic holds my gaze momentarily before returning to his work. "Good. Now, get out of my sight."

I slowly let go, a sigh of relief. All things considered, it could have gone a lot worse.

"Remember," Padraic says as I turn to leave. "I want you both at the annuals tonight."

As if I need reminding. The annuals take place in *my* establishment. Padraic always has a habit of forgetting that the success of Luckies is down to me—especially when it comes to events like this. No, at the annuals, Luckies is his. The fighters are *his*.

But I've had enough years of practice handing him the glory to not sound bitter about it now. "You got a good fighter this year?"

Padraic offers me a rare smile. It doesn't quite fit his face, making it look more like a sneer. "The best."

I nod politely, trying not to seem too unnerved by his expression. "I'll be sure to stop by the bookies, then."

Padraic merely waves me off, and I'm more than happy to get the hell out of there. For one, leaving Aimee on her own was a gamble. It's only been about five minutes, but so much could go wrong in that time. All I want now is to retreat to bed with my fiancé and reassure myself that she's okay. Thoroughly.

My fiancé.

My fiancé is not outside waiting for me when I push open the doors.

I glance up and down the hall. Nothing.

My heart begins to thump rapidly.

I comb through the house, narrowly avoiding Buzz and a disgruntled-looking Morris as I slip into the corridor leading to my bedroom. Hoping, praying Aimee has managed to find her way there.

As I approach, I see the door is ajar. Fuck.

I grab my concealed gun and approach slowly. There's no sound from inside, but that doesn't mean they haven't bound and gagged her–

"I suppose congratulations are in order."

I freeze. Then push the door open.

"Kate."

The blonde sits on my bed, nonchalantly examining her nails. She barely looks up as I enter.

"If you'd bothered to *tell me*, I would have bought champagne."

"Where is she?" I demand quietly.

"Already lost track of your fiancé, Jack?"

"Where's Aimee?"

"I thought it was *Roisin.*"

"Kate!"

She finally leaves her nails alone long enough to look at me. "She's fine; she's with me. Jesus Christ."

"Where?" I take a stride toward her.

"You a broken record or something? She's with me; she's fine," Kate replies, nodding toward the still-open door. "Right now, you need to be worried about telling me what the hell is going on."

I close the door behind me begrudgingly. "There's nothing more you need to know."

"You sure about that? 'Cos if you are, you should know I'm gonna go out there and get the truth from that girl one way or another. And if your stories don't match up, you're a dead man, Jack Duffy."

I run a hand through my hair. God, it's been a day, and Kate's wrath is not something I want to deal with right now. I look at her, the determination in her eyes.

May as well get this over with. She's supposed to be my right hand, after all.

"She's safe?" I ask one last time.

"As houses."

"Fine," I say. "But this might take a minute."

I tell her about Ray tracking Roisin, about bumping into Aimee. About our dates and how we didn't know who the other was. That I didn't put the dots together until it was too late, as the Dead Eyes were already after them. I tell her about our plan, how Aimee accepted my proposal, and how difficult it was to persuade Padraic that it was serious.

"Christ," Kate says, sitting back. "How the hell did you manage to get him to run with that idiotic plan?"

"I'm a persuasive person," I say defensively, leaving out just how far I'd stooped to secure his support.

Kate simply shakes her head and stands up to begin pacing the floor. "You're in love with her, aren't you?"

"What?"

"No sane man would go through all of this just to protect someone he thinks is cute."

I have to look away. If there's any truth to her words, I can't let myself accept them. It was hard enough to listen to Aimee confess her love for me in front of my father.

Even though I knew it was what we agreed. Even though I *knew* it was an act...

... I wanted to hear her say it again.

"It's more complicated than that," I reply finally.

"You could have told me."

Kate stops her pacing as she says this. The accusation she's actually trying to make hangs between us.

"Trusting you is proving a hard habit to keep up," I say weakly.

Her expression softens a little. "Is this because of that time I put bleach in your shampoo?"

"I was thinking of the time you locked me in the kennel overnight, actually," I quip back.

The back catalog of "ways Kate has tortured me" is embarrassingly long. But we were just kids then. Kate's never given me a real reason not to trust her. Everything she's done since Graham's funeral has been to help me find purchase on a slope designed to make me fall.

"I'm sorry," I say quietly.

It seems to take Kate a minute to register what I've said. "What was that?"

"I'm sorry, okay?"

"One more time."

I throw a pillow at her. "You're exhausting."

Kate ducks out of the way effortlessly. "Take the day, Jack. Get your shit together. I'll get Aimee ready for the fight tonight."

"You sure?"

"It's going to be the public announcement of your engagement. You need to be ready for the world to find out."

With those lingering words, Kate turns on her six-inch heels and leaves the room.

Not wanting to dwell on them, I collapse on my bed and hope sleep will catch up to me quickly.

Chapter Twenty-Three

Aimee

The Duffy garage is four times the size of Jack's basement.

I'm thankful for the blacked-out windows of Kate's sports car as I watch the steady stream of Dead Eyes coming in and out. Some drop cars off, others take them. A couple of guys in overalls are replacing a tire on a Mustang with the unmistakable denting of bullet holes along the bodywork.

How my brother thinks he could ever stand a chance against these guys... The sheer amount of *wealth* the Duffys have is mind-altering. The cheapest of these cars could probably buy]the decrepit Maguire mansion two or three times over. If it's even still standing.

Kate said she'd be back in five minutes about twenty minutes ago, but I think I used up all my nerves confronting Padraic, and I don't have any to spare to go looking for her. Besides, it's not like I really care if she's okay, only that she promised to get me the hell out of here.

As if I summoned her with my thoughts, Kate walks into the garage, dangling her keys in one hand and holding two iced lattes in the other. She hands a cup to me wordlessly as she climbs into the driver's seat.

"Thanks," I say, taking a generous gulp immediately. Dear God, that hits the spot.

"You seemed like you needed a distraction."

"What I need is a getaway car," I say pointedly before taking another sip. "But this is helping."

Kate starts up the engine. "So about that…"

I groan. Of course. "Did Jack get to you?"

"Maybe," she says as she pulls out of the garage and back down the driveway to the gates.

I watch out the window as the doorman merely waves Kate through before returning his attention to the three ginormous hounds at his feet. Why does everything in this place feel like it's on steroids?

"If you're not helping me escape," I say, turning my attention back to the road, "where are we going?"

"That would ruin the surprise," Kate replies with a crooked smile.

"So, you're kidnapping me."

"Exactly."

I sink back into the luxurious leather seat and close my eyes, "Well, it's not like my day could get much worse."

"Heard you went toe to toe with Padraic," Kate says conversationally. "Impressive."

"You wouldn't think so if you felt my heart rate right now."

I hear Kate chuckle softly, "He still scares the shit out of me."

"Really?"

"Yeah, well… I'm his favorite for a reason."

I crack open an eye to see if she'll elaborate. Kate catches my glance and lets out a sigh.

"Yes, sir, no sir, three bags full, sir. I've been at his beck and call for years because I'm terrified of making the wrong move," she confesses. "Jack, on the other hand, doesn't seem to have that problem."

Ugh. "I don't want to talk about Jack right now."

"Don't worry; we have plenty of time for you to warm up to it."

***

195

A salon. Kate kidnapped me to a salon.

The large glass doors stand before us. Intimidating in a way to keep the general riff-raff from the street from entering. Glancing at Kate's thigh-high boots and Gucci sunglasses, I suddenly feel entirely underdressed.

"Will they even let me in?" I say a little nervously.

Kate lowers her glasses to look me up and down. "Well, that's why we're here, aren't we?"

Before I have the chance to feel offended, Kate marches through the doors like she owns the place.

Judging by the reactions of the staff, she probably does.

"Ms. St Michael! What a pleasure to see you again so soon." A dark-haired man approaches us, somehow pulling off a highly stylized mullet, and kisses Kate on both cheeks. "Did the nails break already? I can fire someone."

"Craig," Kate says as she steps away from the embrace. "I would like you to meet my new friend Roisin."

Craig's attention is suddenly on me, and I can practically feel his laser-focused eyes analyzing every hair out of place. He seems to float over to me as if drawn to my lack of personal grooming like a magnet.

"Your friend Roisin is cute. Is she single?" Craig says as he circles me.

I see Kate offer me an apologetic smile. "She's actually engaged to my cousin."

"May I?" he asks as he reaches for my hair, and I resign myself to my fate. "You're getting married? Congratulations!"

"Thanks?" I reply tentatively as he continues to poke and prod at me.

Finally, he takes a step back and examines me from afar again. "I can work with this. Shall we get you in the chair?"

He doesn't wait for me to respond before he indicates where he wants me to sit and flies away, presumably to find the numerous tools and instruments he needs to work on me.

"If you wanted to torture me," I say quietly to Kate as we walk over to the chair, "you could have skipped the salon part."

Kate merely pulls up her own chair and sits casually, "If it makes you feel any better, I'm on your side in all of this."

"You haven't even heard my side of the story yet."

"When it comes to Jack? I trust he's somehow in the wrong," she says simply.

I watch as Kate pulls out her phone and begins scanning through a bunch of pictures that look suspiciously like hairstyles.

We're similar in many ways, I realize. Both daughters of organized crime, both doing our best to please the ones we love. It makes me wonder what her relationship with Jack really is. If she was Graham's maternal cousin… that means she's not even biologically related to him. Could it be that once they were more than just allies?

But she's never come across as if she holds him in any high regard. Even now, I don't feel the malice of someone scorned by a lover. Besides, she's the only one who seems to know the truth. The only one that might be able to provide me with some kind of company or even friendship.

Perhaps that's why she bought me here. After all, being a daughter of the mob is a lonely line of work.

"Why do I feel like I can trust you?" I say slowly.

"It's the face, I think," she quips back easily, just as Craig rejoins us with an entire cart of supplies.

"And a beautiful face at that," he says with a grin toward the blonde before turning his attention to me. "Shall we get started?"

I try a smile back. "Do your worst."

He begins picking at my hair again, and I try to settle into the chair. "So, what's your fiancé like?"

"He's an asshole," I reply automatically with a pointed glance at Kate.

"They're going through a rough patch," she says a bit more gently, by way of explanation to Craig. "Roisin was just about to tell me all about it, weren't you?"

I glare at her before letting out a sigh. Without Roisin around, I've had no one to talk to about this whole mess. Maybe it will feel easier if I unload...

"I just..." I begin, then sigh. "I don't know where I stand with him. When we're together and alone... it feels real, like he actually means everything he says."

"Like what?" Kate asks curiously.

I shrug, "Like he cares for me, I guess. Like he wants to protect me."

"Girl, he did not protect you from this box dye," Craig says. "I'm going to have to work double time on this."

"There's no rush," Kate cuts in smoothly. "Besides, Jack is paying."

She waves a matte black card in front of me.

Craig's face lights up. "In that case, I'm thinking highlights?"

"Balayage?" Kate chimes in.

"Yes, yes, yes! Alright, Pippi Longstocking, I'll go mix you up a cocktail."

Craig disappears again, and I throw Kate a concerned look. "It's like eleven AM."

"He means your colors," she clarifies.

"Oh."

"So," she says, leaning in conspiratorially. "Is it just that you don't trust him?"

"Would you? In my situation?"

"No... But then, I'm not you. Am I, Aimee?"

I freeze. "I-it's Roisin."

"Is it?" Kate says, leaning back.

"Well, at least I know Jack trusts *you,*" I say, unable to squash the bitterness of this small betrayal.

"We weren't conspiring together, if that's what you mean."

I snort, "Oh, so it wasn't your idea to marry me off to Jack so I wouldn't help my brother keep his alliance with the Novas?"

Kate's jaw practically hits the floor. "That asshole! He didn't tell me that."

"That's what he told Padraic," I reply. I'd be lying if I said I wasn't even a little satisfied with the validation her reaction gave me.

Still outraged, Kate waves over at Craig. "Hey, Craig? We're going to need nails too."

"Seriously?" I say with a wince.

"I'm going to make sure you look so good tonight, Jack will be on his knees begging for forgiveness," Kate says firmly and without a hint of irony.

I shake the image from my mind. "What's tonight?"

"The annuals," she says, returning to her phone and furiously searching up more references for Craig. "It's a boxing competition that Padraic has been running at Luckies for years."

Oh shit.

I can't believe I didn't put it all together. The annuals... Luckies... BKB and Jack's ability to take a punch. The illegal nature of his businesses...

"I thought the annuals got shut down after that kid died?!" I hiss in alarm.

I remember a day, about seven or eight years ago, when my father read out the news in a rare state of sobriety and good humor. "The Duffys have fucked up for good this time," he'd claimed. My brother had rejoiced; we'd gone out for dinner and ordered sparkling wine. They were sure this would be the scandal that would take the Duffys off the chessboard.

Kate grimaces, "Only made it more popular, I'm afraid. Especially since Jack took it over."

Of course, it did. He's always just so *good* at what he does. The bastard. Now I'm the one who's going to pay the price for it.

"So," I say with a sinking heart. "There's going to be a lot of people there tonight?"

"Yes, and all eyes are going to be on you and Jack."

Great. Excellent. Well, at least Jack will be able to show me off like he wanted.

When we first moved to LA and I used to let my mind wander, I'd sometimes try to imagine what it would be like going back to this life. Maybe as a grown woman, I might have finally been able to avenge my mother. I might have been able to convince my brother to let me work by his side.

They were just the fantasies of a girl who was lost and confused. They fizzled out once I had a taste of what real freedom is.

But never in my wildest dreams did I think I would reenter the underworld on the arm of my family's greatest enemy. To be used as nothing more than bait.

This is going to be humiliating.

Kate seems to sense my dejection. "It's my job to make sure you look the part, are prepared to act the part, and get people interested in the fighting again as soon as possible. Sound good?"

"What do you mean, act the part?" I say, frowning slightly.

"Well… It's been a while since there's been a Duffy engagement, and fiancés tend to get paraded around a bit, I'm afraid." She takes a break from scrolling to give me an apologetic look. "Not to mention that this time, it's Roisin *Maguire*. Whatever she does, people will want to know about it. People will be expecting *something* to gossip about."

"If I slap Jack around the face, would that do it?" I murmur.

"Probably," Kate says before her eyes widen in delight. "But I actually have a better idea…"

"Do I want to know?"

"Probably not."

She turns her phone around.

It's my turn for my jaw to drop.

Kate gives me a devilish grin, "You think you can handle it?"

"Craig?" I say a little hoarsely. "Could we grab some champagne?"

"Way ahead of you," the beautician says as he reappears to hand us a couple of flutes.

Kate raises hers to me, "To Roisin Duffy?"

I clink it with my own.

"To Roisin goddamn Duffy."

Chapter Twenty-Four

Jack

From the VIP box, I can keep a close eye on the audience that floods in through the doors toward the ring. If there's even a flash of red hair, my team has instructions to act immediately. I don't care how many men Padraic has brought with him; tonight, I'm not taking any chances.

And in the unlikely case that a Maguire slips through, I'll be ready.

I've not been back to Luckies since the night of Graham's death. When we sat in this very box, joking about this very night of fighting. How many times have I sat here with Graham, bickering about the bets, scouting the crowds, or even fighting in the ring ourselves when we were younger and had something to prove? This whole situation isn't sitting right with me in the slightest, and I feel like my nerve ends are on fire. Every loud noise has me on edge.

"Hey, Jack!"

I flinch, turning to see Ray leaning against the divide between the VIP box and the lower seats.

"What?" I say, maybe a little too short.

Ray puts his hands up in surrender. "I was just wanting to ask if you'd had a chance to go to the bookies yet?"

"Not today, Ray," I reply a little bitterly, continuing to scan the crowds.

"You sure?" Ray gives me a concerned look. "Kennedy is fighting; you always stick something on him."

That distracts me enough to give him some attention. "Against who?"

Ray nods to Padraic, a few chairs down from me. "Ask him; he's not told anyone yet."

I glance over at the Dead Eye leader curiously. It's not like him to be secretive about his fighters.

"He told me he has someone good," I say, recalling our earlier conversation. "Bad luck to bet against him."

Ray seems to consider this. "For you, maybe. I'm keeping my money on the guy I've seen KO in a single punch. Want me to stick a couple grand on for you? I won't tell."

I shake my head, and Ray offers me a half-hearted salute as he turns away.

The weight of the empty chair next to me feels heavier than it has any right to be.

Only tonight, it's not going to be empty. That, I, at least, can reassure myself of. I've not seen Aimee since our meeting with Padraic. There's so much we have yet to unpack about that little almost-disaster. But where Kate kept her all day, I still don't know. And as if my nerves weren't already fried, the two of them have yet to arrive.

But I'm not the only one glancing at the VIP entrance every few minutes, either. I've seen Padraic's eyes dart over there a few times already. It seems he put out a gag order on our engagement—no one seems to know why he's not yet made his welcome speech or announced his secret fighter. Apparently, he wants our guest of honor to be a surprise.

Just to add to the pressure on our performance.

"You will socialize, delight, and charm as many of our allies as you can. But most importantly, that girl needs to appear as if she's in love with you."

I wish I'd had a chance to speak to her before all this to let her know what she's getting herself into tonight. It's not fair that she has to come out here so ill-prepared for the wolves that will likely descend on her the moment she steps through those doors.

I try to distract myself by resuming my scans of the crowds. Every seat is now occupied, and more than a few are glancing at the clock. No doubt wondering when Padraic will finally begin.

Then it goes quiet.

It's like someone hit the mute button. Every single person turns to look up at the VIP box.

I spin around, half expecting to find Connor Maguire himself poised to stab me in the back. Only for my knees to almost give out from under me.

Kate descends the stairs into the VIP box first—a vision in black, her hair perfectly parted down the middle. Objectively stunning, but no more so than one might expect at these kinds of events.

It's the woman behind her that holds everyone's utmost attention.

Aimee is nothing short of breathtaking. Her restored red hair fans out from her face in soft curls, making it look as if she's been shrouded by fire itself. Perfectly darkened lashes frame her deep chocolate eyes. She gazes out into the crowd, a picture of indifference.

As if she is entirely unaware that there's not a single man or woman in this room that wouldn't want to be her or bed her.

The growling demon of jealousy lurches from my stomach. It wants to claw out every eye that looks at her with even an ounce of desire.

Mine.

She is *mine.* She's my fiance. My wife.

But how can I blame them when she's wearing that dress?

That red fucking dress.

Jesus Christ. She looks like sin incarnate.

The neck falls lower than any dress has any right to, held up by tiny spaghetti straps that look like they could snap under the weight of the attention they're getting from everyone in the room. I try to console myself with the fact the skirt is more modest, but as she descends the stairs toward me, I get a flash of skin. Then another.

The goddamn skirt has two slits in it.

Kate is going to pay for this.

The witch herself reaches me first, just as the murmuring of the crowd starts up again. A coy little grin spreads on her lips as she thumbs something off my face.

"You're drooling," Kate says slyly.

"What did you do to my wife?" I growl at her without thinking, and Kate raises an eyebrow at my slip.

"Your *fiancé* and I have been doing a little retail therapy," she says, handing me a matte-black credit card.

With my goddamn name on it.

"When did you take this?" I choke out.

But by the time my question leaves my mouth, Kate has already moved on. Leaving me face-to-face with my approaching fiancé.

As she gets closer, I can see the warm pink of her flushed cheeks. She practically radiates pure beauty. And she's staring at me. *Me.* With those fuck-me eyes and a smile that makes my heart speed up so quickly, I feel a little light-headed.

I feel like the luckiest man in the entire world.

I can't stand the distance between us a moment longer. I step over my seat onto the row behind to reach her, and she laughs prettily at my antics.

The murmuring around me is getting louder, but I don't care. All I care about is reaching her and bringing her into my arms. There's a glint of something in her eyes that I ignore because she comes to me so happily, so willingly. So eagerly, she presses her mouth to mine, and the little demon inside me finally quietens. Everyone knows now. *Mine.*

She pulls away bashfully and finally seems to notice the crowds staring slack-jawed at the two of us.

But I can't take my eyes off her. "Too much?"

Aimee gives me a brilliant smile and leans in to kiss my cheek. "No, silly. I think it was just enough to keep me sweet."

Her words are like a direct kick to the stomach. The world immediately begins crashing down around me.

I try to laugh it off, "What?"

"Isn't that what you told Padraic you would do?" Aimee says with a tilt of her head.

"Aimee…" I hiss, glancing around at the other people in earshot. Dead Eyes, all of them. Each face reacts to our embrace somewhere on a spectrum from betrayal to amusement.

There's no going back now. I just kissed a Maguire in front of a room of almost five hundred people.

"My name is Roisin," Aimee corrects me. Her smile is still plastered on her lips. "Or did you forget that when you forgot to mention the fact that I'm supposed to be engaged to Arnie Knight?"

I have to stop myself from shushing her. "You really want to do this right now?"

Aimee steps around me to make her way to her seat. "No. I just wanted to see your face."

I'm entirely dumbfounded. This whole thing, arriving late, the goddamn dress, was to show me just how pissed off she was? It would be so cruel if I didn't fucking deserve it. If I hadn't been so selfish.

"A—*Roisin*," I try again, chasing her back down to our seats and ignoring the filthy look Buzz gives me as I pass him.

I watch as Aimee sits elegantly and crosses one bare leg over the other. A picture of seduction itself. I hurry to sit next to her.

"Please, we need to be careful, *chroí*," I whisper desperately.

Aimee simply examines her nails, the way I've seen Kate do a thousand times. "I am. It's you who looks like a flustered moron with something to hide."

"I didn't mean to hide anything from you," I hiss, glancing around the box. There are still more eyes on us than I'd like, but at least people seem to have resumed conversation.

"Oh, please. This was just a power play, wasn't it?" Aimee says as if she's already bored with me. "You wanted to parade me around to infuriate my brother."

"That's not-"

"LADIES AND GENTLEMEN!"

I flinch as the announcement booms over the speakers.

"PLEASE GIVE IT UP FOR THE CHAIR OF THE DUFFY CONGLOMERATE!"

The crowd erupts in applause as Padraic approaches the podium in the VIP box. There's not a person in this room who doesn't know who he truly is, but for the sake of discretion, Padraic is dressed to the nines as the businessman we all know he's not.

In fact, all of us look the part tonight. My own three-piece is more Wall Street than back-alley dealings. Although no one quite matches Aimee tonight, I imagine we make quite the handsome pair.

"Welcome, one and all," Padraic's smooth voice pulls me from my thoughts. "Thank you for joining us for the annuals this evening."

I glance over at Aimee, at the hand resting on her lap, and reach for it. But she pulls it away.

Fuck, am I in trouble later.

Padraic continues, "As some of you may already know, my son, Graham Duffy, was recently taken from us. He was a fierce competitor in the ring and could have one day competed at the annuals himself."

I tense at the sound of his name leaving Padraic's mouth. What the hell is he doing? We all know Graham was hopeless in the ring.

"In his honor, we are dedicating this event to him."

The crowd erupts in applause. A feeling of dread begins to creep into my gut, which is only reinforced when Padraic turns to offer me that same strained smile he gave me before.

"As such," Padraic says once the crowd has died down. "I imagine many of you are wondering who I have chosen for my fighter this evening."

The crowd cheers again. But this time, Aimee grabs my arm.

"Please give it up for my fighter for the 44th NYC annual PKB championship…."

Aimee's fingers dig into my skin.

"… Jack Duffy!"

Chapter Twenty-Five

Aimee

The crowd's roar is nearly as loud as the rush of blood that fills my ears.

I might not know a thing about boxing or fighting or whatever this whole business is, but I know whatever Jack is about to do, he's not going to do it in a three-piece suit.

We share a long, strained look.

No, he didn't know about this either.

Jesus Christ.

Several of the men around us excitedly pull Jack to his feet, and I find myself standing too.

They all turn to me questioningly, and I suddenly feel unsure of myself. What exactly can I do about this? Fight in his place? Throw Padraic Duffy off the goddamn ledge?

Jack's face is expressionless and hauntingly distant. So I do the only thing I can and reach for his hand.

The same hand I so coldly refused him not thirty seconds ago.

The contact seems to awaken something in him. His hazel eyes brighten a little, and he stands a little straighter.

"You better fucking win," I mouth to him. The roar of the crowds is still too loud to say anything of substance.

Jack offers me a small squeeze of my hand before bringing it to his lips. Despite everything and how mad I am right now, the gesture is a sweet reminder of who we are behind closed doors. When we aren't keeping things from each other to gain the upper hand, or dressing ourselves up to play a part we never meant to.

All of our games suddenly seem insignificant as Jack lets go and allows himself to be escorted down to the ring. With one last glance up at me, he disappears into what I assume must be the locker room.

It takes me a moment to register that people are still staring at me. Without Jack by my side, I'm suddenly very aware that the Dead Eye goons aren't taking too kindly to my presence.

"Maguire bitch."

I turn around in alarm, but none of the men behind me seem to want to engage in further conversation.

"Whore." Someone else hisses at me too quickly for me to catch.

I sit back in my seat slowly, beginning to regret this outfit, the hair, and the stilettos that will make it ridiculously hard for me to run if things go south. I try my best to quell the fear brewing in my stomach. Padraic said I was an "asset"; surely he wouldn't let anything bad happen to me?

But then again, he did just send his only son to fight a death match.

The man in question has resumed conversation with the business-looking men around him, pointedly ignoring me. And it seems his goons are more than happy to take advantage of that.

While I stare at him desperately, hating the fact I'm now relying on the man I hate more than anyone else in the world, someone sits down next to me.

"I knew I should have got you a thigh holster," Kate murmurs, and my shoulders sag in relief. "But they would have seen it in that dress."

The blonde turns behind us and gives the men a stare full of daggers before throwing an arm around the back of my chair. I want to tell her that

I'm fine and that I can fight my own battles, but I can't deny that the gesture soothes my growing anxiety.

"What's happening?" I whisper to her shakily.

Kate nods towards the center of the room. "Jack is going three rounds in the ring. Fight ends when either opponent knocks out the other or…"

"Or what?" I say sharply.

"If neither manages to KO, the fourth round lasts as long as it needs to before someone… concedes," she trails off.

I'm already shaking my head. "That has to be illegal."

"Yep," she replies, popping her 'p.'

"Please tell me no one else has died in the last five years?"

"I'd love to."

When she doesn't say anything more, I turn and look at her. Really look at her. In the short time I've known her, I've never seen her look so pale. Her jaw seems to be working overtime as she assesses the crowds and the ring itself below, where what appears to be a referee has begun making his preparations.

She's worried. Really fucking worried.

I swallow hard and stare back out at the ring. "How good is he?"

"Good," Kates says firmly, and I let out a sigh of relief. "He might even make it through the first match."

"There's more than one?"

"If he does well today, there's another fight before the final."

Fuck. "So we have to watch three of these?"

"*If* he does well," Kate reiterates.

I don't want to think about the alternative.

I look over to Padraic again, still rubbing elbows with the people around him. He seems entirely unconcerned about the wellbeing of his son.

Because he *is* entirely unconcerned about the wellbeing of his son, I realize with a start. This whole thing, me being here, not telling anyone about his fighter, was to get revenge on Jack. To show him how disposable he is to the Dead Eyes, to make him pay for not telling him about our engagement. Padraic is practically glowing in his triumph.

That he finally got to show the world that he could put Jack Duffy in his place.

The crowd suddenly roars again, and I watch in dismay as Jack's opponent walks into the ring.

"LADIES AND GENTLEMAN, YOUR FIRST FIGHTER TONIGHT... KENNEDY BROWN!"

The man who lifts his tightly wrapped hands to rally the audience is huge. Even from up here, I can see the veins popping out of his arm muscles. The mouthguard he wears is jet black, giving him a sinister, gapless look. He must have a good foot on Jack, and his thick neck looks as if it could withstand a punch to the face without flinching.

Kate silently grabs hold of my hand.

"AND IN THE OTHER CORNER, WE HAVE NONE OTHER THAN THE PRINCE OF THE DUFFY EMPIRE HIMSELF, JACK DUFFY!"

In my peripheral vision, I see Padraic tense a little at the announcement. If I wasn't so concerned about the shirtless man who steps into the ring, I might have saved a little for the commentator, who will undoubtedly feel Padraic's wrath for introducing Jack like that.

But as Jack walks to his corner, still wrapping his hands, I can't take my eyes off him. Although not as broad or as tall as his opponent, every inch of his bare back is defined with pure muscle. I watch as he stretches them out, remembering how they feel to the touch. The firmness of it as my nails dug into his skin, desperate for him to get closer...

He better fucking win.

Next to me, Kate cheers along with the crowds. "Come on, Jack!"

We watch together as the opponents begin circling each other, sizing the other up. Jack's calmness in the face of Kennedy's provocative sneers has me edging closer in my seat.

Finally, the referee raises a hand.

With the screech of his whistle, Kennedy lunges forward and immediately swings a powerful right hook. Jack manages to dart out of the way by a fraction of an inch.

For the first time, I see his brow furrow in concentration. Clearly, he didn't expect Kennedy to make a move straight after the starting whistle. He gives Kennedy a wide berth as he dances around him, moving so quickly that it almost makes me dizzy just watching him.

Kennedy's patience wears out quickly, and he swings another powerful punch at his opponent. Jack stops his dance to duck gracefully under Kennedy's swing and lands two quick hits to the bigger man's stomach.

But Kennedy barely registers he's been hit. The giant of a man swings again, and Jack is forced to leap away, causing the crowd to protest.

"Jesus Christ," Kate mutters beside me.

The sting of her nails biting into my hand is the only thing keeping me grounded as Jack narrowly avoids another hit. Unphased, he resumes his dance around Kennedy, eyes analyzing his opponent's every move.

"Come on," I find myself whispering.

As if hearing my encouragement, Jack suddenly jerks in a different direction, catching Kennedy entirely off-guard. Jack's punches are swift and accurate. A flurry of his hits land, causing Kennedy to stagger back a step.

Jack takes the opening to punch him square in the face.

When Kennedy falls backward to the floor, there's a beat of silence before the uproar begins.

Jack knocked him out in less than thirty seconds.

Chapter Twenty-Six

Aimee

Kate and I are running down the steps to the locker room before the commentator can even announce the winner.

We pass by streams of people yelling at the ref and the unconscious body of the crowd's favored fighter. But I couldn't care less about the goddamn bookies. Jack won and, more importantly, didn't sustain a single injury.

But I still want to check him over, just to be sure.

By the time we reach the doors, fans and angry Kennedy supporters are already gathering by the entrance, making it impossible to pass through. Let alone for the men stationed outside the locker room to deter anyone from entering.

"This way," Kate says, grabbing my arm and navigating us through the crowds toward a concealed staff door. The man in the Luckies uniform that leans against the wall merely nods at us as Kate pushes through.

"Is it always like that?" I say with a glance over my shoulder at the growing mob of people before the staff door closes behind us.

"Like I said," she replies as she sets off at a brisk walk down the corridor. "Next time, I'll get you a thigh holster."

We don't have to go much further before a flurry of movement rounds the corner.

"Mr. Duffy! Please, you have to wait for a physician!"

Kate and I watch as Jack shakes off a kid trailing behind him, holding his towel and shirt.

"I'm fine," Jack bites out, not slowing his pace, only pausing when he spots us up ahead.

"Jack!" I say, a little shocked by how relieved I sound. I approach as quickly as my heels will let me, reaching for an embrace.

But Jack steps out of the way.

"I'm *fine,*" he says again, just as bitterly.

I shrink back a little. Taking in how his bare chest rises and falls almost aggressively, the hard lines of his brow, the tightness of his jaw.

He's angry. Angrier than I've ever seen him before. His hazel eyes are ablaze with a darkness that seems to consume him.

For the first time, I see the resemblance he shares with his father.

It shocks me enough to take another step back.

Jack watches me closely for another moment before he turns away. Storming back along the corridor from where we just came in.

I can't move, can barely breathe as my body registers the terror that's coursing through my veins.

Suddenly I get it what Kate had said about Padraic.

"I've been at his beck and call for years because I'm terrified of making the wrong move."

At the time, I thought maybe she was just trying to make me feel better. But whoever *that* was, it wasn't my Jack. It was someone else entirely.

"I wouldn't want you to see the person I become when the fighting starts."

A hand touches my shoulder, and I jerk back.

"Hey," Kate says softly. "Let's get out of here."

***

The drive back to the Duffy mansion is a quiet one, despite Kate insisting we hit up a drive-through on our way.

I slurp slowly on my strawberry milkshake, thankful for the sugar intake after such a stressful evening. Coming down from that adrenaline high has completely wiped me out.

Luckily, it seems Kate has developed a habit of anticipating my needs before I realize them. When we enter the mansion, she immediately escorts me up to Jack's bedroom and gives me a key. Shows me how to manage the locks that Jack has installed on his door.

It's a large room with a full-sized private bathroom, but I kind of like his penthouse better. There's something about the old English style of decor that grates on me. Even though Jack has clearly done his best to incorporate some more modern elements, it seems there was nothing he could do to cover up the thick, draping curtains and Victorian paneling.

Someone seems to have already brought up the bags of loot from our earlier spree. Despite spending an extortionate amount of money, I'm glad I at least have my own clothes to wear. Even if the pajamas Kate picked out are a little too revealing to be practical.

"You going to be okay?" she says, lingering by the door.

"Sure," I reply, although it doesn't sound particularly convincing. "Thank you."

With a final sympathetic wave, Kate closes the bedroom behind her, and I lock myself in. Then immediately fall face-first onto the bed.

I must fall asleep because the next thing I know, the clock on the bedside table reads one AM, and I'm still wearing this ridiculous (albeit gorgeous) dress. With a groan, I get up and head into the bathroom.

It takes me longer than usual to clean myself up. With all the new hair products Craig insisted I get and the makeup that needed scrubbing off, it's almost 1:30 AM when I reemerge.

But Jack is still nowhere to be seen.

I try not to feel anxious about it; he's probably just gone back to his penthouse or one of Padraic's fancy hotels. I wasn't exactly subtle about being angry back before the fight began, so he's probably just avoiding me.

But *he* was the one who kept telling *me* to stay close to him. Now he's abandoned me in a house crawling with people who'd love to savage me with words and worse, and my only ally has already figured out I have a weakness for cold, milky beverages. No matter how dead set Jack was on 'protecting me,' I don't exactly feel safe right now—even with all those locks on the door.

I guess I can just add it to my list of reasons to be mad at him. A list that seems to keep growing with every passing hour.

I wait up until three o'clock before succumbing to a fitful sleep.

Bang.

The pounding on the door sounds like bullets, and my body rips me from my pillow into a defensive position by the window. I glance outside. I'm only three stories up; the fall shouldn't kill me.

As the pounding continues, I take a moment to soothe my racing heart. It's just the door, no gunshots yet. But I'm not going to take my chances. I yank open the drawer of Jack's bedside table and search around for something, anything to defend myself with. Finally, I grasp the hilt of a knife. It's not big enough to be much use, but it's better than nothing.

Bang, bang, bang!

My nerves coil tighter with every blow. Four-thirty AM, the clock on the bedside reads as I glance up at it. Somewhere in my sleep-deprived brain, I wonder why Padraic would wait until now to come after me. But I push it aside and adjust my grip on the knife as I slowly approach the door.

Bang, bang–

I swing the door open, taking the perpetrator by surprise, and immediately press the knife into his neck.

"*Chroí.*"

Jack grins down at me. He seems to have lost two of the three pieces of his suit, and his open shirt reveals a little too much of his chest to be considered decent.

He pokes the knife at his throat as if it's only a mild inconvenience. "I'm so glad you're here. Someone locked me out of my room."

"You're drunk," I observe, taking in the scent of hard liquor on his breath.

Jack's smile fades to a pout. "You don't look happy to see me."

"It's four-thirty in the morning."

"Is it really?" Jack looks around as if genuinely surprised that the sun is beginning to rise.

The urge to hit him increases with every moment. "Where have you been?"

"Aww, were you worried about me?" Jack says, a doting smile appearing back on his face as he leans lazily against the doorframe.

"No!" I hiss. "You left me behind while you went on a bloody bender. I'm *angry* at you!"

"Oh no…" Jack slumps down again. "I'm a terrible husband."

"We aren't fucking…." I pinch the bridge of my nose. "Get inside. Now."

He tries to lean in close as he passes, but I take a long stride away from him and point him to the seating area. Jack merely shrugs and follows his instructions. It takes me a minute to secure the room back up with all the locks again. Undoing them hadn't seemed as hard.

"Are you okay?" Jack asks.

I turn to see him watching me quite carefully—despite the fact he's swaying a little in his seat on the couch.

"I thought you were Padraic," I snap.

"Pffft… No, I'm not Padraic. I'm protecting you from Padraic."

I walk over to the couch slowly but stay a good meter away from him. "Well, you did an excellent job of protecting me tonight."

"Did something happen?" he asks.

I falter, "No, but–"

"Then we're good!"

The anger I feel rising inside of me begins to peak. I grab a glass from the side table and march into the bathroom to cool down.

What the hell is he playing at? There are too many things at stake for Jack to run off to drink himself stupid like this. How the hell am I supposed to survive this situation if this is what he's like?

I feel like a prize idiot. Waltzing into this entire situation, believing that the sweet, romantic, possessive, charming man I met at the theater could maybe fall in love with me. That despite all odds, we could make it through this together. How could I be so stupid?

I grab a box of pills from the medicine cabinet. No, from now on, I'm looking after *me*. There's no use relying on Jack when he keeps disappointing me at every hurdle.

With my newfound resolve, I storm back into the room.

"Drink this, take this," I say, dropping the pills and a glass of water into his hand. Jack seems to think I want to hold them, so he reaches for me. I snatch my hands away quickly. "... and don't fucking touch me."

Jack offers me a mock salute. "Aye, aye, captain."

I restrain myself until he's swallowed all the pills before trying to question him again. "Where have you been?"

"Here and there. Oh! Spoke to Padraic about the fight." He continues drinking as if that isn't vital information.

"And?" I press.

"No getting out of it, I'm afraid. I even begged him, you know, didn't want you to deal with all this on your own," he says a little wearily. "Then there was this whole spiel about how I pushed him to do it and how I need to learn some respect and how he'll kill you if I don't play his stupid little games."

What? "*What?*"

Jack just keeps on sipping. "I think he thinks I like you, you know."

My mouth opens and closes a few times before I finally shake myself into an actual response. "It seems there were a few of us suffering under that misapprehension."

"Don't be like that," Jack whines. "Can't we just go to bed?"

I stare at him in disbelief. "You're on the couch or the bathtub. I do not care which."

"*Chroí*, please."

"Don't call me that."

"I'm sorry if I've upset you."

"You just told me Padraic threatened to kill me! How do you think I feel?"

"Tell me about it," Jack says, downing the rest of the water and holding it up pensively. "I think I need to be soberer for this conversation."

I snatch the glass out of his hand and return once I've filled it. "Drink."

He obeys. "I'm sorry."

"Sorry for what, exactly?" I say, taking a seat opposite him. "Forcing me into an engagement to piss off my brother? Ignoring me after the fight? Abandoning me when everyone I meet here hates me? Or are you just apologizing for showing up at four-thirty AM, drunk out of your mind?"

"Yeah, those."

I have to laugh because if I don't, I think I'll cry. "You've betrayed me in so many ways, I don't know where to even start."

Jack stares at me with a little more clarity in his eyes. "I never... wanted it to be like this."

"That's great, but this is how it is. This is happening." I can't laugh anymore. The tears well up and pour out before I have a second to gather myself. But fuck it, he needs to know. "You can't just get drunk every time something goes wrong. You have to be here; you have to hold up your end of the bargain."

Alarm spreads across his face. "Aimee... I'm so sorry."

"Stop it. Stop apologizing!" I close my eyes and swallow hard. "I don't accept it."

"I shouldn't have left," Jack says, and I can hear him get up from the couch. "I should have been with you, protecting you. I was just–"

"I don't care," I manage to hiss at him, shooting him a glare as he attempts to move closer.

He pauses, suddenly looking so unsure of himself that it's almost laughable. "Aimee, please. Please don't cry. I can't stand that I've done this to you."

"Must be so horrible for you," I bite back sarcastically.

"Fuck!" Jack shouts suddenly and beelines for the bathroom. I dry my tears as I listen to him running the tap and splashing his face over and over.

When he comes out again, he seems to have sobered up at least a little bit more because he comes to kneel at my feet.

"Listen to me," he says desperately. "You don't deserve anything that happened tonight, none of it. I hate myself for it; please believe me."

"Then why did you?" I whisper.

He studies my face as if it somewhere holds the right answer. But he doesn't respond. Can't, it seems.

I nod, accepting this bitterly. "Right."

"Aimee…"

"No, this is good; at least I know where I stand with you now. For real, this time," I try to stand, but his hands are suddenly there, pinning me down.

"Please," he whispers. "You have to understand–"

"I understand perfectly. Let me go!"

His lips crash into mine, and for a moment, nothing else matters. Jack clings to me, and I hold on to him just as hard as he deepens the kiss, exploring my mouth. Begging me to submit.

I pull away aggressively. "That's not going to work on me again."

"Please."

"Let me go!" I push against his firm chest, hoping to make any kind of space for me to slip through.

"You said that you loved me!" he blurts out desperately.

"I-" The words get caught in my throat, and it takes me a second to wrench them out. "I only said that in front of *Padraic*! You have *hurt* me, Jack. How could you possibly think that was real?"

Something cracks inside me to say it, but my words have the desired effect. Jack's eyes flash with wild emotion, but he takes a step away. Then another.

"I'll take the couch," he says finally.

I want to exhale in relief, but there's nothing but a hollow feeling inside as I watch him fall onto the couch without another word. After a moment, I stand and crawl back into bed to bury myself in the sheets. Praying that he won't hear my muffled tears.

Despite everything, I only manage to find sleep when I imagine his arms wrapped around me.

Chapter Twenty-Seven

Jack

My head is pounding, and my ears ring on and on in the most irritating way. I try to move, but my back twinges in protest.

That's what you get for passing out on the couch, asshole.

Seems my love affair with whiskey has come to a dramatic end. Or at least we're on a break for a while.

I close my eyes tighter, trying to keep the memories of last night's conversation from coming back to me. But they hit me like a ton of bricks.

You have hurt *me, Jack.*

Fuck. I messed everything up.

I finally turn over and crack an eye open. Someone has left a glass of water and more aspirin on the side table, along with a folded piece of paper.

At least she doesn't hate me enough to let me rot in my hangover.

I drink the water quickly and take a look at the note. It simply reads: "With Kate."

"Kate" is underlined, and I can practically hear Aimee's passive-aggressive voice in my ear.

I know I should have told her where I was going yesterday, but the last thing I wanted was for her to find me. Especially when I was like *that*.

My anger is my curse. It's the one thing I inherited from my father that makes us undeniably related. I make a point of never directing it at someone undeserving, unlike Padraic, and the fighting used to help stave off some of the pressure. But yesterday, I could barely contain it. It bubbled up inside me, the humiliation, the danger I had put Aimee in by bringing her here.

Seeing her face after the match... the way she recognized my anger almost immediately. The way she reacted to my anger. Watching her make the connection to my father almost broke me then and there. I just had to get out, get away.

Padraic was unhelpful and unamused by the state I was in. Threatening Aimee's life was the only thing that held me back from starting Round 2 in his office.

I sigh and get up with a groan. Going back to my apartment had felt like a good idea at the time, and the drinking certainly helped cool me down. But Drunk Jack clearly had other plans when he realized he didn't want to sleep alone.

I grab my phone and key in a text to Ray before heading to the bathroom to clean up. If Aimee wants to disappear on me today, I can't blame her. But I'm sure as hell not going to sit here and stew over the clusterfuck that was last night. I need something to take my mind off it.

By the time I'm out of the shower and feeling more human, Ray has already responded with the contact details I requested.

RAY: *I assume this is also need-to-know?*

JACK: *No one needs to know.*

RAY: *... Kate might know already.*

JACK: *Can I fire you?*

RAY: *Nope*

I run a hand through my wet hair and punch in the digits before I have a chance to second-guess myself.

He picks up on the third ring.

"Jack Duffy! I was wondering when you'd finally call." A silky voice comes down the line, and my eyes narrow on instinct. I'm glad he can't see me.

"I think it's about time we had a chat," I say, equally casually. "Don't you think, Arnie?"

I hear the Italian chuckle. "I know just the place."

***

The place in question turns out to be a quiet dive bar in Lenox Hill. Not usually the kind of place I'd go under my own steam. But if anyone bothered to track me as I left the Duffy mansion after my performance yesterday, it shouldn't be too hard to convince them I was getting blackout drunk somewhere I wasn't likely to be recognized.

Still, I do a perimeter check before I enter. No one pays particular attention to me strolling through the streets of New York with a cigarette in hand. A picture, I hope, of unperturbed casualness that hides the fact every brain cell in my mind is occupied with keeping the dread at bay.

Coming alone probably wasn't the smartest move, but it was the most strategic. In this game, knowledge is power, and there are too many advantages to gaining exclusive information. Padraic may have caught me off guard at Luckies, but I'm going to make damn sure I leave *this* conversation with something I can barter with if it happens again.

I stub out the cigarette, already regretting the dry, ashy taste in my mouth, and head inside.

The interior is as unassuming as the exterior. It's midday, yet the lighting is low, and it takes a moment for my eyes to adjust. The bartender looks more interested in watching football on the monitor behind him than attending to his customers—who are either slumped at the bar watching with him or nursing drinks in one of the leather booths.

The latter is where I find Arnie sitting alone, already halfway through a bottle of nondescript beer.

He shoots me a cocky grin as I take a seat across from him. "You look different," he says without missing a beat.

"Do I?"

"Roisin must be treating you well."

Right. "You want to get into this now?"

Arnie shrugs casually. "Well, you did kidnap my fiancé, so I think we probably should." He waves over to the barmen and indicates for him to bring over two more beers.

"You don't seem too concerned," I say, watching him closely. His relaxed posture hardly screams that he gives a fuck. But I don't know enough about this guy to lower my guard just yet.

"I know you know it's in your best interest to keep her safe," he replies. "But I won't lie to you; my reputation is at risk if I let you go through with the wedding."

There it is, the bite I was waiting for. This is a man perfectly in control of himself. Nothing about him gives away his frustration, yet his words are clearly calculated. I'd be willing to bet *his* anger is icy cold. Perhaps Aimee would be better off marrying him after all. Safer.

The rage I thought I'd stifled flickers again—hotter, more defensive. *My* Aimee.

Except... Arnie didn't say that Aimee was his fiancé. He said he's engaged to *Roisin*. Padraic might not be able to tell them apart but Connor certainly can. There's no reason he'd give Arnie Roisin's name unless...

... Unless Aimee was never meant to marry Arnold Knight.

"Rumor has it, Connor is marrying off his sister to secure the deal." The rumor never specified which sister. I just jumped to conclusions. Shit. The relief comes out of nowhere and I'm blindsided for a second.

The barman places two bottles down in front of us, and I take the moment to recompose myself. This doesn't change anything, for me at least. The real Roisin, however, might have something to say about it.

When the barman's finally out of earshot, I reply. "Are you threatening me?"

"Less of a threat, more of a fact," he says, downing his first beer and moving on to the next. "Roisin is my intended; that's a fact. What I'm *asking* is how you intend to fix this."

I lean forward a little and let him see how *I* play the game. "Have you considered that I'm not the person you should be talking to? Roisin *chose* me. Not you, not Connor. Me. I'm not going to sit here and discuss her choices when they aren't mine to make."

Arnie's mouth curls into a smile, and he sits back in his seat. "You seem confident that she'd deny my advances."

I do my best impression of Kate assessing the men whose hopes she's about to dash before replying, "Have you seen me?"

There's a brief pause before Arnie lets out a laugh and clinks my bottle with his. It's an odd sensation to be so cordial with the enemy, but I seem to be making a habit of it these days. I drink as he does, trying not to wince at the taste of alcohol. Hair of the dog and all that.

"It seems," Arnie says after a moment, "We have a lot in common, you and I."

"Do we?"

"Engaged to the same woman."

"She's wearing my ring," I point out.

But Arnie ignores me and continues, "Both mediators to the two most powerful families in the Irish mob."

"Is that what this is?"

"And we're both bastards," he finishes, using his bottle to salute me.

I frown at this. "You're not legitimate?"

"Oh, I am. They just tell me I can be an asshole sometimes."

I let out a long sigh. "Couldn't imagine why."

"Why did you call, Jack?"

"If we're so similar, I would have thought you'd have figured it out."

"I'd like to hear you say it," Arnie says. "Because the fact you're here means you've exhausted every other option."

I chuckle at that. "You think I'm still trying to figure out who you are?"

His face drops a little.

"Arnold Knight," I continue without missing a beat. "Leader of the disgraced Italian gang, the Novas, after all that business with the Lucas. Position kind of fell into your lap, didn't it? No one left alive to pick up the mantle."

"I manage," he says, sitting back.

"No men, no home, no experience at leadership. You were a hitman before all this, right?"

"I prefer 'assassin'. It's sexier."

Fuck, it's hard not to like this guy.

"So, my question isn't who you are," I say, pointedly ignoring him. "It's: why did you join the Maguires when the Duffys clearly have more to offer?"

"So, you're here to recruit me?"

"I'm here to have a conversation."

"Does Padraic know you're here?"

"What Padraic doesn't know won't hurt him."

"The rumors are true then."

"Aw, has Connor been gossiping about me?"

"Connor likes… information."

I practically grin at his hesitation. "Trouble in paradise?"

"He's made some questionable decisions lately," Arnie says, breaking the rhythm of our back and forth by looking over to the bar. I'm about to push him for more when his guard goes up again, and he turns back to me with a wry smile. "Not least, letting my fiancé fall into enemy hands."

"*My* fiancé," I reply with emphasis. "Would hardly call me an enemy."

"Is that so?"

"I'm taking very good care of her," I say, making sure to imply just how well with my tone. Even though right now, I'm not sure Aimee would even talk to me….

I shove the thought down and focus on the conversation at hand.

"I suppose it's a good job. He has another sister." Arnie takes a casual swig of beer. "Although I hear she may already have had a taste of this life and decided it didn't agree with her. But I do *love* a challenge."

My knuckles go white, gripping my glass. "Aimee isn't in New York."

Arnie examines me closely. "Isn't she?"

"No," I say firmly. "I suppose that means Connor won't be able to hold your interest much longer."

"Perhaps," Arnie replies with a smirk. "But as much as I admire your commitment to getting under his skin, it's going to take a little more than a botched engagement to get me to leave him for Padraic."

I can't help but grin. Even though it wasn't my intention, if making Connor suffer is a side effect of my actions, it makes for a nice little bonus. "Be sure to tell him how comfortable Roisin is with me, won't you?"

Arnie laughs, shaking his head. "You, on the other hand…."

"What do you mean?"

He pulls out his wallet and shakes his head, placing two crisp twenty-dollar bills on the table. "Let's stay in touch, shall we?"

"I'm not sure how happy Connor would be with that." I don't bother pointing out that Arnie has just drastically overpaid for our beers.

"What Connor doesn't know won't hurt him." Arnie parrots my earlier words back to me, and I smirk.

When he offers me his hand, I don't hesitate when I shake it. Wild card or not, Arnie's intriguing. He has this ability to talk so much without saying anything at all, playing the game to a standard I can't help but appreciate.

"Until next time," I say as I let go and move out of our booth. I'm not entirely satisfied what I've learned, but I'm curious about the opportunities a man like Arnold Knight could present.

I've already turned my back when Arnie calls out again.

"Oh, and Jack?"

I look over my shoulder to see Arnie's brow furrowed as if contemplating something. I wait patiently for him to find the words.

"It's not my alliance with Connor you should be worried about," he finally says before finishing his drink. Helpfully cryptic.

"Two drinks, and you're already spilling secrets?"

He shrugs, "Just wanted to give you a heads-up."

It doesn't look like he's willing to share any more, so I don't push it. Instead, I bow my head fractionally and continue on my way.

***

I ruminate on the last part of our exchange the entire drive home. Could Connor somehow have other support out there? If so, who haven't we considered yet?

The other Irish mobs are smaller and have sided with the Duffys for years. None of them feel like they could pose a threat to us on their own. Unless Connor somehow managed to convince multiple groups. But even then, they wouldn't have the money needed to go up against us.

Unless Arnie was alluding to a gang outside the mob. But would he have bothered warning me if he'd used his own connections to get the Italians involved? Besides, it's not like the Novas were getting picked first for the Italian Mafia dodgeball team. I'd be surprised if any of them would want to be associated with Tony Nova willingly. Even if it is only his nephew.

I'm still scouring my head for clues as I enter the mansion, and it takes me a moment to realize what's different about the place.

The whole entrance is decorated to the nines - flowers, ribbons, string lights, and even a water feature is partially installed in the gap under the twin staircases. There's only one time a year the house looks like this outside of Christmas. I just didn't think it would ever happen without Graham here.

The sting of pain at his loss still rattles me as Padraic appears from one of the side doors. Two attendants follow behind him.

"I suppose there's no point asking where you've been?" Padraic says spitefully when he notices me.

I choose to ignore him. "The gala is still happening?"

Padraic simply sneers. "Worried the dancing might ruin your form in the ring?"

I turn away before he can get me riled up, striding as quickly as I can toward my room.

"Make sure Roisin wears something more appropriate this time," Padraic calls after me.

My teeth grind together as I change my course to the gym.

I need to hit something. Hard.

Chapter Twenty-Eight

Aimee

I stare at myself in Kate's oversized mirror and barely recognize the woman looking back. The pale gold satin of my dress hugs every curve and ripples romantically around my feet every time I move. The matching stilettos make my legs look long and elegant, though they show through the slit in the satin far more than I'd like. But at least it's more reserved than the red dress.

Kate brushes my curled hair over my shoulder, and tiny strands of gold glitter through it as the light catches them. Her beautiful handiwork over the last few hours was to patiently and painstakingly attach and braid in each one.

The effect is astounding, but I can't help but think the amount of effort put in corresponds with Kate's new agenda: *Keeping me the hell away from Jack*.

"You look a bit like a Disney princess," she muses as she stands back to admire her handiwork.

I give her a theatrical twirl that's ruined by the sarcastic twist to my voice. "Just don't expect me to sing."

Kate smirks. Her own black gown falls elegantly from her shoulder and is pinned in place with a silver brooch. In the two days since the match at Luckies and our spontaneous shopping trip on Jack's credit card, I've not seen the women even entertain another color in her outfits.

But looking at us both in the mirror, we look like night and day. A spectacle in our own right.

"You look great," Kate says as if sensing my hesitation.

"That's not what I'm worried about," I say. "Everyone stared last time."

"And they'll stare again."

I turn to her. "And if I'd rather just fade into the background?"

Kate merely shrugs. "Wear your jeans if you have to. But you should know, Padraic hated your last dress."

I smirk at that. "Really?"

"Almost as much as Jack loved it."

My expression must sour because she shakes her head at me. "He might be an idiot, but at least you know he has good taste."

"I just don't see why I need to even be at the gala," I say for perhaps the fifteenth time.

It's not the idea of getting all dressed up to dance around and make small talk with people that make me feel nauseous. In fact, these events were probably the only good part about growing up in the mob.

It's the idea of getting all dressed up for *him* and spending the evening pretending that we're stupidly in love so that Padraic doesn't take me to one of his 'interrogation' chambers.

Kate filled me in on her uncle's favored pastime when I told her what Jack said about him threatening my life. It seems the rumors I'd heard as a child about the leader of the Dead Eyes paled in comparison to reality. The thought of being alone with that monster has my stomach in knots.

That fear is currently at war with my *need* to hit the man in the face. Hard.

"The guest list is fairly exclusive, so at least you won't have to deal with the riff-raff this time," Kate says casually. "All you need to do is show your face and smile."

I glance at myself once more before taking a deep breath and marching to the door.

"Where are you-"

"To this stupid gala," I say over my shoulder.

Kate bites her lip, "Padraic said he wanted to wait to introduce you—"

"Fuck Padraic fucking Duffy, I want to get this over with," I say as I yank the door open. "It's like you said; I just need to show my face and smile. If Padraic wants me to be a spectacle, I'm going to do it on my own terms."

As I stride across the hallway, I can already hear the murmurings of guests and the pleasant hum of a live quartet. People had been arriving for the last hour or so, but hanging around in Kate's room was making me restless.

The blonde eases off her protesting and quickly falls into step beside me.

"Remember, let Jack do the talking and try to avoid anyone that might remember you from before," she says as she takes my arm, guiding me toward the dual staircase for our grand entrance.

"If no one has said anything by now, I assume they're either dead or don't care. Or both," I mutter back.

"Still, be alert," Kate whispers as we reach our destination.

The foyer is quite beautiful. The decoration plays into the traditional architecture of the room, and a newly installed water fountain trickles happily in time with the band. If it weren't for the modern dresses and all the skin on show, it would feel like I'd stepped into Regency era-Britain.

I take a step down the stairs, then another. I'm not arrogant enough to presume the guests will stop to watch my arrival, but with the blonde by my side, it's a little satisfying to see some of the women move their husbands on by a little quicker.

As we take the final step, Kate squeezes my arm and nods toward where Jack has emerged from the crowd. His hazel eyes are glued to me, even as he approaches the both of us.

"*Chroí.*"

"Jack," I reply curtly.

Kate glances between the two of us a little nervously. "I'll leave you guys to it."

Jack doesn't stop staring at me as Kate makes her exit. "You look as beautiful as ever."

I offer him a sweet smile. "You still look like an asshole."

Just as he narrows his eyes, a server walks past with a tray of champagne flutes. I reach over to grab two and turn back to find Jack holding his hand out expectantly for it.

I stare at him for a moment, then down one of the glasses in one. Then put the empty flute in his outstretched hand.

"Shall we get on with it?" I say, taking a dainty sip from the other glass.

Jack's jaw tightens, but he doesn't rise to the bait. "With pleasure."

He takes my arm and leads me through the room. More than a few guests turn to stare at us as we pass by, but I keep my head held high. Focusing on what I assume is Jack's destination, the bar.

But suddenly, he jerks and changes course. My heart sinks as we approach a gaggle of overdressed, over-painted young women.

"Jacky!" The apparent leader of this pack of frills and puffy sleeves says as she leans in to kiss his cheek. "Where have you been?"

The way her hand lingers on his arm makes my blood boil, and I can't help but "tsk" loud enough for Jack to hear.

But he ignores me. "Business has kept me busy."

"I heard the most awful rumor," the leader chirps. "They're saying you're *engaged*."

I stiffen as the woman's eyes dart toward me, then at the arm tucked through Jack's.

"Guilty," Jack says with a sly smile. "I'd like to introduce my fiance, Roisin Maguire."

Some of the girls don't even attempt to hide the disgust on their faces when they hear my surname. I roll my eyes. "A pleasure, I'm sure."

"This has to be some kind of sick joke, right, Jacky?"

Jack lets out a dramatic sigh. "I wish it were. But Roisin here is just so in love with me; it's been hard to shake her from my side."

I turn to face him slowly. "Is that so?"

"It's almost a bit desperate," Jack continues without looking away from me. "I only proposed so she'd stop harassing me about it."

The girls explode into fits of giggles as my mind runs through all twenty-three ways I could murder Jack with a stiletto.

"Truly," I say when the laughter dies down. "The feelings I have for this man are… indescribable. Please, excuse me." I yank my arm away from Jack and storm toward the bar.

The bar staff must see me approach, as there's already a glass of champagne waiting for me when I arrive. I sip it slowly, letting the bubbles fizz out on my tongue. Trying to imagine my anger fizzing out with every mouthful.

"Well, aren't you something?" a voice says beside me.

I turn to see a lanky man has sat himself beside me. He's not wholly unattractive, but it's hard not to feel revolted by a man who can't take his eyes off my chest.

"Can I help you?" I say politely, trying to catch the eye of the barman in case there's any trouble.

The man, however, finally looks up at me and offers his hand. "Lars O'Neil."

"Roisin Maguire," I reply, taking it.

"You know, the O'Neils were Maguires not too long ago," Lars says conspiringly. "We're practically on the same side of all this."

Over Lars' shoulder, I spy a flash of hazel eyes, intently watching our conversation. Oh, *now* he's paying attention to me. Okay then. I knock back the rest of my drink.

"It's always nice to find allies in a place like this," I say sweetly, making sure to flutter my eyelashes a little too much. "Do you dance, Lars O'Neil?"

Lars seems to glow at the suggestion. "Has your *fiancé* not shown you the ballroom yet?"

"No," I reply tragically. "I was so looking forward to seeing it."

Lars rises from his chair and offers me a ridiculous bow that I make sure to laugh too much at. "Then allow me the honor of escorting you, ma'am."

Without so much as a glance Jack's way, I take his hand eagerly and allow my new friend to escort me to the dance floor.

As the music picks up again, Lars begins to lead us through a basic waltz. We laugh together as I pretend to get used to the footwork, but Lars is at least a patient teacher, and soon I reward his work by moving as fluidly as the other dancers around us. All the while, I can practically feel Jack's eyes burning into the back of my dress as Lars places a hand a little lower on my waist.

"It's quite unusual," Lars comments as we sway. "For a Maguire to marry a Duffy."

"Truly, I hadn't noticed," I reply, my tone dripping in sarcasm he doesn't pick up on.

"Very much so. In fact, I think you'd be much better off marrying someone more loyal to your family name," Lars continues. His arm slides further down my waist.

I try not to panic. "Like who, exactly?"

"Well—"

"May I cut in?"

Lars staggers us to a halt, clearly frustrated, but pales instantly when he realizes the cause of the interruption.

Jack towers over us, looking twice as large as Lars in his tailored three-piece. The anger in his eyes is thinly veiled by his cool exterior.

"The song's not over yet," Lars replies weakly.

"I don't care."

Lars glances at me as if hoping I might intervene. "Well, you see, the lady agreed to–"

"How's your wife, Lars?" Jack cuts in.

The two men stare at each other before Lars relents, handing me over to my fiance without further protest.

But, as Lars goes to leave, he leans in close to me. "Perhaps we could discuss my suggestions later?"

Jack pulls me into his chest before I can answer, and suddenly we're flying across the room. As far away from Lars O'Neil as we can get, it seems.

"What the fuck was that?" Jack hisses in my ear.

I let him twirl me around before I reply, "An alternative marriage proposal, I think."

"What?"

"You interrupted, so I can't be sure," I say, matching his every step as he strides confidently around the dancefloor. "But it felt like it was going in that direction."

"We are supposed to be *in love*," Jack bites on the last word bitterly. "You can't go waltzing with another man in front of everyone."

I pretend I don't hear him and carry on. "It was certainly going to be a more romantic proposal; perhaps I should have stayed to hear him out. Considering the amount of *protection* I've received these last few days."

"Can you not be petty about this for five minutes?"

I scoff as he dips me low. "Then what was that with all those girls earlier?"

"They are my *friends*, Aimee. God forbid I introduce you to people."

"Friends? You've got to be kidding me," I say, forcing myself to smile at a couple we pass by.

Jack suddenly pulls me in close, a dangerous smirk on his lips. "Oh, I get it, you're jealous."

"Of who, *Jacky*?" I bite back.

I watch the fire in his eyes burn brighter and brighter. The music is fading, and the people around us disappear.

"I can't believe I ever thought you and I were a good idea," he whispers so softly I barely catch the insult.

"Oh no, did proposing to the girl you barely knew backfire on you?"

The music stopped several beats ago. But still, we stand there in the middle of the dance floor. Chests pressed together, heaving with the strain of our dancing. My heart beats frantically in time with his.

I could kiss him right now. It would taste like sweat and anger and *passion.*

He glances at my lips. Fuck. If he kisses me now, I won't have the restraint to stop. I'd let him have his way with me. Anything to release this tension between us.

"All right, you two, save some for the honeymoon," Kate's voice breaks through the echo chamber of our ragged breaths.

We jump apart quickly as she approaches, and I busy myself fixing my hair. To my despair, it seems we've attracted something of an audience. Even Padraic, sitting up on the second-floor balcony that overlooks the dancefloor, is staring at us. The men around him whisper in his ear as they smoke cigars as thick as my arm.

"Your performance seems to have satisfied Padraic," Kate mutters to us both quietly.

I try to ignore the fact we weren't attempting to perform as I answer. "Does that mean I can go?"

"Give it five, but yes. Good job." The blonde turns on Jack and narrows her eyes. "And you. Try to act for five minutes like you're thinking with the head on your shoulders."

Jack merely nods silently in response. I watch them for a moment before leaving the dancefloor, trying not to make eye contact with anyone as I silently count back from five minutes in my head.

"Roisin Maguire. My, how you've grown!"

It's like someone poured iced water down my back. I turn to see a woman with thick black hair approaching me, her gray roots confidently on display and a smug grin on her face. Her dress is tight in places it shouldn't be, but the effect is wholly intimidating. She's older now, but there's something about the arrogance in her eyes that hasn't changed a bit.

"Eda."

My father's contact with the cartel.

"My condolences," she says, coming to a stop in front of me. "I'm sorry I couldn't be at your father's funeral. But rumor has it, neither were you."

"What do you want?" I whisper, every warning bell in my head going off.

"I merely wanted to pass on my regards to an old friend. Although I'm surprised you remember me, the state you were in the last time I saw you."

I grimace. "I'd hoped you'd be rotting at the bottom of the Hudson by now."

When Eda laughs, it sounds more like a cackle. The memories it triggers pierce through me like a thousand knives, and I almost stagger back.

Though I try to keep my face schooled into a neutral expression, his eyes light up at my reaction. "Still as feisty as ever, hmm? How's your sister these days? I always thought she would be the one to marry into mob royalty."

"Leave my sister out of this," I whisper, suddenly very aware of how much weight my body is holding up.

"I've missed our little chats, Roisin," Eda coos. "You should come to visit me some time; you can't imagine the delicacies I have in stock these days."

I think I might vomit. Even the thought of Roisin talking to this woman again has my vision spinning. This woman destroyed my sister. It took five years and giving up my entire life to get her to a place of recovery. But now we're both back in New York, and Eda seems just as powerful as ever.

What the fuck have I done? I breathe in and out. Why did I let her come back to New York? This is my fault. My fault.

As I begin to spiral, someone steps up beside me. I barely register he's there until his arm wraps around my waist, and I'm pulled to his side. Without missing a beat, he takes on the weight that threatened to buckle my legs a moment before.

Jack kisses my forehead lightly before turning to Eda with a sneer. "What's this, *chroí?*"

Eda's eyes go wide at the sight of my fiancé. "My name is Eda, Eda Romero," she says a little too eagerly, holding her hand out to Jack.

Jack stares at the outstretched hand in disgust, "Well, Eda Romero, I'd appreciate it if you didn't speak to my fiancé or her sister again."

Eda's smile falters, "We're just old friends, aren't we, Roshe?"

"No," I whisper before finding my voice again. "No, we aren't."

Eda glances between the two of us as if something has just clicked, then reaches out to touch me. Perhaps to stroke my arm or grasp my hand to try and prove our affection. However, before she has a chance to even graze me, Jack has moved, snatching her arm and pulling her in close so he can hiss in her ear.

"And if you even think of touching her, the DEA will be on your ass before you can even spell it." He steps away but does not release her from his iron grip. "Are we clear?"

Jack throws her arm away, and she instantly rubs the skin where his fingers had been. Her dark brows furrow as she backs away. "I'll be sure not to bother your fiancé or her *sister* again, Mr. Duffy."

With that, she turns on her heel and stalks away.

I sag against Jack in relief, aware that more than a few people seem to have noted our interaction.

He kisses my forehead again, this time lingering so he can whisper, "Are you okay?"

His voice is so full of concern I almost believe it.

Instead of responding, I pull away and smooth my dress. Throwing the on-lookers a tight smile before taking off down across the room. I just need to leave, go somewhere I can be alone. There must be a thousand unoccupied rooms in this goddamn house.

I know Jack is hot on my heels because he keeps calling after me, but I ignore him. I can't bring myself to respond, knowing that my voice will probably crack under the weight of the emotions storming through me.

Finally, I reach a quieter corridor and beeline for a set of double doors. I push them open and find myself in a dark dining room that I barely have time to register before Jack yanks the door open behind me.

"*Aimee!*" he hisses.

"What do you want?" I say, gulping down the emotion threatening to spill from me at any moment.

He looks at me as if I've grown a second head, "What is going on with you? Who was that woman?"

"It doesn't matter."

He crosses his arms. "Clearly, it does."

"I don't owe you an explanation," I say desperately, backing away.

Jack is already shaking his head by the time I finish speaking. "Goddamn it, Aimee, I'm trying to help you right now."

"Now you're trying to help me? Why? Is keeping me sweet back on your priority list after you avoided me the last few days?"

"I haven't been avoiding you–"

"Then where have you been?"

"Where have *you* been?" he says, taking a step closer.

I don't back down. "You're seriously deflecting right now?"

"You've been avoiding me just as much as I've been avoiding you."

"You're fucking infuriating!" I practically shout, even though his face keeps inching closer.

"Yeah? Then you're the bane of my fucking life."

His lips are crashing into mine before either of us seems to register it's happening.

My body reacts instinctively. Curling into him, gripping onto his neck to pull him closer and deepening the kiss with my tongue.

He groans as he tugs my hair and wraps his arms around me even tighter. He's everywhere. My waist, the top of my thigh. My neck. God, my neck.

When he pulls away, his breath comes out in rapid pants, and he rests his forehead against mine. Cradling my face in his hand as he just breathes me in.

"I've missed you."

The words make me crash back down to earth with a nauseating jolt. We've been here before. I've fallen for this before.

I pull away, even though every cell in my body screams at me to stay.

"I can't do this," I whisper as I back away.

The vulnerability I see flash across his moonlit face almost makes me reconsider, but I continue my retreat defiantly. One step, then another, and I'm out the door, and I force myself not to glance back at him.

This time when I leave, he doesn't follow. When I find another empty room, the doors don't crash open behind me.

But as the tears begin to fall, I can't help hoping that maybe they might.

Chapter Twenty-Nine

Jack

I must have sat in the *Luckies* locker room a thousand times. Whether it was to train or to try and goad Graham into a fight or even take part in a few low-stakes matches, this place has always felt like a second home.

But tonight, I feel like a stranger here.

The roar of the crowds seems louder than I ever remember it before. As I wrap and re-wrap my hands, I try to tune it out so I can focus.

My first match against Kennedy had been simple, fueled by the rage I felt for Padraic. The fact I'd seen Kennedy fight before made it easy to take him down, even though he was by no means an easy opponent. He won this very competition only last year.

Living at the Duffy mansion this last week should have made it easier to pick up on clues to my next fight. But the only name Ray and I managed to find was "Quinn." There were close to a dozen low- to high-profile fighters in the eastern European circuit, so it didn't exactly help.

Nonetheless, I spent a sleepless night in Ray's office scanning crappy handheld footage of anyone fighting with that name.

"You're tired," my old coach observes from across the room as I stand up and stretch out my muscles again.

He's not wrong; I can already feel the fatigue starting to set in. With Aimee making a habit of locking me out of my room these past few days, it's been difficult to catch any discreet shut-eye. Morris already made a joke about me being in the doghouse, and there's only so much… separation we can get away with before Padraic starts to notice.

I know she'll be in the crowd somewhere today. Kate, at least, has taken it upon herself to text me her location since the gala. It does little to settle my nerves, and there's been a few times I've had to stop myself from outright stalking her. I'm constantly reminding myself that she rejected *me*.

Sulking like a teenage boy about it feels pathetic.

"Not as tired as you, old man." I try to say it lightly, but it comes out in a dull monotone.

He approaches to clasp me on the shoulder, a gesture I know he's only rarely performed. "Be careful this time, okay?"

I nod, finally satisfied with my hands, and give them an experimental flex.

"Watch your left foot; I saw it slip a few times against Kennedy," Coach gives me a small pat before walking away.

"See you on the other side?" I say to his retreating form.

He's saved from his response by a booming announcement crackling over the speakers. The crowds immediately quieten. There's no speech from Padraic this time, only a brief welcome before my name is announced.

The crowd goes berserk. That's my cue.

I head toward the door and step out, up the stairs, and into the ring. Even though I tell myself I'm not going to look for her, I still do. My eyes scan the crowd for her red hair as the commentator reads out my weight and class.

Finally, I spot her. A vision in emerald green perched on her seat in the VIP box. Deep, chocolate eyes watching me intently.

I give her a mock salute.

For the first time in a week, I see the ghost of a smile on her lips.

Something deep in my chest cracks, and a dull pain envelops my entire body. Like someone has punched me straight in the rib.

I've missed that smile.

"Aaaaaannnddd, in the other corner, we have three-time European champion Quinn Matisse!"

It takes me a moment to tear my eyes away from her to size up my opponent.

Of course, Padraic would import a BKB champ to fight me.

Quinn and I are physically much more evenly matched than Kennedy and I. He's a similar height, and his strength seems to be in his core instead of his arms and shoulders. Lighter on his toes, too, I notice as he skips quickly from one foot to the next.

A glance back to my corner to look at my coach's grim expression tells me all I need to know. This is going to be a rough fight.

We circle each other slowly. Quinn's face is a mask of pure professionalism. I notice him glancing at my left foot and immediately adjust to compensate, cursing myself for giving a weakness away.

Watching him move at this distance, however… I come up short. There's nothing there to exploit, no obvious weaknesses. This man is built like a goddamn machine.

The referee finally raises his hand, and I brace myself for Quinn to make an immediate attack.

Only when the whistle goes it doesn't come.

Quinn is on the defensive.

It takes me a split second to come up with my plan. If he wants to play defense, I'm going to let him. I need to go in with quick, tight hits, keep him guessing and hopefully overwhelm him before he can get a read on my preferred attacks.

I lurch forward on an off-beat and aim low.

Quinn moves like a flash. Quicker than I ever thought he'd be able to manage. He dodges effortlessly and lands two light punches to my side.

I leap away quickly to keep him in front of me. The crowds are already getting excited.

My opponent's face is unreadable as we begin circling each other again. Okay, new plan.

Again, I lurch off-beat and feign a left attack—only to move in on my right foot. Just as I think I'm about to land, Quinn is suddenly there to block, and I'm rewarded with a punch to the gut.

I stagger back to the tune of the crowd's 'ooohs' and try to pretend the blow didn't almost wind me. Pulling up my hands defensively, I try to discern any kind of tell in my opponent. But he simply stares blankly back.

Ding, ding, ding!

Saved by the bloody bell. I head back to my corner.

"Stop attacking," Coach says as soon as he hands me a bottle of water. "Let him come to you."

"He hits hard," I admit quietly.

Coach merely shakes his head, "You've taken harder. Don't let him see you flinch."

I nod and throw the bottle back to him before heading toward where my opponent is already readying himself for round two.

"Jack!"

I look back over my shoulder at Coach.

"Left foot!"

Ding, ding, ding.

We start our dance again.

This time I hold back as instructed, watching Quinn intently. I register every flicker of movement he makes, positioning and repositioning to take on any offense he might take.

When it comes, I'm ready for it… until I'm not.

I dodge, and his first swing goes wide—only for his other fist to collide with my jaw. Hard.

My feet barely hold me up. Stars scatter through my vision as I try to evade my opponent. But suddenly, he's there again.

Two punches to the gut and another to the jaw. As I fall to the ground, I feel something snap.

Faintly in the audience, I hear someone scream. But as I lie there, all I can focus on is the bright lights above me. Until the ref blocks them out.

Five fingers up. Then four. Three.

Shit.

I scramble to my feet, shaking off the way the world spins around me, and hold my head high. The telltale taste of iron fills my mouth, and when I spit, blood splatters on the pale floor. I wipe my chin off it as I glare at Quinn.

The ref watches me a moment longer before conceding. I'm still in the game.

Quinn immediately darts forward, hoping to take me off guard, but I evade, landing awkwardly on my left foot. In the brief second of instability, Quinn is there again. Another punch to the side.

My balance fails, and I realize I'm going to fucking fall again.

Ding, ding, ding!

At the last second, I stumble forward and catch myself. Jesus Christ.

I try to shake it off on my way back to the corner, but Coach's face is spinning in front of me.

"Hey, hey!" he snaps, chucking water in my face. "Look at me."

I obey; however, I'm not sure which coach I'm meant to be looking at.

"Fuck." Both coaches say in sync.

The effort of keeping them both in my line of sight is suddenly exhausting.

"Jack Duffy, keep your goddamn eyes open; you hear me?" Coach roars, and I jerk awake with a start. Only to be greeted with another faceful of water.

Thankfully, it clears my head a little, and the two coaches combine into one.

"Keep low, don't let him hit your face again," he hisses as he throws a towel at me. "And remember your–"

"Left foot," I finish. My voice is weaker than I'd like it to be, but Coach nods in approval.

I towel off quickly before the ref calls me back in for round 3.

Ding, ding, ding.

There's less tension in Quinn's shoulders this round. I must look like shit, because he clearly thinks he'll be able to finish me off.

When he skirts toward me, I match his step. It's awkward, and the retreat stings my pride, but I successfully avoid another blow to the head.

For the first time, I see a flash of annoyance in Quinn's eyes.

There you are.

He strikes again, this time faster. I'm not quick enough to avoid a blow to my shoulder, but I can take it. I don't even flinch when I block a third hit with my forearm.

Quinn retreats, reevaluating his approach.

Just as I see an opening.

I lurch forward on my left foot, and Quinn automatically blocks my right, thinking I'm feigning.

Only I follow through on my left.

The hit to the chin catches him entirely by surprise. He staggers, arms flailing.

This could be my only opportunity. So I hit him again and again. Each time my fist makes contact, it feels like my brain rattles in my head. The pain is almost unbearable, but I keep going, ignoring the blood dribbling down my chin.

The crowd is alive and electric as Quinn is backed into a corner, only able to crouch and cover his head under the barrage of hits.

As my final hit reverberates through my body, a jolt of pain pierces my head, and I almost black out.

Quinn takes the opportunity to peek around his cover. I watch in slow motion as my fist automatically fires out and smacks him square in the face.

There's a beat. Then another.

Quinn hits the floor first.

I stay on my feet long enough to be announced the winner before I fall right next to him.

Chapter Thirty

Aimee

"Get the hell out of my way!" I roar as the crowds begin to swarm around the entrance to Jack's locker room.

The staff room exit will take twice as long, and they're already dragging Jack out of the ring.

Thankfully, the crowds part for me, and soon, the only thing blocking my path is one of Padraic's goons stationed at the door.

"Let me through," I demand, already reaching for the door.

But the man throws up his arm. "Can't."

I blink through my rage. "Do you know who I am?"

"Yes,." The brute narrows his eyes slightly.

"Then would you rather answer to my brother or my fiancé about this?"

The man's demeanor instantly changes. His back straightens, and he removes his arm as if I'd just threatened to bite it.

I waste no time pushing through the door and into the locker room.

It's the coach I see first, a man with a tight, grim expression as he holds Jack down on the table at the back of the room. Jack seems conscious, at least, but he keeps trying to sit up despite the yelling of the older man. Looks like he listens to other people just as well as he does to me. I glance around for a sports medic or at least some kind of physician but only find two attendants flurrying around, going between the entrance and the table brandishing towels and water.

"Where's the medic?" I demand, striding over.

The coach glances up at me with wide eyes. "He's not here."

"I don't need a medic," Jack groans, but we both ignore him.

"What do you mean he's not here?"

"He's attending Quinn," the coach replies, wrestling Jack back down when he tries to get up again.

I stare at him in disbelief. This place is a goddamn death trap that has been "successfully"running for years. "You only have one fucking medic?"

"Ow!" Jack moans, flinching away from my shriek.

As much as he might deserve it, I take a second to cool down and keep my voice level.

"Can you keep him lying down?" I say to the coach before I turn on the two attendants. "Give me those towels. I need a first aid kit, a flashlight, and some rubbing alcohol. If you don't have that, get the highest proof vodka from the bar. Nothing flavored."

They stare at me blankly as I tie my hair out of my face. So I clap at them. "Now!"

That seems to do the trick. A moment later, they're running out of the room, and I'm able to turn back to my patient.

I try not to bite my lip at the bloody graze I find along his side.

"Burn from the floor," the coach clarifies as I take a moment to assess the damage. It's not too deep, but it needs proper cleaning to stave off infection. I'm more worried about his concussion and the fact he's breathing unevenly.

"Jack?" I say, finally gathering my courage to drag my eyes to his face. His lip has split at the bottom, and there's an already darkening bruise forming along his jaw. As gently as I can, I open his mouth and take out his mouthguard. He flinches a little when my finger grazes his mouth.

There's more blood in there than I would like, but luckily it looks like his teeth are all still intact. I'm a lousy emergency dentist.

"Aimee?" Jack mutters as he stares up at me.

"No," I say firmly, moving to unwrap his hands. "I'm Roisin, remember?"

I ignore the odd look the coach gives me and finish my task. "Can you stretch out your fingers for me?"

Jack obeys.

"Good; now, can you squeeze my fingers?"

I hold my hands up for him, and he gently weaves his fingers through mine and squeezes.

"That's not what I meant," I say, feeling the blush blossoming on my cheeks.

The two attendants reappear, and I snatch my hands away quickly. They must still see, since they drop everything they managed to gather at my feet and scurry away again.

I grab the flashlight from the pile and hold it up to Jack's face. "Okay, look at me? Watch my finger."

Surprisingly, he does so without a fuss. I don't like his pupil dilation, but at least he's able to follow my finger.

"You're very pretty, you know that?" Jack says suddenly, and I realize he's given up on my finger and is instead just staring shamelessly at my face.

I roll my eyes and glance up at the coach. "He has a concussion and maybe a cracked jaw. His breathing is concerning, too; I'm just hoping it's just a broken rib."

"And the graze?" He nods toward Jack's chest.

"It needs disinfecting, but it should heal over time. If I can find some gauze in here, I'll bandage it, but best to take it off when he gets home. Aspirin for the pain, then maybe some soothing gel after it's had a chance to dry up. Then it's just bedrest for a few days."

The coach looks at me weirdly again, "But you're going to do all that, right?"

Right. I'm his fiancé. "Yes, sorry, I was just… thinking out loud."

"That's my Roisin," Jack says with a laugh. "The thinker."

"Jesus," I say, rummaging through the supplies until I find the rubbing alcohol. "I need to clean you up. You promise me you're not going to move?"

"Scouts honor," Jack replies with a mock salute.

The coach backs away from him slowly, but Jack thankfully stays still long enough for me to douse a towel in rubbing alcohol and press it into his graze.

"Jesus fucking Christ!" he yelps, and the coach has to place a hand on his shoulder to keep him steady.

"I thought you were a tough guy?" I goad as I press into him again.

Pride effectively wounded, Jack shoos away the coach to hide his hiss of pain.

I look up at the other man. "Thank you. I can probably take it from here."

"You sure?"

I nod, "If you see Padraic out there, tell him I'll kill him."

The coach chuckles humorlessly. "I like you, so I won't." He turns to Jack. "You do what she says, you hear?"

Jack makes a non-committal noise, and I say nothing until I hear the door close behind him.

"You're a prize idiot, Jack Duffy," I mutter, attacking him again with the towel.

He hisses out a breath. "Guess I deserve that."

"You should have stayed down."

The scream that came out of me when he fell in the ring… every part of me begged for him to get back up, to give me some kind of sign that he was still alive. Hindsight is a funny thing.

Jack doesn't seem too interested in reliving the fight either. He watches my hands as they deftly attend to his wounds. "You learn how to patch a guy up like this in medical school?"

"I've patched guys up more times than I can count." Before I even got to medical school. But I don't need to say this out loud; Jack already seems to understand.

"Handsome guys?"

I smirk a little, fingers lingering on his muscled chest. "Sometimes."

Jack's answering smile is slightly obscured by his swelling lip, and I can't help chuckling at how ridiculous it looks. The laughter takes root quickly. Maybe it's just the ridiculousness of the whole situation or the fact the adrenaline is still coursing through me, but I have to bite my lip to stop the waves of giggles that threaten to spill out.

Then Jack starts laughing too. It's a wonderful sound, so familiar and yet so *missed*.

The floodgates open, and we sit there like two crazy people laughing in the locker room together. By the time we're done, tears have started streaming from my eyes.

Jack suddenly winces and grabs his chest. "Ow."

"Stop laughing!" I say between residual giggles. "You've broken a rib."

"That would do it," he says with a wry smile before lying back with a sigh. "I don't like fighting with you."

I return to the task at hand, "Well… I don't like watching you fight."

"I'll stop if it makes you happy."

"There's still one more round," I point out.

Jack deflates a little. "Right."

"Do you think Padraic will stop punishing you after that?"

"Maybe. Depends."

"On what?"

"If I win, it's a good look for the family—but I'll be celebrated, and that means Padraic is no longer the center of attention. If I lose, I'll be humiliated like Padraic wants, but he risks being ridiculed by other families. It's a game of pride versus ego."

"Then throw the next match," I say a little too passionately. "I don't care about Padraic's fucking pride."

Jack looks at me curiously. "You think I can't take it?"

"You won on a technicality! If you'd fallen a second earlier, you'd have both lost."

"Picked up a few of the rules, did you?"

"I'm serious, Jack. You could have been seriously hurt."

He watches me for a moment before concluding, "You were worried."

"Do you see anyone else in here tending to your wounds?"

"Aimee…"

The way he says my name sends shivers down my spine. It's like every part of him is calling to me, inviting me in. And dear God, have I missed this. Being apart from him, then seeing him get hurt in the ring pained me more than I could have imagined.

But right now, he's my patient, and we're not out of the woods yet.

"The sooner we get you clean, the sooner we can leave," I state quietly, and he seems to get the message. Not here.

***

Getting Jack into the car and back to the mansion was an ordeal in itself. Between insisting he could walk on his own, then promptly getting too dizzy to stand straight, we only just managed to stumble back to his room in one piece.

"Lie down," I instruct, and Jack promptly falls into bed with a groan.

I wander into the bathroom to find some aspirin, but when I return, Jack is looking at me expectantly.

"You're not sleeping on the couch tonight," he states, determination and stubbornness written over his face.

I walk over and hand him the pills, but back away when he tries to reach for my hand. "I'll stay in Kate's room."

"Please, Aimee…" His hazel eyes bore into mine. "Let's not fight anymore."

There is so much I should say, confess, and apologize for. But tonight, he needs to recover. *I* need to recover.

I back away.

"Don't leave me again," he whispers. The vulnerability in his voice almost shatters my resolve, but I stride forward and flick off the lights, grabbing the door handle determinedly.

This is the right thing to do. It's too complicated to sort through everything right now. I'm being smart and careful. I'm looking after *me*.

"I…" I hesitate in the doorway. "I missed you too."

My words hang in the air, and my heart starts to beat faster and faster.

"Come here," Jack whispers into the darkness.

My feet move before I have a chance to process his words. He reaches for me as I approach the bed, and I meet his embrace, easily slotting into the crook of his arm as I lie next to him. Then carefully, avoiding his side, his jaw, we wrap around each other so tightly, it's impossible to say where he starts and I begin.

His hand strokes the back of my head, and my fingers scrunch into his shirt. My mouth gasps in his scent as he nuzzles into my shoulder. Our intertwined legs tangle and detangle, then tangle again.

We cling to each other like a lifeline.

All the anger, all the doubt, and all the denial melt away in the intensity of the embrace. Everything suddenly feels so stupid. Why were we avoiding each other? Why were we fighting? Why were we denying ourselves *this*?

"What can I do to help you trust me again?" he whispers against my skin.

Nothing. Everything.

"I don't know," I answer truthfully. "I want to."

Jack squeezes impossibly tighter, "I want you more than I want to play Padraic's stupid games. I want you more than the fighting between our families. I want you more than I want revenge for my brother. Aimee... please. Please believe me. This last week without you—I've barely slept. I've never wanted anything more in my life. I know it's fucking complicated; I know I should have told you so many things; I know I've fucked up. But I've missed this. So fucking much."

The sting of tears fills my eyes at his confession. I've never heard him sound so broken, so desperate.

"I thought I was going to lose you today. When you went down that first time, I thought... People die in that ring, Jack. I couldn't bear it. There was nothing I could do except watch helplessly from the sidelines." I breathe in and out. "I don't want to sit on the sidelines anymore."

"I won't ask you to pick a side," Jack replies. "But maybe we could... be our own team? Not Duffys, not Maguires, just us."

"Just us?"

"Just us."

I give in. Every muscle in my body relaxes into him. There's no fight left, only us. We're exhausted, overly anxious, and in an awful situation. But at least at this moment, we have each other.

"I think I'd like that," I whisper back.

Chapter Thirty-One

Aimee

I've never slept so well in my life.

For the past few nights, curled up against Jack's firm chest, it's been impossible to tell apart the sweet dreams from reality. Although we've barely even kissed, the intensity of this closeness is like nothing I've ever experienced.

Last night was no different. With a barely bruised rib and a healed-up lip, Jack had been more attentive than usual. Eager to hold me, prove to me that he's recovered. My dreams only made his touches more tantalizing.

Even as I begin to register that I'm waking up, I can still feel the ghost of his hands lingering in places I only ever want him to explore more. The feeling of his lips against my stomach makes me squirm further into the numerous pillows around me.

I don't want to wake up. Not yet. Not when his lips keep kissing lower and lower. When his hands cup my breast and tug lightly on my nipple.

"Mmm," I murmur my content into a pillow.

The kisses suddenly stop.

"Good morning, *Chroí*," Jack's words vibrate against my thigh.

I freeze. This isn't a dream.

The kisses resume, moving closer and closer to my center. I suddenly become aware of how wet I am, my core already begging for my dreams to become a reality.

"You seem eager for me," he hums, his mouth moving to the top of my pajama shorts and tugging at the fabric with his teeth. "Did you sleep well?"

I look down at him, resting between my legs. His muscled back is splayed out before me, and I fight the urge to comb my hands over his shoulders to feel how strong and firm they are for myself.

Instead, I reach for his hair and push it back out of his eyes. "Perfectly."

A cocky smile spreads across his lips. "You were moaning my name."

I bite my lip, trying to ignore the blush I know is currently spreading across my cheeks.

"Was I?" I say as innocently as I can as he places a tantalizing kiss on my bare stomach.

"It made me jealous," Jack hums. "What was I doing to you?"

I try to shrug, but Jack's hands are suddenly lifting me up and sliding off my shorts. The cool air flashes over my nakedness until Jack lowers himself onto me again, resuming his soft kisses across my abdomen.

"Just touching me…." I reply, trying to sit up to watch him work, but his hands hold me firmly in place.

His kisses trail down me again, and my breathing hitches.

"Where?" He asks as his mouth lingers at the top of my shaved pussy, brushing his bottom lip across the light stubble.

Something inside me tightens, and I lose patience with his teasing. I drop my hand down to my throbbing entrance and start working myself. Reveling in the release with a groan.

"Here," I bite out.

Jack chuckles. "So impatient."

His hand is suddenly on mine, working me harder for a wonderful, delicious moment before removing it. Before I can protest, he puts my finger in his mouth. His tongue swirls around it tantalizingly, lapping up the juices eagerly.

The sensation makes my breathing come out quick and ragged. Jack seems delighted by my reaction. He sucks up and down my finger while he stares up at me, distracting me from where his own fingers have started creeping up my leg.

A moment later, I feel him enter me and groan in pleasure. He moves in synchronization with his mouth, and I have to bury my head in the pillow at the overwhelming sensation that envelops my entire body.

"I want to hear the sounds you made, *Chroí*," Jack says, finally releasing my finger and adding another inside me.

He glides in so easily I barely register the adjustment until the third finger goes in. "Oh fuck!"

"That's it, good girl."

Jack begins kissing me again, leaving a trail of bites along my thigh before soothing them with his tongue. Getting closer and closer to where his fingers relentlessly work me harder and harder.

"Did I kiss you here?" He purrs against the top of my pussy, placing an experimental kiss just above the bundle of nerves that are practically screaming for him to touch.

"Yes!"

He needs no more encouragement. He takes me in his mouth, and I scream. Jack curls his fingers inside me, and I cry out at the intensity of the pressure that builds there.

The pleasure is indescribable. I barely remember my own name as he works me again and again, bringing me to a climax that feels like it stretches out for eons. A shrill cry fills my ears, and it journeys with me through the waves of pleasure.

My throat feels hoarse when I finally come back down to earth, and I realize it was me who was crying out.

Jack hovers over me, looking more than a little smug.

"Did it feel like that?" he says, his eyes raking over my body and darkening with desire.

I can only nod as he lowers himself onto me again. He licks his thumb slowly and lowers it to my now-spent core. He circles it lazily, brushing over my clit gently until my body tenses in response.

"Did I fuck you here?" he says, pulling away to unsheath himself.

I will never not be amazed by the size of Jack's cock. Especially now, when it's already thick with wanting. I reach for it, trailing my hand along to his girth, then back down again. It's Jack's turn to tense up.

He moves quickly, flipping us over so I sit on top of him. My pajama top falls back into place.

"Take it off," Jack demands, and I obey. Slowly. Making sure to push out my chest as the fabric passes over my nipples. My fingers brush against something, but I don't have time to question what it is.

His mouth is on my nipples before my shirt hits the ground.

"Oh God, yes!"

Jack's fingers dig into my skin, lifting me slightly so I can position myself over him. My cum drips down his cock before he can even enter me as he relentlessly worships my tits.

I push down onto him. Hard.

I don't give myself time to adjust to his size before I start moving, loving the sounds he makes at the pleasure of my tightness. The friction is unparalleled.

The moan that escapes my mouth is practically feral.

"Louder," he says gruffly.

"Fuck!"

"Good girl."

He starts matching my movements, and suddenly the momentum isn't enough. I need him *harder*.

At my whimper, Jack reaches up and grabs something seemingly out of thin air. He places the end of the rope in my hand.

"Hold on to this."

I glance up. At some point in the night, Jack must have attached the rope to the ceiling above his bed. It just dangles there, innocently waiting for someone to hang on to it.

I do as I'm told, using every ounce of strength to hold myself up as Jack starts to slam into me. Harder, harder, harder.

The slap of our skin is background music to the stars that fill my vision. No one has ever used me like this. No one has ever made me cum like this.

I use the momentum of the rope to meet him mid-thrust, and he groans as I explode around him. My arms start to go limp. I'm not sure how long I can hold on.

But Jack lets out a groan, and his body shudders, finally reaching his own climax.

I collapse on top of him. Completely spent. Breathing hard.

Jack holds me to him and kisses my forehead. "The next time you dream of me like that, I want you to wake me up. I want you to ride me like that until you cum."

I nod into his chest, not trusting my voice to answer him coherently.

We lie like that until our breathing returns to normal, and Jack starts to move again.

"Come on, you need to get dressed."

"What? Why?" I pout.

"I'm taking you out on a date."

***

Jack removes his hands from my eyes, and I gasp in delight. On the rooftop of a building overlooking the Brooklyn Bridge, a picnic bench has been set up—adorned with flowers and fairy lights and a basket seemingly filled to the brim.

I dart over to the wall, the barrier between us and a seven-story drop, immediately. You can see the entire ecosystem of New York from here. The cars, boats, and people traveling to and from their destinations.

"This is gorgeous!" I call back to Jack, who watches me, bemused.

"I knew I had to find somewhere with a view," he says fondly. "I'm sorry it's not as fancy as the hotel."

I tear myself away to join him at the table. "No, this is perfect."

He's already extracting a bottle of champagne from the basket and pouring it out for us. When he hands it to me, he clinks it with a sweet smile. "To just us?"

"To no more secrets," I tease back.

We take a sip, and I watch as Jack grimaces and looks away from me.

"In that case, I should probably tell you something," he admits, not looking me in the eye.

I take a deeper gulp of alcohol. "Hit me."

"I met with Arnie Knight the other day."

Ah... I forgot about that. "I know, Kate told me."

Jack sighs, "It seems our intel wasn't... specific."

"What do you mean?"

"Your brother promised his sister to Arnie Knight in exchange for their alliance; we just didn't know *which* sister."

It takes me longer than it should for it to click what he's saying. "I was never engaged to Arnie, was I?"

Jack shakes his head, "I mean, technically, as you're posing as Roisin, and he's still very much interested in getting you back."

For fucksake. "I'm going to murder Connor the next time I see him."

"You're not upset at me?" Jack asks cautiously.

"Should I be?" I shoot back.

He swallows, "Part of the reason I suggested this engagement was because I didn't want Arnie to get his hands on you. It was selfish of me, I know that. But the safety thing remains true."

"You were jealous?"

"A little," Jack smirks a little sheepishly.

"Then let's call it a happy accident and leave it at that," I reply, refilling my glass.

Jack takes out some of the food and passes it to me quietly.

I take it with a sigh. "What?"

He hesitates. "I just want to make sure that this is actually what you want."

"I want you."

"I know, but I'm… I'm not a good person, Aimee," Jack holds onto my hand and squeezes. "After the first fight… I swore to myself that you would never see me like that."

The memory of Jack storming down the corridor at Luckies, the spitting image of his father, fills my mind. I gulp a little. "It's fine."

"No, it's not," Jack says firmly, staring intently into my eyes. "You were terrified. And I did nothing to stop it; I just left you there. God… I never wanted you to be scared of me. That's why I started drinking. I couldn't make myself face you again any other way."

I match his stare. "I don't want you to hide from me, Jack. Can you promise me that?"

"I can try," he replies, and I see the truth of his words in his resolve.

"That's all I ask," I say before I let out a long sigh and return to my food. The sound of the city around us, the faint beat of helicopter wings, makes it feel cozy even with the expanse of space around us. "Let's talk about something less heavy."

"Like what?"

"Tell me about… music?"

Jack looks at me, amusement returning to his face. "Music?"

"What's your guilty pleasure?"

He blows out a breath, buying himself a bit of time. "I don't know, Aerosmith?"

"Seriously?"

"You said guilty pleasure!"

"I'm trying to imagine you belting out *"I Don't Want To Miss A Thing"* in one of your fancy sports cars."

"That song was designed to sing alone in your car," Jack points his fork at me. "You can't tell me you've never done it."

I shake my head, "More of a Stones fan, I'm afraid."

"Of course, you'd side with the British," Jack mutters under his breath. Despite all the noise from the helicopter flying nearby, I still catch it.

Okay then, he went there first. "Hey—the Maguires did what they needed to do to survive the famine, asshole."

"Including selling out the Duffys for a couple extra English crumbs?" Jack counters.

"The English betrayed us too, you know."

"Aye, but you betrayed us first."

"Me personally?" I counter, brow raised.

Jack smiles at this and shakes his head.

"Isn't it crazy that a couple Irish guys made some bad decisions a few hundred years ago, and we're here today still suffering their consequences?" I say conversationally.

But Jack's smile fades a little. "The mob doesn't forget," he says with a sigh.

"But what if it did?"

"It doesn't."

"Why?"

Jack puts his utensils down. "It might have started with a couple bad decisions, but this *war* between our families... Aimee, people have died for it. That makes it our consequence too."

"It doesn't have to be; we could start fresh."

But Jack is already shaking his head. "If we wash over everything that happened, that means they died for nothing."

"They'd have died for peace, Jack," I say quietly. "Are you telling me that's not what Graham would want?"

"What would peace even look like?"

"I don't know... A nice house out in the suburbs?"

"Seriously?"

"Fine. An apartment in the tallest building in New York City, a steady job in the ER where I make up for all the lives my family has taken. A Chinese joint that knows my order before I even need to place it." I glance down at my plate. "A husband who loves *me*. Not my family name or the power he can gain from it. Just me."

"Any man would be lucky to have just you."

"Then what does that make you?"

Jack's entire body shifts before I even register what's happening.

It all happens in slow motion.

He throws himself across the table and pushes me to the ground. We land on the concrete, hard. Glassware shatters around us, but I can barely hear it over the sound of the helicopter. I ignore the bite of pain as Jack drags me back toward the wall.

Just as a spray of bullets pelts through the wood of the table we'd been sitting at only seconds before.

Chapter Thirty-Two

Jack

Being attacked by a fucking helicopter wasn't exactly on my to-do list today. As I watch the picnic table get blown to smithereens, I wave goodbye to the matinee tickets in my back pocket.

As much as I want to focus on the task at hand, my mind can't get over the absurdity of the situation. A goddamn helicopter is gunning us down in *New York City*. This doesn't happen unless someone has one hell of a lot of cash to bribe the cops to look the other way. And Homeland Security to boot.

Aimee clings to my arm as I shield her from the debris, and I shake the thought from my head. We can figure that out later. Right now, my priority is getting us out of here safely.

I plot a route in my head. The stairs lead directly down the alley below, where we can make our escape. Only the door to that staircase is on the other side of the building. A few hundred yards of open space between us and cover.

The barrage of machine-gun bullets winds down slightly. "Are you hurt?" I whisper to Aimee.

"No," she replies a little weakly, but her face is set and determined.

"We need to get to that door. On my mark, you run there, okay?"

Aimee grabs my arm urgently. "What about you?"

I unsheath my gun and load it up. "I'll provide some cover."

"Jack-"

As she tries to protest, the machine gun stops firing completely, and the unmistakable click of the reload reverberates around us.

"Run. Now!"

Aimee, thankfully, scrambles to her feet and takes off across the rooftop while I turn to face our attackers.

The sound of the helicopter propellers this close is almost deafening, and I have to force myself not to shield my eyes as I take aim at the open side. Three men, all in black, stand around the gun, loading it up expertly.

Bang. The shot misses entirely, but the pilot notices me and tries to move them away from my line of fire. I aim at his window.

Bang. The bullet barely dents the glass. Fuck. I return my attack on the men I can actually hit.

Bang. This time, I hit one of them in the arm, and he staggers back.

I glance over my shoulder. Aimee is already by the door. I begin my own retreat.

Bang. Bang. Neither shot lands its mark, and I watch as one of the men slams the final compartment of the gun closed.

Double fuck.

I turn around and sprint.

The machine gun splutters to life; the chamber rotates slowly at first, then rips around faster and faster. I'm only a few feet away from the door now. I can see Aimee's panicked look as she watches in horror.

A spray of bullets follows my feet, and I leap at the last moment through the door. Aimee slams it shut, and I'm insanely grateful it's made of solid metal when we hear the bullets ricochet off the other side.

"Did you get hit?" Aimee says, a few octaves higher than normal.

I check myself over just to be sure. There have been a few times in my career when the adrenaline has kept the pain away, and I can't afford to be bleeding out right now.

"No."

Aimee punches me in the arm. "Don't you dare do that to me again!"

I shoot her a crooked grin that probably levels my nerves more than hers. "We're not out of this yet. Come on."

I take her hand, and we begin our descent. The stairway is dimly lit and square, making each corner we take more nerve-wracking than the last. We must be halfway down when we hear the gunfire.

We duck instantly. I gesture to Aimee to stay put as I quietly reload. Before she can stop me, I lurch forward and out of cover.

Two men are coming up the stairs, a floor below us. Both are dressed head to toe in non-descript black, the same as the men on the roof.

Bang. The first goes down. The second sees me and starts firing off, but I duck easily and start descending the stairs in a crouch. When I turn the next corner, the second man is right in front of me, still shooting at where I'd been a moment earlier.

Bang. The second man goes down.

Just as I feel the barrel of a gun pressing into the back of my neck.

Bang!

I flinch, but the pain doesn't come. Slowly, I turn around to find a third man slumping to my feet. A few stairs up, Aimee holds a smoking gun. Her face is completely expressionless.

She shakes herself off and begins moving again. "You need to watch your back, Duffy."

"Where the hell did you get that?" I say, still in shock.

"Thigh holster," she says, running past me down the stairs.

I gape after her. "You brought a gun to our date?"

"I didn't know how well it was going to go!" she shouts back up, and I have to jog to keep up.

"You were going to shoot me?"

She scoffs as we round the final corner. "You brought your gun too!"

"People like trying to kill me."

"Me too, apparently!"

We come to a stop when we reach the bottom floor. The door to the alley is closed in front of us.

I gesture toward it. "I'll go first. There's a third exit out the alley if they have both ends cut off."

She nods and expertly counts her bullets, so I do the same. Seven left. Better make them count.

"On my signal," I continue. "You run to the other side and take cover. Got it?"

Her gun makes a satisfying *snap* noise as she reloads it. "Got it."

Fuck, if that doesn't turn me on.

I reach forward and grab her neck, guiding her mouth up to mine. She responds eagerly for a moment before biting down hard on my freshly healed lip..

"Focus, Duffy," she says, albeit a little breathlessly.

With a grunt, I pull myself away from her to lean against the door. It's quiet on the other side, but that means very little. I gesture for Aimee to stand to the side before I wrench the door open.

Nothing. I step out tentatively, gun out and darting my aim between both entrances. It's clear.

"Okay, you can-"

Bang. Bang. Bang.

I drop to the floor, narrowly avoiding being hit by a cascade of bullets from above.

"Fuck!" I yell.

But suddenly, Aimee is there, standing over me and aiming high.

Bang. A guy falls out of the window one story up. Fuck, that was our third exit.

She runs to the other side of the alley and takes cover as instructed. We glance at each other, and I point toward the far end of the alley. It's 50/50 at this point which side might be surrounded, but at least that exit is closer to our car.

We move in sync, staying low, ducking behind cover, and slowly making our way down. I take a tentative glance behind us.

Four men have entered the alley on the other side. I fire off a warning shot.

They duck out of the way, and I gesture for Aimee to keep running. I follow just behind.

Bang. I hit one of the men square in the head as he moves out from cover.

The other three immediately go on the offensive, and I find myself speeding to catch up with Aimee.

Instead, I almost crash straight into her. We've reached the end of the alley… to find that the entire exit is surrounded. Bastards have been herding us.

I push her to the floor just as a burst of automatic fire flies over our heads. We roll in separate directions, Aimee squeezing herself into a doorway, whereas I manage to block line of sight with an industrial-sized garbage can.

I take the opportunity to grab my phone and key in an emergency SOS. If we're lucky, there will be a Dead Eye patrol running nearby. But I'm not holding my breath. There are still the three men who were herding us down the alley behind, and they're getting closer every second.

Bang. My shot goes wide.

Aimee notices what I'm doing and begins firing on the men behind us as well.

Ignoring the barrage of automatic fire, I take down one, then another. Aimee takes down the third just as my gun clicks empty. Shit.

The downed men are too far away for us to grab their guns.

Aimee looks over at me with wide eyes. The danger behind us might be dealt with, but she must be low on bullets, too, and we've not even started picking off the men in front. She nods toward better cover just in front of her, big enough for us both to hunker down.

It's better than nothing. Aimee stands up quickly, her aim deadly as she strides forward, and I take the cover to run toward the spot.

Men crumple with every step—dead, wounded, I don't care as long as they're not an immediate threat.

Bang.

"Fuck!"

Only a meter in front of me, I watch helplessly as Aimee slumps to the ground.

Chapter Thirty-Three

Jack

The roar that erupts from my lips doesn't sound human.

I don't give anyone time to react. I reach for her and drag her behind cover in half a second.

"Aimee!"

She blinks up at me, clutching her arm to her chest.

"They shot me," she whispers, her face pale as she looks down at herself.

"It's going to be okay." I'm babbling now, touching her face, her beautiful auburn hair. "You're going to be okay."

She groans as she sits herself up, and for the first time, I see the blood oozing out her arm. "I need a tourniquet," she says, wincing.

I immediately tear off a strip of my shirt, wrapping it around the top of her bicep as tightly as I can. When I'm satisfied, I remove what's left of my shirt and press it against the bleeding gash.

"Hold that there, all right?" I say gently, leaning in to kiss her forehead.

When I pull away, she's rolling her eyes. "I'm not dying on you."

"How many bullets do you have left?" I say, distracting myself from the very idea. That was too close.

"Three," she hisses on an out-breath.

I grab her gun from the floor and test the weight in my hand, "You keep talking to me, okay?"

"You're being dramatic."

"Aimee."

"Fine!"

I glance around our cover and aim at one of the men holding the automatic.

Bang. He goes down. But the responding fire is aggressive, and I turn back to Aimee to cover her body with mine.

There must be at least ten more men out there, and we only have two bullets left.

"We need to find more ammo," Aimee says, panic starting to leak into her tone.

"We're pinned down," I say evenly. "I might be able to run back down, but there's not enough consistent cover."

Aimee shakes her head. "You'll be full of holes in seconds."

She's not wrong.

I pull my phone out desperately. No one has responded to my SOS.

No one is coming to save us.

"Aimee…" I begin to say.

"Don't," she hisses. "This is not how we die."

I kiss her hard as another barrage of bullets barely skims over us. If we're going to die, this is how I'm leaving this godforsaken world. Her tears merge with the dirt on our faces, but I don't care. All I need is her.

"Aimee, I do-"

A motorbike screeches down the alleyway behind us, revving its engine as it pulls back onto one wheel. Charging head first at our attackers.

Three more bikes appear behind it and follow suit, and we hear the yells of the men in black as several more arrive behind them. The spatter of gunfire is quickly redirected, but when I finally glance around our cover, the bikes are quite literally running rings around them.

In less than a minute, the remaining men in black are either retreating or on the ground. The biker gang whoops and cheers at their success.

I pick myself up just as one of the bikers approaches. A giant of a man made entirely of muscle and leather, with a sly grin I haven't seen in years.

"You're not too good in an alleyway, are you, Batman?" he booms by way of greeting.

"Brute," I say after the shock wears off. "The hell are you doing here?"

"Saving your ass, apparently," the leader of the Old Dogs replies easily, giving us a once-over. "Although, to be fair, we've been tracking these so-called 'black coats' for a few days."

I glance over at the carnage left behind. "They had a fucking helicopter. Who are these guys?"

Brute shrugs. "We're not sure. Don't seem to be hailing from any particular family. Italians are just as stumped."

There's a rustle next to me, and I turn to help Aimee up.

"I'm fine; I can stand," she says testily as she wobbles to her feet. But when I silently offer her my arm, she takes it.

Brute watches her. "And you must be the infamous Roisin Maguire. Jacky-boy clearly needs to keep a better eye on you, eh?"

Aimee bristles a little. "I can take care of myself."

"All the more reason," Brute says with a mischievous grin.

I don't like that look. "Why would they attack *us*?"

"I don't know; got any enemies?"

Aimee and I exchange a glance. Too many. Could this be Connor's handiwork? Padraic's? There could be any number of people in the mob who'd rather we weren't around.

"People have been hearing rumors about a Maguire/Duffy alliance," Brute says slowly after thinking about it a moment.

"What?" I say, suddenly confused.

Brute's eyes flicker between us both, "Well, you are getting married."

"The alliance was between my brother and the Novas," Aimee says. "A Maguire/Duffy alliance was never on the table."

The realization hits me like a ton of bricks. "But that's not what it looks like, does it?"

Roisin Maguire was supposed to marry Arnie Knight, but instead, she's apparently marrying me. Quite happily, it seems. It's not exactly a stretch to assume the proposal was orchestrated by Connor as well.

"You seriously didn't consider that?" Brute says, somewhat surprised by our expressions. "The Irish mob has been divided for centuries, only ever as strong as its biggest faction. If they ever made peace among themselves…"

"We'd pose a threat to the other families," I finish for him.

Aimee frowns. "But that's assuming Padraic would even name you heir."

"Well, you got my vote, son." Brute says, stretching out his arms and glancing back at his men. "I reckon it would be useful to have the leader of the reformed Irish mob owe me a favor."

I give him an incredulous look. "Do you know?"

"You and your bride-to-be aren't dead, are you?"

"Thank you for your help," Aimee chimes in quickly. "We're not trying to set up some sort of hearts-and-rainbows unity bullshit, but Jack would be more than happy to owe you a favor, right?" She gives me a pointed look

"Right," I say through my teeth.

Satisfied, Aimee turns back to Brute. "And for what it's worth, I'm also in your debt."

"Thank you, Miss Maguire,." Brute bows his head. "But your beauty is all the payment I need."

"Watch it," I growl.

Brute lets out a booming laugh and slaps me on the back. "You Irish are so easy to wind up." He takes a couple steps backward toward his men.

"We best get this mess under control before the cops start sniffing about. It's been a pleasure, Jack, Miss Maguire. I hope we meet again."

With that, he offers us a dramatic bow and takes his leave.

Aimee smirks at me. "He seems nice."

"You need to go to a hospital," I counter, ignoring her attempt to goad me into a fit of jealousy.

As I walk us back to the car, she leans heavily into my side. "It's a gunshot. There will be too many questions."

"We have a couple guys I could take you to... At the veterinary clinic?"

But Aimee is already shaking her head. "Going to need antibiotics. Maybe..."

"What?"

She looks at me nervously. "Could you take me to Lenox Hill?"

***

We pull into the car park of the ER twenty minutes later. Aimee looks paler than before, her head bobbing up and down every time we hit a bump.

"Stay with me," I say for what feels like the thousandth time as I cut the engine.

Aimee looks over to me. "You're not wearing a shirt."

"That's not exactly the problem right now, is it? Where are we going?"

She points in the direction of the staff entrance. "Go in there and ask for Aisha in Anesthesiology; tell her you have someone in the car. Give her this number..." I listen intently as Aimee reels off what sounds like a pager number.

"I'm not leaving you here," I reply stubbornly.

"If you carry me in, it will cause a scene," she points out. "Please, Jack. Just trust me on this."

I look her over once more. "Fine. I'll be two minutes."

With a final kiss on her cheek, I get out of the car and march straight over to the staff entrance.

The whole place makes me feel uncomfortable and out of place. My shirtless state doesn't help, but I don't get more than a few puzzled glances as I stride up to the only desk I can find.

"Excuse me, sir," the woman behind it says as she looks up at me. "This is a staff entrance; kindly enter the building elsewhere."

"I'm looking for Aisha? She's in Anesthesiology?"

She purses her lips, and her gaze lingers on my chest. "You a stripper-gram or something?"

I grit my teeth and force a smile. "Sure."

The woman barks a laugh and hits something into her pager. "Dr. Lous is going to lose her shit over this."

A minute later, I'm spared the humiliation of being ogled by every woman the receptionist calls over by the appearance of a young nurse. She approaches me cautiously, "Who hired you?"

"Aisha?" I say and quickly recite the pager number Aimee gave me.

The nurse looks taken aback, "Yes, that's me… How did you–"

"Aimee Maguire sent me. She's been hurt."

"What?"

I shush her. "You need to help get her in here."

I see the moment the woman goes into nurse mode when she grabs my arm forcefully. "Where is she?"

"Outside, in the car."

"How much blood has she lost?"

"Too much."

Aisha turns from me and snaps her fingers at a passing hospital porter dragging along an empty gurney. "I'll take that."

Together, we push it back out through the entrance toward the car.

"You're not the one who was stalking her, are you?" Aisha asks as we get closer.

"No, I'm her—I'm helping her," I land on just as we reach the car. I step forward and yank the door open.

But Aisha is already there.

"Aimee? Can you hear me? Do you know this man?" She looks up at me emotionlessly. "I've got 911 a button away."

I'm about to protest when Aimee's voice calls out, "Jesus, Aisha, are you really going to call the cops on my fiancé?"

Aisha visibly recoils in shock. "He said he was a stripper-gram!"

"Aimee, we have a gurney. Can you stand?" I say, trying to restore some urgency to the situation.

She shuffles around in her seat but hesitates when she tries to stand up. I swoop in instantly, cradling her against my chest before lying her down on the gurney.

Aisha is looking at me with narrowed eyes. "You can't come in without a shirt. Here." She passes me her jacket, and I throw it over my shoulders. It doesn't close over my chest, but at least I'm slightly less exposed.

"I'm sorry, Aimee," Aisha says, turning to her colleague. "You're going under the blanket. Lous filed a missing persons report on you, and I'm not filling out that paperwork."

With Aimee's face concealed, the three of us make our way back through the hospital. Heads down and walking with an urgency that might help deter questions, we finally make it to a quiet examination room.

I close the door behind us as Aisha immediately gets to work, attaching Aimee to a drip and reapplying the tourniquet.

"How long since she was hit?" she says.

"Maybe half an hour?"

Aisha grimaces and slowly removes my bloody shirt from the wound.

Aimee looks down at it, too. "Looks like a graze."

"There's no exit wound," Aisha replies, shaking her head. "And there's shrapnel."

"I would have felt it if the bullet was still in there," Aimee counters, albeit wearily.

I look between them both. "What does that mean?"

"It means she should be in surgery," Aisha says matter-of-factly.

"It's *fine*," Aimee replies more forcefully. "I just need it sewn up."

Aisha throws her hands up in exasperation. "How are you going to do that by yourself?"

"What the *hell* is going on in here?"

The three of us freeze as we turn to see the door is now wide open. In it is one of the most terrifying women I've ever seen.

Chapter Thirty-Four

Aimee

Dr. Lous stares at us down like we're petulant children.

"Well? Who's going to tell me?"

Aisha opens her mouth and closes it again. Jack looks torn between jumping to our defense and making a run for it.

Dr. Lous slams the door behind her. "Dr. Maguire, where the hell have you been?"

"It's a long story," I say, trying not to sound like I'm in too much pain. The bleeding has stopped, but with the adrenaline out of my system, it stings like a bitch.

"Your sister phones me every day, your landlord is missing rent, and your brother showed up last week demanding your paperwork."

"What?" I say in alarm.

Jack seems to make up his mind and blocks my line of sight to my superior. "Doctor, I appreciate your concern, but we're dealing with a time-sensitive matter here."

Dr. Lous looks him up and down, "Who are you supposed to be? Dr. McDreamy?"

"Dr. Lous," Aisha cuts in. "She's been shot. Can you come look at this wound and tell me if the bullet is still in there?"

Despite the sour expression on her face, Lous walks toward my arm and examines it carefully. "It's just a graze, but it's messy. Aisha, hook her up with some local anesthetic and send a prescription for antibiotics down to the pharmacy."

"McDreamy." Lous looks up at Jack and gestures to the side. "Bring that station over here."

I watch as Lous prods around my skin and wipes away some of the dirt. "You better have a damn good explanation for this."

"My brother," I say quickly. "What did he want?"

"Did he do this to you?" Lous asks.

"No! It was… well…"

Jack pulls up a chair and sits next to me. "There are certain things that I think Aimee wouldn't want you to feel incriminated by," he says, trying to gauge Dr. Lous' reaction. "What's your stance on doctor-patient confidentiality?"

Dr. Lous stares at Jack, and her lips form a thin line. "I need to know if my employee is in danger."

"Probably," I admit. "But not from my brother. Or him." I nod toward Jack with a smile. "Dr. Lous, this is my fiance."

"Mazel Tov," she replies dryly, just as Aisha returns.

Jack reaches for my hand and squeezes it gently as the physicians flutter around my wound, poking and prodding it until we finally hear the *ting* of shrapnel landing in the metal dish.

"Aisha, please return to work and make sure people know I'm tied up right now," Dr. Lous says once she puts down her tongs and begins work on the stitches.

Jack, however, stands up and blocks her way. Aisha looks up at him, challenge written all over her face.

"No one can know we're here," Jack says to her sternly.

Aisha narrows her eyes but glances at me for confirmation.

"It's safer for everyone," I answer her quietly. "I'm sorry for dragging you into this."

"If people find out, it won't be because of me," Aisha replies, raising an eyebrow at Jack, who lets her pass without another word.

Dr. Lous watches her leave before sighing loudly. "I suppose you want my silence as well?"

"Yes. I'm sorry I can't tell you everything, but it's better for everyone if you pretend you don't know anything," I say as earnestly as I can.

The attending physician chuckles to herself. "Your brother offered me half a million for any information I had on you. I could retire on that kind of money."

"You didn't, did you?" I say, my heart beating at record-breaking speeds.

"Of course not; he was being too pushy about it," Dr. Lous said. "Besides, I didn't *know* anything, did I? You disappeared. Your sister thinks you're back in LA right now."

The wave of guilt washes through me like a tidal wave. "She what?"

"She said you stopped answering her calls weeks ago. Shethought something bad might have happened, and she asked me to file a missing persons report."

Jack returns to my side and touches my arm gently, a reminder that he's here with me. I shoot him a grateful look.

"So why does she think I'm in LA?"

"Your brother's friend said he'd heard a rumor you'd been scared off. So I mentioned it to her - we thought it might have something to do with that stalker you had," Dr. Lous explains as she pulls through the last stitch.

"So Roisin thinks I abandoned her?" I whisper, more to myself than the others.

I feel like an idiot. I never answered Roisin's calls because I didn't trust myself to be able to lie to her. I didn't want her to worry. Now she likely hates me for leaving without saying goodbye.

Jack, however, ducks down to press his lips against my good arm. "She doesn't hate you," he says as if reading my thoughts.

"How am I going to explain any of this to her?" I say a little hysterically.

"We'll figure it out, okay?" Jack says firmly. "One thing at a time."

One thing at a time. Like getting to safety, figuring out why those "black coats" were after us, surviving the next fight, and convincing Padraic to leave us alone. Hell, why not throw in figuring out how my brother knew I was even here?

Dr. Lous takes off her gloves and leans back, "The antibiotics I'm going to give you will only last a few days. You need more; you're going to have to come back."

"Thank you," I reply. At least "dying from a bullet wound" can be struck off my to-do list.

Jack glances over to the doctor. "Would you prefer cash or credit?"

Dr. Lous narrows her eyes at him, "How much are you offering?"

"Connor said he'd pay you half a million?" He looks down at me and offers me a gentle smile. "I'll double it."

"Jack!" I say in shock.

"You can retire twice over and never look back. But we were never here; you don't know where Aimee Maguire is, who she's with, or that she was shot. When her sister calls you again, you tell her that the police suspect that she's still in New York, but you're too busy to keep looking into it."

Dr. Lous purses her lips and stands up, "I'm not leaving New York, and my wife would never believe I came by that kind of money legally. You'll pay for the care and the resources I just used so we can keep our books balanced."

Jack nods, "And what about what you saw here today?"

Dr. Lous shrugs and heads toward the door. "Just another day in the office."

I watch her leave in pure amazement, not knowing if it's her loyalty or her tenacity that impresses me more.

"Oh, and Dr. Maguire?" she says, looking back over her shoulder. "You're fired."

I deflate a little as the door slams behind her. Well, it's not like I didn't expect this to happen, but it still stings that the only normal part of my life is now gone.

"Hey," Jack says quietly, returning to my side. "We can get you another job."

I shake my head, "It's okay, really. It's not like I'm able to help anyone right now."

"I mean it. I know how important this is for you."

"Let's just get out of here."

Jack wordlessly helps me up and out of the gurney. My legs shake a little to begin with, but I can stand up on my own now the pain has subsided. I know the anesthetic will wear off soon, but right now, the numbness is blissful.

"Jack?" I say as we approach the doors. "Can I ask a favor?"

"Anything, *Chroí.*"

"Can we get milkshakes on our way home?"

***

An hour later, we pull into Jack's garage. We never discussed going back to his penthouse instead of the Duffy mansion, but I get the feeling that neither of us has the energy to deal with Padraic today.

Despite the milkshakes, exhaustion hits me like a bus the minute the engine is cut, and I realize I'm going to have to walk again.

"Let's go to bed," Jack says with a sigh. I see the tiredness setting on his own shoulders, but he rallies himself to get out of the car and come to open the door for me.

He takes one look at me and begins to slide his arms under my legs.

"What are you doing?" I say in alarm.

He ignores me, moving my arms to hold onto his neck, and lifts me out of my seat. Pressed against his firm chest, I allow myself a moment to relax in his arms before beginning my protests again. On principle.

But Jack simply kicks the car door closed and carries me to the elevator. There's clearly no fighting him on this, so I let out a sigh and close my eyes for just a minute.

When I open them again, Jack is sliding into bed next to me. The curtains closed, the lights were off, and his silk sheets were wrapped around me.

"Mmm?" Great job, Aimee; very coherent.

Jack's arms wrap around me gently, avoiding my arm, which now rests to one side.

"You fell asleep," Jack clarifies. I can't quite make him out in the darkness, but I can feel his steady breaths tickling my cheek and his chest rising and falling against my side.

I snuggle in closer. "I figured."

"You should sleep more; it's been a long day."

Dear God, do I want to. But the events of the day begin playing through my mind. "What the hell happened today?"

Jack sighs, "I don't know. These 'black coats' are clearly a well-armed and well-funded militia, but they could be anyone."

"Or hired by anyone," I point out.

He doesn't disagree. "Padraic might know," Jack says after a moment. "But is it worth asking if he might be the person who sent them?"

"Surely, if he wanted us dead, he would have done it already?" I counter although I can't deny the thought has crossed my mind. "He's had every opportunity to do so under his own roof, not to mention in the ring."

"He doesn't like wasting money," Jack concedes. "Besides, I need to talk to him about this so-called 'alliance' between our families. Whoever is spreading this rumor is no friend of ours. If the cartel or the Italians feel threatened, we could have a war on our hands."

I shudder at the thought, then another hits me harder. "Do you think... Connor might have hired the 'black coats'?"

Jack's hand cups my face, and he strokes my cheek with his thumb. "And risk losing you?"

"It's been five years." I whisper my fears aloud. "A lot can change."

"*Chroí*, he was at the hospital looking for you," Jack reminds me, reassurance lacing his tone. "I have little regard for your brother, but he doesn't strike me as the kind of man who would risk his sister's life just to get to me."

The memory of Connor's face flashes to the forefront of my mind. He was always there for us, a step behind me and Roisin whenever we went to the park or the store. Always watching, making sure we didn't get into any trouble.

"He always wanted to keep us safe," I admit quietly.

"The question is," Jack says, dropping his hand, "how did he know you were at the hospital?"

I frown at this. "I suppose the Dead Eyes found me pretty quickly."

"By accident. If you hadn't treated that guy, we'd never have thought to look for you," Jack points out.

"But Connor thinks Roisin is in New York, right? Maybe he figured out I couldn't be far behind."

Jack thinks on this for a moment, then sighs. Moving so that he can pull me in closer, he rests his forehead against mine.

"Let's not think about it now," he says. "Get some rest."

I instantly relax into him. His very scent settles my nerves, and soon the buzz of unanswered questions that swarm my brain fades into the background.

"Thank you," I whisper.

"For what?"

There are a thousand answers to that question, I realize. Jack has saved me so many times in more ways than one.

"For getting me out of there today," I land on.

Jack exhales through his nose, "You did most of the work."

"I froze up there," I admit, my body shaking at the memory. "You knew what to do and had a plan instantly—if you hadn't been there—"

"Shh…" Jack whispers, kissing my nose, my cheeks. "We got out of there. It's over now."

He comforts me until the shaking stops, and a new fear enters my head. "I killed those men."

Jack squeezes me impossibly tighter. "And you saved my life."

"They would have had families, people who loved them—"

"Their fate was sealed the moment they tried to kill you," Jack breathes into my ear. "Trust me, the world needs you more than it needs any of them."

I gulp back tears. "Does it get any easier?"

"Yes and no," Jack says after a moment. "But don't you dare, for even a moment, tell yourself that your life isn't worth it."

"But—"

"No," he says firmly, pulling away from me.

Now that my eyes have adjusted in the darkness, I can make out the hard line of his jaw, the firmness of his expression.

"I thought I lost you today," he confesses in a tone so broken I reach out to comfort him. He leans his head into my hand. "And the world became so much darker."

"Jack…"

He kisses my palm and pulls away. "I never want to lose you. I don't care who comes for us next; you are more important than any of them."

My heart breaks at his words, the pain in them.

New words bubble up in my throat, threatening to spill out into the silent privacy of our little darkness. They glow brightly in my mind, so obvious now, and I realize they've always been there. Just waiting to be acknowledged.

I let out a shaking breath.

I can't. Not now.

Chapter Thirty-Five

Jack

I finally found Padraic at the shipping yard warehouse.

As I approach the looming doors, both Morris and Buzz are lingering outside—it's not the kind of place I tend to hang around for that reason alone. But I know there are more sinister things lurking behind those walls that put these two sociopaths to shame.

"Well, if it isn't 'Rocky,'" Buzz says in greeting.

"You lost me a lot of money, Duffy," Morris goads as I get closer.

I ignore them and nod toward the door. "You boys get bored already?"

"The boss is having a bit of one-on-one time," Buzz said.

"Who?" I ask.

"Cartel, I think," Buzz replies with a shrug. "Hard to tell."

"Jesus," I say. If they're fucked up that badly, it's going to be a gruesome conversation.

Buzz nods at me, "You going in?"

"Got a report," I say as I pass them, beelining for the doors. Hopefully, I can avoid any more conversations.

Unfortunately, Morris seems to have other ideas. He flings an arm carelessly around my shoulder, and I flinch.

"Hey, listen, I just wanted you to know if you were to die in the next round," Morris sneers in my ear. "I'd personally take very good care of your missus."

"You even look at her again," I say calmly, "you're a dead man. Are we clear?"

Morris laughs, "Aye, that's fair. But if you die, who exactly is going to stop me?"

I tackle him to the ground before he can let out another wheeze of laughter. With my knee against his neck and his arms restrained by my own, he begins choking immediately.

"What did you say?" I hiss at him.

Behind me, I'm vaguely aware that Buzz is approaching. "Jack, leave it!"

"What did you say about my wife?"

Morris groans, and I ease up slightly on his neck. "She's not your wife yet," he wheezes.

I press back down harder. Morris begins to choke even louder.

"Jack!" Buzz yells as he strides forward to try and push me off.

But I stay put. "You're a dead man, Morris."

He squirms beneath my grasp, and I falter slightly. Long enough for Buzz to get a good shove in. My arms fly out to balance myself, but Buzz catches them, dragging me away from the Dead Eye grunt.

"You're fucking dead, you hear me?!" I shout at him, despite the fact Buzz has pulled us apart.

"Jesus, Jack." Buzz lets me go with a shove. "You're insane, you know that?"

Trying to picture Aimee's face, the way she looked at our picnic, in my bedsheets, I swallow the rage. It comes out in a tight grunt.

"Stay the hell away from me." I point at Morris over Buzz's shoulder. "Both of you."

I storm away and push open the warehouse doors, not wholly proud of my actions but unable to regret them.

The "holding room" hasn't changed in the decade I've visited it. The smell of bleach burns the inside of your nose, and the scratches that stretch the length and breadth of the walls look like scars. When I was younger, Padraic used to make me clean out the drains if I misbehaved. The things I'd find down there used to give me nightmares. But it built up my resilience.

This means when I walk into the scene before me, I don't vomit instantly.

Padraic has hung his jacket on the back of a chair. His white shirt is still immaculate but loose around the neck and rolled up to his elbows, exposing the tattoos that snake around his arms. As I approach, he doesn't look up from his task at hand—wiping down a ruthless-looking blade with a blood-stained rag.

"My bastard graces me with his presence."

"Padraic," I say calmly in greeting.

"I'm in the middle of something."

I glance over to the other occupied chair and swallow down the bile that rises in my throat. "Dead men don't talk."

"Aye, but their widows do," Padraic tosses me something.

I catch it easily and open my palm. It's battered and splattered with blood, but there's no doubt what it is.

"Consider it a wedding gift," Padraic says with a dry smile. "If you'd like, I'll find you a matching set."

The gold band in my hand suddenly feels too heavy, and I place it on the side. Aimee on the rooftop, Aimee in the infinity pool.

I clear my throat, "I have a report."

"You weren't assigned anything to report on," Padraic informs me as if that's the end of the conversation.

But I stand my ground. "Have you heard anything about a bunch of guys in black coats?"?"

"Why are you hiring them?" Padraic scoffs.

"Who do they work for?"

Padraic shrugs, throwing his rag down and turning his attention to the blade itself. "They're an imported mercenary group. I can't remember who brought them over, but I imagine they're dead now. The 'black coats' are only happy as long as you pay them and they aren't above screwing you over for the next highest bidder."

"They tried to kill me."

Padraic snorts. "Who would anyone pay that kind of money to have you killed?"

"I guess someone who was bored of waiting for me to die in the ring," I counter bitterly.

It's the wrong thing to say. Padraic puts down his knife to look at me properly. "You die in that ring, you disgrace this family. Haven't you done enough damage?"

I feel my jaw tense. "Father." I watch as Padraic flinches at the name. "They came for us both, me and Roisin. They knew where we were and that we'd be alone."

"The Maguires have a funny way of settling their scores," Padraic says dismissively.

"You said it yourself, the 'black coats' only answer to the highest bidder," I point out. "When was the last time the Maguires had that kind of money? Besides, Roisin says her brother wouldn't do something like that."

"Her brother murdered yours, or did you forget that along with your pride when you started fucking that whore?"

"Don't. Call her that."

Padraic brushes me off with a wave of his hand. "I know who Connor Maguire is. He's a power-hungry little shit who will do anything to make his mark. Your *fiancee* hasn't seen him in years."

"Brute said that rumors have been circulating about a Maguire/Duffy alliance," I say as evenly as I can. This is why I'm here, to do my duty to my family, then I can leave. "If people see our marriage as a threat, we could have a war on our hands."

"What's that pissant biker got to do with anything?"

"*Brute* and his men helped us escape the 'black cloaks.'"

"You needed help from a biker gang?" Padraic's face twists in distaste.

I blink. *That's* what he cares about? "They came at us with a helicopter!"

"I don't care if the 'black coats' came at you in a fucking tank, Jack. You deal with it, and you don't run around owing favors to that mindless swarm of Italian leftovers."

"They saved our lives."

"That was your mistake." Padraic raises his voice. "You keep disappearing from the mansion without any kind of backup; of course, you're going to get attacked."

"Because I don't trust any of your men to have my back!" I argue back.

"Not my problem."

I throw my hands up in exasperation. "Then what the hell am I supposed to do?"

"Don't you dare ask me that question, boy," Padraic snarls. "You got yourself into this mess. You can get yourself out."

It's like I'm a petulant teenager, and he's scolding me for being late to Mass.

"I was only trying to warn you to do my duty to this family," I try again. "The annuals are almost over, you can't bench me forever, and our family could be on the brink of war. We need to settle this now. People will die if we remain divided."

"You think you can come in here and *threaten* me?"

My eyebrows shoot up, "I'm not threatening you; I'm just laying out the facts."

"You're not my fucking heir," Padraic says, spitting on the floor for good measure.

Somehow, the words don't sting as much as they used to. "I didn't say I was."

"You're a joke, Jack. No one wants you to lead them because they don't trust you to. If you're not hooking up with Maguire whores, you're rubbing elbows with biker scum."

"Stop calling her that."

"You're weak. Everyone can see it," he lets out a cold bark of a laugh. "They saw it in the ring, and they'll see it again when you face your next opponent. There's nothing left for you here."

I step forward. "Our entire family is at risk because of your ego."

"My family wants nothing to do with you anymore." Padraic steps forward, too, this time brandishing the knife and pointing it directly at my chest. "Even if you win your next match, you'll be disowned. If you lose, well, it'll save me the trouble of announcing it."

I'm suddenly exhausted. I always suspected this might be the end result, but to hear him say it out loud hammers the final nail into my coffin.

I'm alone. Always have been, was always going to be. There was never a future for me in the Dead Eyes. Even if Graham were still alive, Padraic would have found a way to get rid of me. I was never good enough for him or his wife. I'm not good enough for Aimee, either. I'm just a bastard without a claim to anything.

"I am your only son," I say, barely believing the words myself.

"Graham was my only son. And after everything you've done, he would have stood by me on this."

My pity party ends with that one sentence.

"I don't believe that."

"You proposed to the sister of his murderer out of *spite,*" Padraic laughs again. "And you say my family is at risk because of my ego?"

"I love her."

He looks at me, and a cruel grin spreads across his face "And it will be the death of you."

Chapter Thirty-Six

Jack

The only relief I have from Padraic's words echoing through my head is when Aimee wraps her arms around me as soon as I enter the apartment. I inhale her sweet scent greedily, letting it calm my nerves.

"How did it go?" she asks against my chest.

The exhaustion hits me instantly. "Are there tall buildings in LA?"

"That bad?"

I don't even know how to answer that. None of this seems to matter anymore. The only thing I can control is making sure Aimee stays the hell away from all of this. There's no way Padraic won't come for us both if things go south tomorrow at the fight.

As I kiss her forehead, I realize that *this* right here is all I care about.

And I need to protect it at all costs.

I pull away and reach for my phone. "I need to talk to Ray. We don't have much time."

"Time for what?" Aimee says cautiously as she watches me cross the room to the window.

The view from here is beautiful, but there's no telling how quickly Padraic would be able to find us if he wanted to. I've not exactly been careful about coming here, and Kate's name is also on the documentation.

Ideally, we need to start somewhere fresh, where tracking us down just isn't worth the effort.

I hit 'dial' and bring my phone up to my ear.

"Jack?" Aimee says just as Ray's voice booms down the receiver.

"Jack!"

"Secure the line," I say sharply, glancing over at Aimee. Concern is written across her face as she takes a seat on the couch, watching me intently.

Ray doesn't hesitate, and after a moment of tapping, he comes back to the phone. "What's happening?"

"Can I trust you?"

Ray groans. "Did you fall out with Padraic again? You know, in the divorce, I'm picking you, right?"

"Ray," I warn through my teeth.

"Yes, you can trust me," Ray says a little sarcastically, but I can hear the truth in his voice.

Satisfied, I place a hand on the receiver and glance over to my redhead. "Aimee, what's the tallest building in LA?"

She looks even more confused by the question. "The Ritz-Carlton, maybe? There are a few big banks that have–"

That's all I need. I turn back to my phone. "Ray, I want a penthouse at the LA Ritz-Carlton by yesterday."

"Jesus, just say you're a billionaire," Ray mutters but begins tapping away at his computer. "Under what name?"

"Aimee Maguire." I risk a glance at the woman in question.

She mouths, "What is going on?"

I turn away to look out the window again, suddenly aware of the muted scuffling sounds on the other end of the line.

A cool female voice sounds down the line. "I want the room next door."

I freeze. "Am I on fucking speakerphone?"

"Maybe?" Ray replies weakly.

"Goddamn it, Ray."

"You're moving to LA without telling me?"

"Kate, I don't have time for this," I say, pinching the bridge of my nose. Of course, she'd be listening in; I don't think I've had an ounce of privacy from the woman since the first fight.

"I'm coming with you," Kate insists.

I stand my ground. "You're not moving to LA with us."

"We're moving to LA?" Aimee chimes in. Shit.

Kate won't let it go. "You can't just disappear on me like that."

"Why would we move to LA, Jack? What is going–"

"I hear it's not all it's cracked up to be," Ray adds.

"Everybody, just shut up!" I say a little too loudly, causing Aimee to cross her arms in anger. "Ray put a down payment on ONE penthouse at the Ritz-Carlton and move 5 mil into my off-shore account. Kate, I'm sorry, but you're not coming. It would only put a target on your back. Aimee–"

"We're not moving to LA," Aimee says stubbornly.

"*Chroí,*" I beg. Now is not the time for this. We can deal with the practicalities later.

But Aimee isn't having any of it. She stands abruptly, walking over to me. "Roisin is still here. I'm not going anywhere without her."

There's a beat as we stare at each other, a battle of wills.

"I thought *she* was Roisin?" Ray says down the phone, apparently overhearing our entire conversation.

Fuck it. I put them on speakerphone.

"Ray, meet Aimee Maguire. Aimee, this is Ray."

"Hi, Ray," Aimee says without breaking her stare. "I'm not Roisin, and we're not moving to LA."

"I thought you didn't look like your profile picture," Ray chirps, finally putting everything together.

"You were looking at my sister's profile picture?" Aimee frowns and finally breaks eye contact to shoot a glare at my phone.

"Jack was stalking her."

I gape as Aimee's glare turns to me. Traitor.

"Shut it," I say to Ray before gathering my thoughts. If they all insist on getting involved, then fine. I'll lay it out for them. "This is the situation. Padraic is done. I'm either dead or disowned after the last fight, so I need to make preparations for the worst-case scenario."

Aimee's hand reaches up to touch my face, her eyes suddenly wide. "Jack-"

"I'm sorry, *Chroí,*" I say as I plant a kiss on her palm. "I dragged you into this, but I won't be able to protect you here for much longer."

"And you think you can protect her in LA?" Kate chimes in, clearly unconvinced.

"Better than here," I reply honestly. "I can't ask you to come with me, Kate. Ray is risking his life enough as it is."

Ray mutters, "A heads-up about that would have been great."

"There's no way in hell I'm being left here on my own, Jack," Kate counters.

"I understand you're panicked, Jack," Aimee says. "But there has to be another option."

I sigh, "Don't you want a normal life? A Chinese takeout that knows your order by heart?"

She smiles sadly. "Yes, but I can't do any of that without Roisin."

I nod at her. "We'll pick her up on our way out."

"I'll have to call her," Aimee replies, biting her lip nervously.

"Do what you need to do."

She hesitates. "What do I even say? She thinks I've abandoned her here in New York!"

"Does she trust you?" I ask quietly.

Aimee leans into me. "I-I think so?"

"Then trust her to believe you."

Kate's voice suddenly comes down the phone. "I have a safe house in Brooklyn."

I stop short. "Since when?"

"Since Graham," she says as if that's enough of an explanation. "Let's get an apartment in LA as a backup, but after the fight, we move to the safe house. We only call Roisin *if* we need to leave."

"You keep saying 'if' like there's a possibility the world won't go to shit after the match," I groan.

"I think you underestimate how many people would take your side if Padraic were to disown you," Kate explains in a bored tone. This is entirely new information to me.

Ray takes the opportunity to pipe up. "I've got at least three men who will follow me wherever I go."

"And I can double that number," Kate adds.

Aimee stares at me with an unreadable expression. This is a dangerous conversation; Padraic would consider it treason if it ever got out. There is no way I can risk Aimee's safety like that. It's already too dangerous.

"We are not staging a coup," I say firmly.

"Why not?" Aimee whispers.

I look at her in disbelief. Realizing that it's not fear or anger in her eyes. It's *calculation*.

"You said you wanted peace," I whisper back.

"What if we could be the people to usher it in?" Aimee says, her mouth stumbling over her words in her excitement. "I could negotiate meetings with my brother; we could work together."

My jaw practically hits the floor. "This would be your life, Aimee. No more working in the ER. No more anonymity. Every day you'd be risking your life."

"For peace? I'll do it."

I shake my head. No. She's already given up too much for this world. "Forming an alliance between the Duffys and the Maguires will make us even more of a target."

"I said I'll do it," she snaps. The determination in her eyes would be so fucking sexy if she wasn't so terrifying. "We keep Roisin out of this. But I'll message her, prime her to be able to leave at a moment's notice without giving away the details. Ray, spend the 5 mil on local assets."

He hesitates. "Jack?"

"She's going to be my wife; she speaks for me. Do it."

For just an instant, Aimee's smile is dazzling. Then she's all business once more. "We don't want that much money off-shore. We'll need it nearby and ready to liquidate. Kate, how many people did you say you could bring?"

"Six," she says through the speaker.

Aimee nods. "Make that twelve, and I want three drivers waiting for us after the match. We all take separate cars and rendezvous at Jack's apartment before going to the safe house."

"Roger that," Kate chirps.

"How big is it?"

"Spacious."

"Your twelve, Ray's three, and the four of us make 19?" Aimee says.

"Easy," Kate replies with a chuckle. "We could double it and still swing a cat."

Aimee turns to me. "Is that enough to move your cars from the basement, Jack?"

I stare at her, completely overwhelmed by her being just so… Aimee. It's breathtaking. "Are you sure about this?" I say quietly so the others can't hear.

"Yes," she hisses back.

"Then that makes 22," I reply louder. "I'll vet the drivers and make sure they're outside to pick us up. And yes, that's enough for the basement. Although I might need to come back for the bikes."

"We're not coming back for the bikes," Aimee and Kate say simultaneously.

I smirk at Aimee, and she offers me a smile that could light up the darkest of rooms. For the first time since I met her, I saw a flicker of hope in her eyes. And I know I will do whatever I can to make sure it doesn't disappear.

"Fine," I say casually. "You have your orders. If anything goes wrong, fall back immediately. Protect the safehouse at all costs—if the location is compromised, we're all fucked."

"Pleasure doing business with you, Jack," Ray replies sarcastically. "As always."

Aimee takes the phone off me. "We'll see you on the other side."

She hangs up and throws the phone to the side, immediately wrapping her arms around me.

I draw her in close, breathing her in. "Are you sure about this?"

"Please stop asking me that. We need to do this; you and I both know that running away is no way to live."

I can't help it; I kiss her square on the mouth.

She gasps a little against my lips before responding enthusiastically. I feel her fingers wrap around my neck, and I hoist her up onto my hips. The pressure of her sitting right *there* has me growling in frustration.

Our kisses suddenly feel desperate, like we can't quite get enough. I lose myself in her embrace, in the sweetness of her tongue as she explores my mouth earnestly.

I tear at her shirt, and a moment later, it's on the floor. The only thing in the world that matters right now is her skin against mine. I wrap my arms around her, pulling her in closer.

"Take your shirt off," Aimee gasps out between furious kisses. It's like she instinctively knows what I need.

I throw her down on the couch and strip down as efficiently as I can, eager to close the distance between us again. She meets me there, wrapping herself around me with the same amount of desperation.

Never would I ever believe that Aimee would embrace me like this? Not just physically, but this life, our *lives* together.

And god fucking damn, is it hot when she takes command like that.

I tug at her skirt and slide it off her body, pressing my thigh into her core.

She groans, and I do my best to swallow every sound.

"You're so wet already," I purr against her, rubbing her up and down.

"I want you to fuck me so hard," she growls back, squirming against my leg.

I don't need telling twice. I pick her up again and bend her over the back of the couch.

Her ass lifts eagerly into the air, and I feast on her cheeks, burying my nose beneath her panties to get at her soaking-wet pussy. Nothing tastes as good as this. Her nectar is the sweetest I have ever tasted. My tongue circles her over and over, lapping up every drop.

"Fuck!"

She whines when I withdraw, removing her panties with my teeth.

"I'm going to fuck you now," I say, surprised by how deep my voice sounds. Every inch of my body is overwhelmed with my desire for the woman in front of me.

My cock is already hard and throbbing in my hand as I guide it into her. Her gorgeous gasp is like a drug, and I slowly push in further and further.

"You're so fucking tight," I groan.

She gasps again, taking my full length. I pause there for a moment, waiting for her to turn around. To let me know she's okay.

When she glances over her shoulder, her eyes are fire.

My fingers tangle in her hair and pull her head back. She submits entirely, stretching up onto her toes to give me better access. Her delicious ass bounces against my thighs with every thrust.

I slap it, earning me a whimper.

"Good girl, you like that?" I praise her, earning me another one.

I slap her again, this time hard enough for the skin to turn a beautiful pink.

This time she groans loudly and arches her back. It drives me deeper within her, and I have to concentrate hard not to come instantly.

Instead, I concern myself with wrapping her auburn hair around one fist so I can push her further over the sofa with my other.

She's so willing to please me, so desperate to obey every touch and command.

I slap her again. This time my handprint lingers there for a moment.

"J-Jack!"

I feel her tighten and contract around me as the orgasm hits. Her cry of pleasure is the most angelic thing I've ever heard, and I measure my breath so I can keep up my rhythm. Guiding her through the shudders of ecstasy as her walls relax around me.

Aimee collapses onto the sofa, unable to hold herself up on her toes a moment longer.

I withdraw, admiring my handiwork on her perfect ass. The possessive male inside me is proud to have made my mark there. My fingers reach for my rock-hard cock as I look at her, completely spent. Completely *mine*.

After a moment, she picks herself up and turns to me. Her eyes zone in on my hand, and she sinks to her knees.

"Aimee..." I grunt as she reaches for me.

"Please," she murmurs against my thigh, kissing up toward my crotch in the most tantalizing way.

I don't need to answer. One looks down at her huge chocolate eyes, and she knows I consent to this.

As if any man in the world would say no to her perfect lips wrapping themselves around his cock.

The noises I make are ungodly. She takes me deeper and deeper, expertly working me at a rhythm we've become so familiar with. I want to do nothing but live in this moment forever.

My fingers curl into her hair and grunt out a warning just as I come undone in her mouth. The orgasm hits me in waves as she swallows everything I give her. Licking so delicately around my most sensitive parts.

I sink to my knees next to her.

When I kiss her, I taste myself. It's a filthy, desperate kiss that has us curling into each other, and I lower us to the floor. The thick carpet cushions my spent body as I hold onto her tightly.

She lies across my chest, and we just breathe together. In and out. The words I want to say fill my mind, almost winding me with the force they appear. It all feels so clear now, why Aimee is so important, why I'm willing to do all this. Love is such a foreign concept to me but for her? I'd do it. I'd do anything for her.

But right now? In the small moment of calm before the inevitable storm, I can't bring myself to say it.

"You're the only thing that matters to me now," I say instead.

She kisses my chest.

"I know," she whispers back.

Chapter Thirty-Seven

Aimee

Jack and I walk into Luckies hand in hand.

The underground boxing ring looks exactly as it did the last two matches—but somehow, the atmosphere feels more electric. Like every person in every seat is anticipating something huge. I suppose it is the final match, so it shouldn't be surprising.

But it could also just be me. Our plan to start a coup feels more real with every step we take, and the buzz of adrenaline feels like it's radiating off my very skin.

The dress isn't helping, either. This time, it's a flowing black silk to match Kate's signature look. The short skirt tickles my thighs with every stride, giving me goosebumps.

We come to a halt by the locker room, and Jack tugs me toward him. Our kiss goes on longer than is probably acceptable in public, and I can feel more than a few pairs of eyes on us.

But I don't care. Not today.

When we finally pull apart, there's no one else in the world apart from us.

"Are you sure?" Jack says quietly.

I look up into his beautiful hazel eyes and know there's only one answer to that question. I knew it the moment I met him, and no matter how many times I tried to deny it, it's still there. I'd give up my entire world for this man.

"Yes," I reply simply with another peck on his cheek. "You better come back to me in one piece."

He smirks. "I'll do my best."

"I mean it."

Jack leans for a final, sinfully soft kiss. "I'll always come back to you."

Without another word, he pulls away and steps through the doors out of sight.

I let out a shaking breath and take a moment to compose myself before facing the music. Whatever happens now is totally out of my control. All I can do is wait and trust that Jack will keep his promise.

I walk up the stairs to the VIP box to find that Kate has already saved me a seat. She offers me a small smile as I take a seat next to her.

"Padraic's been pretty tight-lipped about the next fighter," she says conversationally. "Although I don't know how he's going to top a champion fighter."

I hum in response, digging out my phone from my purse and checking it for the thousandth time. Still nothing.

Scrolling back through my messages with Roisin fills me with shame.

ROISIN: *Are you okay??*

1 missed call from Roisin.

ROISIN: *I haven't heard from you in days???*

3 missed calls from Roisin.

ROISIN: *I'm getting worried, Aimee, don't make me call the cops.*

ROISIN: *I'm serious.*

8 missed calls from Roisin.

ROISIN: *Please pick up.*

12 missed calls from Roisin.

And on and on and on. They stopped only a few days ago, lining up with the timeline Dr. Lous gave us. When she was told I'd gone back to L.A.

My measly response looks pathetic in comparison.

AIMEE: *I'm sorry, don't worry about me. Still in N.Y., but we may need to leave soon. Stay safe. I love you. Sorry.*

The only glimmer of hope I have is the fact there's a little blue tick next to the message. She's seen it, at least, even if she hasn't forgiven me for not replying. At least she knows I haven't left the state.

Still, I'd feel better if I could hear her voice. If I could know she was okay… Jack told me about his contact at Julliard, and I have enough faith in him to know that he picks his friends wisely.

But I'm not only worried about the mob getting their hands on her. She'd been partying a lot in the weeks leading up to all this. The last time I saw her, she was suffering from a hangover.

Our agreement was always ironclad—if she ever needed me to pick her up, I'd be there in a heartbeat. Want if one of her calls was her asking for help? What if she felt unsafe and I wasn't there to protect her?

Kate's hand brushes against mine gently. "Hey."

I look up at her and see her looking at me intently.

"One thing at a time, yeah?" she says with a nudge to my shoulder. "She's safe."

"Being safe is different from being *well*," I mutter, locking my phone again. My hand pulls through my hair and tugs at the roots. Of course, Kate's right. There's nothing we can do right now, and I have Jack's word that as soon as it's safe to do so, we'll be checking in on Roisin. Still, the nagging, sisterly part of my brain won't stop filling me with dread.

Which is doing nothing to help the dread I already feel for the more pressing matters.

"I wouldn't put it past Padraic to choose an actual bulldozer at this point," I say through gritted teeth.

Kate lets out a humorless snort as we glance over to the man in question.

Padraic is keeping court with multiple older members of the Dead Eyes as well as a few faces I don't recognize. Each of them is wearing tailored suits and watches that catch what little light there is in the room every time they throw their hands up in heated discussion.

"The Italians don't usually come here," Kate comments under her breath. "Padraic must be expecting a show."

I try not to gulp audibly. "Jack is going to be okay, right?"

"Always is," she says quickly, although her eyes never leave the Italians.

What the hell is Padraic up to?

I try to distract myself by surveying the audience, but they seem even more energized than before. Constantly moving around, laughing, chatting animatedly. I wonder if they notice us up here, still as statues.

But our silence is interrupted by Ray, climbing the stairs toward us two at a time.

Kates's face darkens as she leans over the barrier to greet him. "Where the hell have you been?"

Ray tries to catch his breath, but Kate cuts him off before he can begin his explanation.

"If you say the bookies, I swear to God, Ray."

"Not the bookies," Ray pants. "I found out who Jack's fighting."

I'm suddenly alert and sitting on the edge of my chair. "Who."

Ray looks at me with a frantic gleam in his eyes before glancing to Kate for confirmation.

"Spit it out!" she says, leaning to shake his shoulder a bit.

Ray opens his mouth, then closes it again before finally composing himself enough to look at me again.

Just as he says the name, the sound is lost in the announcement that Jack is entering the ring. The sudden eruption of the audience drowns out anything else.

But my attention is on Ray.

No.

He couldn't have said what I thought he said. My lip reading isn't what it once was.

It couldn't be.

Kate sits back in her chair and grabs my hand tightly. The only time I've ever seen her lost for words.

"Jack Duffy, ladies and gentlemen!" The commentator's voice booms down the speakers as Jack does a lap of the ring.

I watch in horror as he looks up at the VIP box to find us. He must see the concern on our faces because a frown furrows on his brow before he retreats back to his corner. His coach mutters final advice as Jack keeps glancing back over to us as if trying to decipher our thoughts.

"Kate," I whisper—how she hears me in the crowd, I'll never know.

"It's going to be okay," she says in my ear.

I shake my head, "It can't be true."

"It's going to be okay."

In front of us, Padraic tears himself away from his mafia companions to offer me the most horrifying grin I've ever seen.

He did this.

"Aaaaannnddd in the other corner…." The commentator roars as a figure emerges from the other locker room, a towel hanging from his head.

With every step he takes toward the ring, the more I have to suppress the urge to vomit. Kate's hand tightens around mine as he ducks under the rope and removes the towel.

Standing a half foot taller than Jack and at least a few inches wider than I last saw him. Arms dangerously huge and without an inch of fat. A fuzz of beard is trimmed to his tight jaw. Chocolate eyes laser focused on Jack.

His shoulder-length red hair is tied up in a messy knot.

The commentator doesn't seem to believe it either.

"… Connor Maguire?"

Chapter Thirty-Eight

Jack

It's like tunnel vision.

One minute the crowds are cheering my name; the next, there's only silence.

And Connor fucking Maguire.

I've not seen him since that night in the alleyway. But he's still wearing that crooked little grin on his face.

There is nothing that could cool the fires that rage inside me. Anger courses through my very veins as I watch him enter the ring. The man I swore I would kill for ending my brother's life.

"You better fucking kill them for this."

This is the man that murdered Graham. This is the man responsible for all the torment that followed. Every shitty thing that's happened since that night is *his* fault. I was disowned because of *him*. Aimee's life now hangs in the balance because of *him*.

"Surprised to see me, bastard?" Connor leers as he stretches out his tree-like arms.

In the silence of rage, clarity hits me like a freight train.

Because how could Connor be here? In a Duffy establishment? *My* establishment? Not only that but in the ring as a competitor?

It doesn't make sense until it does. Memories storm through my mind so quickly it's almost painful.

"It's not my alliance with Connor you should be worried about."

"You're weak. Everyone can see it... They saw it in the ring, and they'll see it again when you face your next opponent."

"People have been hearing rumors about a Maguire/Duffy alliance."

It was never an alliance between Aimee and me.

It was between Padraic and Connor.

The rage turns cold as hell.

Connor smirks at me from across the ring, clearly enjoying my torment. The realization that I'd been betrayed by my own father. For the man who murdered his son.

I never thought I would see the day that Padraic would do something like this. Would lower himself to an alliance with the family he swore was our greatest enemy.

Isn't that what you did? I ignore the voice in my head as Connor begins to circle me.

No. The only reason Padraic would form an alliance with the Maguires would be if...

"Nothing to say? So much for the bastard prince of the Duffys," Connor goads at me.

… If I actually threatened his position as head of the family.

What if Kate was right? What if Ray was just one of many who would willingly join me? To prefer me to lead them over my father.?

A memory stirs in my mind. Arnie sitting across from me at a dive bar.

"... it's going to take a little more than a botched engagement to get me to leave him for Padraic... You, on the other hand..."

I am the rightful heir to the Duffy empire.

I let the killing calm take over my body, showing Connor the true face of the man who will take him down permanently.

314

"It was a mistake to come here," I growl, stepping forward to square off against him.

Connor meets me in the middle. "Your brother isn't here to take a bullet for you this time."

His eyes are nothing like his sister's. That earthy brown is colder, harder, with a vicious tinge that would make a lesser man shrink. But I won't back down. Not when the monster within me is begging to be unleashed.

The ref puts his arm out between us. Brave man.

"Keep it clean, boys." The ref steps between us, and with a final glare at my opponent, I turn away.

Over my shoulder, I hiss back, "Nova money isn't going to save you in the ring."

I hear Connor's laugh as I tighten up my hand tape. It digs into my skin hard enough to draw blood if I'm not careful. But I don't care. I won't need my hands after I've finished pummeling Connor to death.

When I turn back to my opponent, his smile has widened. "No." Connor looks over to where Padraic is sitting, but I can't stand to follow his gaze. "But *Duffys* might."

My roar is drowned by the sound of the starting bell.

I don't waste any time.

Right hook, left hook, uppercut, all make contact with Connor's jaw. Each land with a satisfying thump that has Connor retreating.

His footwork is fairly lethal, and he's quicker than he looks–

I double over, winded from the blow Connor dealt to my stomach. He hits hard too. Goddamn it.

"That was for my sister," Connor is saying when I return to my stance again. "What the hell have you done to her?"

I dodge his next hook and land a flurry of hits to his shoulder.

"Did Arnie not tell you?" I reply, evading his responding blow. "I just gave her something you never could: satisfaction."

My left hook is about to collide with his face when suddenly Connor's hand is there. Catching my fist in his own and absorbing the impact.

"You stole her from me. For that, you're going to pay with more than your measly life."

I don't have time to retaliate when Connor's head suddenly smacks into my nose with a hair-raising crack. I go careering backward, staggering awkwardly to avoid landing on the floor.

Connor laughs and begins circling me again. "Man, am I going to enjoy taking you down."

I lunge at him without warning. One, two, three tight, hard hits to the stomach, then a final blow to the face. He groans, and the monster inside me rejoices.

Just as Connor looks as if he's about to move to offense, the bell rings to indicate the end of round one.

I pull away but can't take my eyes off my enemy.

"Jack, come on. You need to concentrate," I'm vaguely aware that Coach is talking to me as he lathers petroleum on my broken nose. "You're too emotional."

"I'm fine," I snap back. I watch as the man in Connor's corner—Arnie, I realize with a start—dabs a cold press to his busted lip.

As far as first rounds go, it's been pretty evenly matched. Connor has clearly done this before; he's no amateur, and his left hook stings like a bitch. But I'm faster, and I have a home-ground advantage.

The crowds around me chant my name. Padraic miscalculated; people like me more than they fear him. I can't look up at the VIP box to see his reaction, not when I know who will be sitting behind him. But I imagine the grimace twisting his mouth, the anger in his eyes, and it energizes me.

The bell goes off for round two, and I stand immediately.

I waste no time. Uppercut, uppercut, retreat. I switch my stance from Orthodox to Southpaw to mess with him, and it works instantly. He's thrown off balance, swinging wide in order to dodge my foot.

My fist collides with his eye with a satisfying crunch.

I know his orbital socket has gone before his face even begins swelling. There's a piercing cry in the audience, but I can't focus on it. Won't let myself focus on it.

"You fucking asshole," Connor says, already wincing in pain. He's clearly suffering, and I can see the holes in his defense since I switched stances. He barely blocks another punch to the face.

So I hit him again.

My fists pound into his forearms relentlessly. With each blow, Connor has to fight not to step back—but slowly, I back him into a corner. I'm digging deep into my energy reserves to keep up the attack at this ferocity.

But it works.

Connor feels the rope at his back, and I see the panic in his eyes.

Got him.

I feign another blow to hit his defense but instead swing low. My fist hits him directly in the gut.

"Fuck!" He doubles over in pain.

It's a simple knee-jerk reaction, but Connor falls for it. His guard drops entirely.

So I hit him again.

This time, the force of my right hook has him flying to the floor.

I stand over him as the crowds begin chanting my name. The ref is somewhere, counting down to the KO.

But all I can focus on is the rise and fall of his chest.

He's still alive.

I fall to my knees, breathing heavily in and out. My mind doesn't care how much it took out of me to bring this man down. Only that my mission isn't complete yet.

Connor grunts as he feels my weight on top of me but does nothing to block me as my fist collides with his face again. And again.

"This is from Graham."

I spit at him between blows. Blood starts pouring from his nose, his split lip. My knuckles turn red.

Vaguely I'm aware that someone is trying to pull me off. But I push them away. I hear a rib crack, then another. Pain and rage. That's all I can hear, all I can *smell*.

"This is for Graham," I hear myself saying.

Connor keeps slipping in and out of consciousness. Not good enough. He needs to know why he's dying. He needs to know what he has done.

I grab him on the shoulders and shake him awake. Only one of his eyes opens. Good enough.

"This is for Graham!"

I punch him to the floor. His head bounces on impact.

That's when I hear it.

Through the pain and the rage and the revenge, a single voice calls out my name.

Broken, hoarse.

Crying. She's crying.

"Jack! Please! Stop!" Aimee sobs.

I don't know when she made her way down to the ring. I don't know how much she saw, but she sees me now. The monster is about to murder her brother.

I can't take my eyes off her. Radiant, like an angel in mourning, uncaring about anything else in the world except what is happening in this ring. What *I* am doing in this ring.

I'm hurting her.

With every punch, every bone I break of Connor's, I hurt her.

My hands finally hesitate.

Reality begins to crash down around me. The concerned cries of the crowd, the Dead Eyes encouraging me to finish the job. I glance up at the VIP box. Padraic hasn't moved an inch. His stony, white face tells me one thing: I was not supposed to survive this. I meet his eyes and feel my face pull into a feral grin. *Pray that I die, old man. Because I am coming for you.*

"Jack, please," Aimee says again.

Her voice is like a beacon; I'm so helplessly drawn to it. I scramble off the unconscious man and begin crawling to her. My adrenaline ebbs, and my limbs are suddenly spent with the effort it took to take him down.

But the darkness is behind me, and Aimee is there in front of me. Reaching her arm out encouragingly.

We could run away now, start our own life a thousand miles away. We could be safe together; we'd survive this.

"I'm sorry," I manage to get out, still crawling pathetically.

"It's okay."

"I'm sorry."

I'm almost there. Almost to the cool touch that will soothe my anger, and the cool mind that will back me to the hilt. She reaches out. "It's-"

Terror suddenly flashes over Aimee's face.

"Jack!"

My name echoes around my mind as everything goes black.

Chapter Thirty-Nine

Aimee

"Roisin! Stop!"

"Roisin!"

I ignore everyone around me as I push forward, launching myself up onto the ring from the sidelines. It's not graceful, but I don't care.

Not when my brother is about to kill Jack.

The anger in his eyes as he drags Jack's unconscious body to the middle of the stage would send chills down my spine if I wasn't already hyperventilating.

My foot finally finds purchase, and I push up into the ring.

Only for a pair of firm hands to drag me back.

"Roisin!" A man's voice sounds in my ear. "You can't. It's too dangerous."

I step on his foot. Hard. "Let me go, you fucking asshole!"

He lets go as if bitten by a snake. I get a quick glimpse of dark hair and notably Italian features before I scramble back up the side of the ring.

I look up to see Connor standing over Jack, his back to me. Kicking him over and over. The crowd boos him, but his confidence only seems to grow.

"Is this your prince?" Connor shouts out to his audience before delivering another blow to Jack's stomach. "He is nothing!"

I scramble to my feet, throwing off my ridiculous heels in the process and sprinting toward them.

"You deserve a real heir," Connor roars again, landing another blow. "Someone with true Irish blood!"

I don't think, I just jump between them.

I don't register the pain at first. Just the fact that I've reached him, and he's still breathing. Barely, but it's enough.

It's not until Connor has reeled back in shock that the wave of agony washes over me. I hold onto my stomach, desperate to hold back tears.

The crowds gasp in shock. Connor has just kicked his own sister. I hear them whispering, crying out for me. "Roisin! Is Roisin okay?"

I finally find the strength to stand. Pushing myself up painfully from the floor whilst still keeping myself between the two fighters. I turn on Connor, venom on my tongue...

... until I see his face.

His eyes are filled with tears.

He falls to his knees as he takes me in. As I take him in.

His face is ruined. Both eyes are now swelling around his broken orbital socket, and blood still drips from his nose, leaving red spots all over the floor.

But beneath it all...

"Connor," I say, unaware that my own tears are starting to fall.

It's been five years. The grief hits me harder than any blow he could deliver.

"Aimee?" he replies in disbelief.

I can't help it. I step forward, reaching for him.

"Aimee? You're okay?" Connor says, pulling me to the floor.

The embrace is everything and nothing at all.

Even blood-stained and sweaty, he smells like Connor, like home. I remember Connor as a boy, standing up to the kids that made fun of my hair. Of the teenager who scared off men from giving me unwanted attention. I remember my brother—who was, in many ways, the only positive male role model I had growing up.

"Where is Roisin?"

"She was never here. She's safe."

"It was always you?"

"Yes."

"I've been looking for you... looking for you both. I thought they'd... I thought *he'd* captured you. I thought they were torturing you."

The nothingness seeps into the embrace. It was there before, but the more I remember it, acknowledge it, the worse it becomes. Connor's face when he told me Roisin was overdosing. When he said he wasn't leaving with us for LA. When I found out he had murdered Graham Duffy in cold blood.

This is not the boy I knew. This is a stranger in a man's body.

I pull away. "I'm fine. Jack told you I was fine."

I can barely force myself to look at Jack's unconscious body behind us, but I risk a glance. Still breathing. Good. I stand to go examine him further.

"Forgive me for not believing a word out of his bastard mouth."

I turn on him, irritated. "But you'll happily side with Padraic, then?"

He stares at me in disbelief, "I only did that to get you back! Aimee, please. We need to leave. Now."

Connor reaches for my hand, but I snatch it away.

"No."

In my peripheral, I see a skirmish beginning at the edges of the ring. Dead Eyes and Maguires clash as some attempt to enter the ring.

"We don't have time for this."

Connor doesn't give me a choice. He looms over me and grabs me by the arms, lifting me clean off the floor.

"No!" I screech as he starts to carry me away from Jack. "Let go of me!."

"What, to stay with the bastards who kidnapped you? Have you lost your senses, Aimee?" He doesn't stop.

"Put me down, you gobshite!"

Connor only hesitates a split second before beginning to pass me over the rope to someone on the other side. The dark-haired man from before seems to have managed to fight his way to the side of the ring.

I'm not sure whose hand it is, but I bite down on it. The Italian man yelps and is suddenly lost again to the skirmish. I try to slam my head back against Connor's broken face.

"Aimee!" Connor says, desperation lacing his voice. "We don't have time for this."

I try to wriggle loose. "I'm not leaving."

"Yes, you are. It's not safe for you here."

"He won't hurt me."

Connor grunts in frustration, "He's a *monster*. Why can't you see that?"

Finally, I manage to break free of his grip, landing awkwardly but still upright as I face off against my brother.

"Because I love him!"

Connor looks at me as if I've grown a second head. "You can't be fucking serious."

"Deadly."

Connor roars. This time, I have a moment to brace myself before his arms lift me up again.

This time I scream. I shout. I scratch. I bite. Anything. Everything. "No! No!! Let go of me!"

But his grasp only tightens. Through the skirmish, I see the Italian again waiting for me to be manhandled out of the ring.

"No," I whisper helplessly.

No. No. No.

"I'd appreciate it," a voice says from behind us, "if you would let my fiance go."

I sob in relief. Filled with new defiance, I wriggle free of Connor's shocked grasp.

I run to him. Tears streaming down my face when I see Jack standing there, ready to fight my brother for me. Our bodies collide roughly, and my hands seek out his face immediately.

"Are you okay? Do you remember your name? What year is it?" I say as I scan his eyes, looking for any sign of concussion.

Jack gently takes my fussing hand in his. "You said you loved me."

"I..."

The kiss is soft and unprovocative. Yet it tastes sweeter than anything else. When he withdraws, he places his forehead against mine.

"I love you too."

It's hardly the time to be swooning, so I simply stare at his face. Committing it to memory so that I will never forget this moment. Bruises and battle scars be damned.

"What the fuck did you do to her?"

Jack immediately takes a defensive position around me, shielding me from Connor's view. "I didn't force her to be here."

"You've manipulated her!"

I try to step around Jack. "Connor, please. This has nothing to do with you."

"It has everything to do with me! You're a Maguire, Aimee. You belong with me at home."

There's a roar from the sidelines, and a gunshot goes off. Padraic is shouting orders from the VIP box, gathering Dead Eyes to him to mount a counterattack.

Jack pulls us both to the floor instinctively. We need to move now—before the fighting gets any worse. The cars should still be waiting for us outside.

A dark figure finally breaks through the side of the ring and approaches Connor.

"We're leaving."

Connor sneers at him. "I'm not going anywhere without my sister."

"You stay here, you're dead. *I'm* dead," the Italian says harshly. "We can fight about this another day."

Connor turns to me, torn. "Aimee, please."

"Go," I say firmly, crawling out from under Jack. "Leave."

For a moment, I think he's going to try again. Fight Jack and drag me kicking and screaming through the unruly crowds back to the house I never wanted to return to.

But then he turns away.

"I'll see you again, bastard."

Before Jack has a moment to respond, Connor slips away into the crowds.

Epilogue

Aimee

Alexas, Kate's hand-picked driver, manuevers us through the city at astonishing speed. Not that either one of us seems to really notice.

No, as I cradle Jack's head on my lap, the only thing I can think about is just how many stitches he's going to need.

Even after his fight with that European champion, he's never looked this bad. And from his uneven breathing, I'd say he's broken at least one rib. But all I can do right now is stroke his hair and admire his hazel eyes that stare up at me in wonder.

"You chose me over your brother?" he whispers quietly.

I sweep across his bloodied brow with my hand gently. "I know," I reply just as quietly.

"I thought... that's what you would want?" he says carefully, trying not to let me see the vulnerability in his eyes.

"So did I," I say, honestly. "But when I saw you there on the floor, I just... Something just cracked."

"Cracked?"

With a sigh, I try looking out the window to try and find the words. "Whatever I feel about my brother is... complicated. Some part of me thought he'd always be my big brother, ready to protect me, but that illusion's shattered."

Jack doesn't speak, letting my words hang in the air.

"I realized the only way I wanted to do any of this was with you. That you were the only person I cared about protecting in that ring." I conclude quietly.

"I was going to kill him," Jack says after a moment. "You stopped me."

I think about that for a moment, revisiting the fear I felt after Jack threw the first punch. After I saw Connor go down and Jack's relentless rampage.

"I don't want anyone else to die. Least of all, anyone who you might regret killing later," I reply truthfully. "It's true, I don't want my brother to be killed, but it's you I worry about."

Jack smirks a little at this. "That's a bit fucked up."

"Yeah," I say with a huff. "But it's the truth."

"Thank you," he says earnestly. "For stopping me."

We pass by a row of brightly lit storefronts and then duck into an alleyway. Wherever we're going, I get the feeling that Kate has made sure only a handful of people know the location. I'm so disoriented I can't even tell which direction we are heading, let alone where we've been.

"Do you think…" I say absently before trailing off.

"What?"

I bite my lip. "Do you think Graham would have liked me?"

Jack reaches up a hand to stroke my cheek, "Of course, he would. He was a better man than me."

"Even though I'm a Maguire?"

He pulls me down to kiss him gently. "He'd come around. Quicker than I did, probably."

I pull away with a sad smile. "I'm sorry I never met him."

"Me too."

We take a final jerk to the left and suddenly plunge into darkness. The driver turns around in his seat.

"Mr. Duffy? We are almost here."

'Here' turns out to be a little further down the dark tunnel we just entered. A few seconds later, lights begin to flicker on, guiding our path toward some industrial-sized garage doors.

They open with a shudder, and the creeks echo throughout the tunnel around us. But as it rises, the more I can't tear my eyes away.

Behind the door is what looks to be a car showroom more than a garage. Already, almost half of Jack's cars have been lined up in rows along the gigantic room. The whole place looks like some kind of warehouse, except...

"We're underground?" I say, looking back down at Jack.

"It would appear so."

Waiting for us in the garage is a small group of people—two of them standing next to a gurney. Thank God.

To their left, another group of people gets out of the car. They must have arrived just a few moments before us. Among them is the signature blonde hair of the safe-house owner herself, Kate St Michael.

The way she maneuvered us out of Luckies had been beyond anything I had ever seen. The woman must have made a deal with the devil in order to move like that. Pushing through the crowds efficiently and without drawing attention to the two people she'd shoved into oversized hoodies. Hoodies both Jack and I are still wearing.

She truly thought of everything.

When Alexas comes to a stop, he exits the car and runs around to the back seat of the SUV, beckoning the gurney over.

"This is going to sting like a bitch, isn't it?" Jack says, wincing a little as he tries to sit up.

"Yes," I say honestly. "But I hear your doctor is pretty cute."

***

It takes several hours to clean Jack up and fully assess the damage done during the fight. By the time I've finished strapping him up and prescribing him painkillers from the impressive collection Kate seems to have amassed, all sixteen of our new family have arrived and settled into the safe house.

Jack insists on a brief meeting, even though I put him under strict bed rest—so we compromise by moving to a lounge next door, equipped with a fully stocked bar that everyone eagerly makes use of.

"I'll keep this short," Jack says once everyone settles down. "As it's been a long day, and I imagine some of you feel worse than I look."

This earns him a few chuckles, and I smile at him fondly.

"I want to first thank you for trusting me and for going along with all this. What you saw tonight was the result of Padraic's careless revenge. Weeks, maybe even months in the making." Jack says solemnly. "For a while now, Padraic's goal has been to remove me from the picture by any means necessary. Even if it meant collaborating with his own son's murderer."

I duck my head as a few of the men begin to murmur to themselves.

"Understand, my fiancee and I never intended for any of this to happen," Jack says, looking at me with a small smile. "And it's my fault for not anticipating Padraic's reaction to our engagement."

"It's not your fault," Kate speaks up suddenly. "You had every right to his empire, to be named heir, but he was never going to give it to you. Your engagement was just an excuse for him to latch on to."

She turns to the men, only a flicker of anger showing under her practiced calm and perfect makeup.. "For too long, we've played this game under a leader who's willing to sacrifice his men to fulfill his every whim." Kate glances back at Jack. "I think it's about time we put our faith in someone who actually gives a shit."

The men launch into whoops of applause, much to Jack's apparent surprise.

"Thank you," he says once it finally calms down. "At present, our only objective is to lie low for a couple of weeks. That means no contact with the outside world, no leaving the property. Take this time to rest and make yourselves at home. I'll be putting together a group of you to form my inner circle, and we'll keep you informed about any new developments. I also want to hear all your thoughts, ways you think we can streamline operations or outsmart the Dead Eyes."

Despite the weariness we all seem to share, the men look at Jack in admiration, seemingly keen to ask him a hundred questions about this new faction of the mob and how he intends to lead it. But the best part is the way Jack is looking back at them—he's tired and he's hurt, but he's thinking. I can almost hear his mental wheels turning, bursting with ideas to form and reform this new organization. Sixteen people against the Dead Eyes… but with Jack, I think there's a chance.

I take the opportunity to step in. "However, tonight you are all prescribed bed rest. So, if you'll excuse us…"

Jack looks at me with a grateful smile, even though the men seem equally as thrilled by this announcement.

I help Jack up, even though he stubbornly insists on walking by himself, and we slowly make our way to the room Kate assigned to us.

Despite being underground, I'm pleasantly surprised by the amount of light Kate has managed to wire into this place. The decor is earthy and inviting, and it takes Jack all of two seconds to collapse onto the bed.

I don't bother undressing before falling down right next to him.

We lie together in silence for a moment, both of us presumably thinking over the last 24 hours. It's not until I turn my head to see Jack staring at me that I realize I may have taken a little too long.

"What are you worried about?"

I wince a little. "Everything?"

He chuckles, a little wryly. "You're not the only one, *Chroí*. You worry to me, I'll worry to you, and we'll keep the family—our family—from worrying at all."

"It's just… everyone knows I'm not Roisin now. What if people start looking for her again? What if *Connor* starts looking for her again?"

"We won't let that happen to her," Jack says, squeezing me a little. "If we get even the slightest notion that people might be after her, we'll bring her down here."

I bite my lip.

"What is it?"

"Should we have picked her up already? I mean, who knows how dangerous it is out there for her now? I mean–"

Jack silences me with a kiss. "Once we've gotten a secured line available, you can call her and catch her up on everything. Then she can make her own choices."Besides, I thought you wanted her to have a normal life?"

"I do," I concede. "I just wish it wasn't this complicated."

"I know, I'm sorry," Jack says, empathy lacing his words.

I rest my forehead against him. "I just miss her, that's all."

"You'll see her again, I promise," Jack says, holding out his pinky finger.

I smile at his childishness and take his finger in mine. "I'll hold you to that, Mr. Duffy."

"Oh, *Chroí,* I'm counting on it."

***

THANK YOU FOR READING FORBIDDEN ROMEO

DON'T MISS THE FREE SIZZLING BONUS CHAPTER

Jack lowers his face closer to mine, but I place a hand in front of his lips. "Please tell me you didn't clear out the meeting so that you could fuck me in private."

"I thought we already established, Chroí," he says, bypassing my hand and kissing me anyway. "I'm not going to share you with anyone."

"Jack…" I groan, already feeling my cheeks color again. "Someone will walk in."

He pulls away with a mischievous grin. "Actually, I have a surprise for you."

Half a second later, he's pulling me out of the room and down the corridor to the left. We pass a few people milling about who offer us a friendly smile or wave. But eventually, we come to a stop by a door I'd not noticed before—tucked away just behind the garage.

I say nothing as Jack reaches into his pocket and pulls out a keycard, swiping it along the almost invisible seam.

The door pings open, just like…

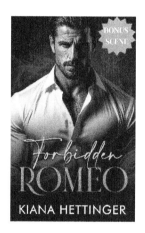

Can't get enough of Aimee and Jack? Download the free bonus scene for one more steamy chapter.

Download the FREE bonus chapter here -
https://geni.us/forbiddenrbonus

What's Next?

Wow, I hope you enjoyed *Forbidden Romeo*. Your support means the world to me!

By Kiana Hettinger

Forbidden Romeo is a Dark Irish Mafia Romance Standalone.

Mafia Kings: Corrupted Series

#0 Cruel Inception

#1 Corrupted Heir

#2 Corrupted Temptation

#3 Corrupted Protector

#4 Corrupted Obsession

#5 Corrupted Vows

#6 Corrupted Sinner

#7 Corrupted Seduction

Standalones

Stolen Bond

Brutal Oath

Forbidden Romeo

Calling all Kittens! Come join the fun:

If you're thirsty for more discussions with other readers of the series, join my exclusive readers' group, Kiana's Kittens.

Join my private readers' group here -
facebook.com/groups/KianasKittens

CAN YOU DO ME A HUGE FAVOR?

Would you be willing to leave me a review?

I'd be over the moon because just one positive review on Amazon is like buying the book a hundred times! Reader support is the lifeblood for Indie authors. It provides us the feedback we need to give readers what they want in future stories!

Your positive review would mean the world to me. You can post your review on Amazon or Goodreads. I'd be forever grateful, thank you from the bottom of my heart!

Printed in Great Britain
by Amazon

30806973R10188